GORDON R. DICKSON

BEYOND THE DAR AL-HARB

A TOM DOHERTY ASSOCIATES BOOK

First printing: November 1985

A TOR Book

Published by Tom Doherty Associates
49 West 24 Street
New York, N.Y. 10010

Cover art by Alan Gutierrez

ISBN: 0-812-53550-2
CAN. ED.: 0-812-53551-0

Printed in the United States of America

IN THE CHAMBER OF
THE WHITE FLOWER

The way Jami followed led to the room where the Flower of Passion slept. Softly, he withdrew his sword from its scabbard, and held it up to the room. In the bright metal he saw reflected a golden, animal-like body flecked with silver. Its muscles were enormous, and it had a huge head with a massive mouth showing a glimpse of great canine teeth.

Jami had seen—in Europe, before he had come to this land where the making of images was a religious crime—a drawing of a creature called a *sanaja*, a magical creature whose glance, like the basilisk, could kill.

He lifted his sword in both hands, took one long and silent step within, closed his eyes as the creature whirled to face him, and struck downwards . . .

BEYOND THE DAR AL-HARB

Contents

BEYOND THE
DAR AL-HARB

A CHANGE IN THE CHORUS OF SOUNDS THAT MADE UP THE voice of the bazaar was the first warning, a sudden silence from farther up the walled and dome-covered street that contained the bazaar shops in the walled city of 'Ayla. The change was registered unconsciously by both Umar al-Hafiz, the jeweler, and Jami al-Kafir Jamie the Infidel—but neither reacted because at the moment the attentions of both were occupied elsewhere.

Umar sat cross-legged on a scarlet cushion, his white caftan tucked primly about his small body, his turbaned head bent low with concentration as he delicately weighed some pearls in a scale. Umar was wealthy and could have afforded a magic balance that would have given him the value as well as the weight of what he measured; but he preferred the old methods and was not a man to spend money unnecessarily—though in other ways he was generous and charitable to a fault, as Jami had reason to know.

Jami himself stood behind Umar in the shadows with his hand lightly resting on the hilt of his sword. He had been watching an individual he took to be a Sufi holy man. The fellow had been lingering on the other side of the dirt street that ran between the closely packed rows of shops. Dim

9

sunshine filtered down on the bazaar through the skylight in the dome above them—for the day was nearly spent.

There was something about the holy one that made Jami uneasy. His ragged and dirty blue robe, patched as most holy men's robes usually were, had a strangely contrived air about it, almost as if the patches had been sewn on as a design, instead of being the natural result of wear and use. Beyond this, he was blind in one eye and the lid over the empty socket had sunken in in an ugly fashion. There was a certain cringing but arrogant air about him, as if he was ready to crawl or attack, depending upon the strength of the person he faced—an attitude that did not fit his tattered garb.

Now Umar finished his weighing and scooped the pearls from the pan into his hand. He lifted his head. By this time the silence had extended itself down toward them and, going ahead of it, like the first strong wave up the beach ahead of a sudden breath of storm, a whisper . . .

"The Desert Men . . ."

There was a hissing detestation in the message as it was passed around the brick walls separating shop from shop. The Bedouin, the Men from the Desert, were not loved by the city dwellers; nor did the Bedouin love those of the city.

Umar automatically lowered his hand, so that the pearls would be out of sight. He frowned. The first faint puff of the hot evening breeze blew down the covered street ahead of those whose coming the whispers heralded.

It was in such a time of year as this, always, the time of the hot winds from the wastelands beyond the walls of 'Ayla, that the Bedouin sometimes came to the city. As Jami and Umar watched, the first of them rode into sight— like cloaked demons, slim men on prancing, fine-legged horses. They wore the typical voluminous robes of the wastelands, and headcloths rather than the turbans that were the mark—and the privilege—of all true believers in God and the Prophet. They sat proudly, ignoring with a fine disdain the merchants they passed, who looked back at them with open hatred.

Umar sat, stiff and unmoving on his cushion, watching the delicate hooves of the horses turning the muck and earth of the street.

Jami also watched, the sight of the riders bringing back deep-buried memories and a savage feeling of anger, of which even Umar, his patron in 'Ayla, knew nothing. Once he had ridden with some of these very men who were passing—though none of those identified him now among the shadows into which he had drawn, at the back of Umar's shop. Once he had sworn revenge on their leader, who should be along at any moment now, and that oath still lived.

The silence was profound now, except for the muffled noise of the horses' hooves and the creak of the saddle leathers as the riders passed. They rode two by two, neither speaking to each other nor to those they passed. The animosity from the shops around them was a solid thing in the dim air under the domes; and their disdain of it was an equally solid thing.

They passed more quickly than it seemed they might, for their horses did not linger. And then came one rider, the sight of whom made Jami's breath catch in his chest. This one was surrounded by what were obviously guards. His robes were a clean and shining white, and his headcloth—also white—was held in place by a circlet of gold. A gold sash cinched the robes around his narrow waist. Above those robes, his shoulders were broad, his face was middle-aged, dark and brilliant with piercing brown eyes and a harshly beaked nose over a straight line of a mouth and a small, sharply pointed gray beard. This resplendent rider did not glance toward Umar's shop any more than the others had; but Jami felt his guts suddenly knot with the fury he had carried secretly inside him for more than two years now.

A gray parrot was perched on the leather band encircling the chief rider's right wrist, a parrot hooded like a falcon. As the rider passed, the bird turned its blinded eyes toward the shop of Umar.

"Marauder!" it shrieked suddenly, loud in the stillness, "Look to your goods! Marauder!"

"It is written," muttered Umar, so softly that only Jami could have heard him, "that Gehenna holds a dwelling place for the proud."

The little jeweler continued to sit unmoving, watching the passing riders, a statue in his white caftan with the bands of inscriptions woven into the borders at wrist and hem. With his snowy turban and black velvet carpet slippers, he made a rich contrast to the plainness of Jami, who bulked taller and even wider-shouldered than the Bedouin leader, in the shadows behind Umar.

In variance with the garb of Umar, Jami's clothes were strictly practical. His thigh-length tunic was of unbleached cotton, and under it he wore narrow, brown cotton trousers that disappeared into knee-high boots of cloth. Since Jami was an infidel in Moslem eyes, one of the things forbidden to him in law was the turban. Instead he wore a flat cap he had deliberately had made in a shape not unlike the bonnet of his Scottish boyhood.

A plain leather swordbelt supported the scabbard holding the sword he was specially licensed to carry under the surety of Umar and the religious fellowship to which Umar belonged. Otherwise, as a non-Muslim visitor from the Dar al-Harb—the House of War that lay beyond the known and civilized world of the Dar al-Islam—he would have been permitted no such weapon. Infidels who went armed in Muslim lands risked the pain of grievous punishment.

Umar, however, had gone personal surety for Jami's being allowed the weapon—on the grounds that Jami was employed by him and his fellow jewelers as a guard for them. Jami, who had been born a prince in a tiny Scottish kingdom, would have been shocked to learn that Umar and his fellows thought of him as an object of charity—infidel though he was. But this, the little jeweler had never let him guess; any more than Umar could himself have guessed the reason Jami had stepped back out of sight with the passing of these particular desert riders, or their connection with Jami's coming to 'Ayla, two years before.

It was a large thing Umar had done, going surety for that sword; and it spoke well of his trust in Jami, for if the tall infidel should misuse the weapon, the consequences would recoil upon the jeweler as well.

Under the cap, the ends of Jami's rebellious dark red hair curled up. His very coloring marked him for what he was—an infidel, a "Frank," as Muslims commonly called anyone from the Dar al-Harb to the north.

The desert men continued to ride by. Umar continued to sit motionless, propped on his scarlet cushion above the brightly carpeted floor of his shop. He made no move to pour another glass of pomegranate juice from the carafe on the silver tray beside him. In his studied immobility, in the dimly-lit store, Jami thought, he might have been mistaken for some heathen idol.

The last of the horsemen passed. Umar's hands began to move busily, gathering his valuables together in preparation to locking up the shop. He sorted his gems by colors and shapes, into small black velvet bags, and stacked ingots of precious metals on a square of heavy white silk.

"They are proud, indeed, those sons of Iblis," muttered Umar as he worked. "You know who they are? You know the Sheik al-Birain—he with the parrot on his wrist?"

"The Sheik of the Two Wells—" Jami's tongue echoed the Arabic words Umar had spoken, but his mind translated the words into his birth language. "Yes, I know him—of him."

The last two words made a hasty correction. But Umar, busy gathering up his valuables, did not seem to notice.

"As always they will be staying at the house of the merchant Sulayman Tufeek," said Umar, "and doing business with him—much good may it do either them or Sulayman," said Umar. "You can give me a hand with the shutters once all this is locked away—what are you staring at?"

Umar had turned his head as he spoke and caught Jami's eyes again on the holy man who was still lingering across the street.

"It's only al-Muqla," growled Umar contemptuously.

The name translated to "The Eyeball." It was not complimentary. Jami looked at the jeweler in some surprise.

"It's not like you to misspeak a holy man," he said. "Particularly a Sufi, like yourself."

"Al-Muqla a Sufi? Holy?" Umar snorted. "As holy as those he lives with in their *khaniqah*, on the Street of Silence—those who call themselves the Brotherhood of the Flower! You're an infidel and I suppose shouldn't be blamed for not being able to tell a true holy Sufi from such as they. See the skillfully arranged patches, and the other parts of the robe worn thin with a stone to make them seem like the wear sustained by one who truly walks in the way of the Prophet!"

"That robe did look a little too good to be true to me," said Jami, slowly. "That's why I was keeping an eye on him. I thought he might be a thief, dressed up—"

"Thief! They're worse than thieves, the Flowery Brotherhood!" snorted Umar, tying up the ends of his wrappers to tightly contain their contents. Jami stared at his small friend and employer, a little bemused at the heat of Umar's attitude toward al-Muqla. Jami himself knew little of the Brotherhood of the Flower, beyond its name and the location of its *khaniqah*, which he had always assumed to be nothing much more than a Muslim counterpart of the monasteries he had been used to in Christendom.

However, it was all one to him—a Christian. He stopped

himself just in time from shrugging. But something of his attitude must have shown in his face, since Umar went on to further denunciation of the Flowery Brotherhood, which he, as an orthodox Muslim and a devout Sufi, plainly found shocking or worse.

"What is a true holy man?" snapped Umar. "One devoted to prayer, good works and preaching from the words of the Prophet, blessed be his name—"

Jami thought of the Blue Friars, or the Companions of St. Giacomo in Europe, Christian equivalents of the organized Sufi orders. However, Umar was continuing.

"But the Islam this Brotherood of the Flower offers is a sham and a lie. They substitute the vain imaginings of men for the holy law of the Prophet, on whom be everlasting peace. They forget the favor of God and grasp instead for the pleasures of Shaitan-inspired music, and songs by gazelle-eyed young men. In my own Brotherhood of Jewelers it is otherwise, as even thou knowest, Jami . . . but I waste breath on one who knows not Allah. Only, take my word for it that the Brotherhood of the Flower—that Flower they pretend to be so secret it may not be named—is in no way holy, nor are any of their practices holy.

"Take the metals, the package is heavy and better suited to your muscles than mine. I will take the gems and we will put them in the safe cabinet."

He tied together the ends of the cloth with the jewels as he spoke, and picked it up. Jami did the same with the white cloth holding the scraps and bars of gold and silver. As Umar had said, the latter had weight despite its lack of bulk. Together they went to the back of the shop to what seemed to be merely an intricately carved chest of wood that stood about knee-high. With his free hand, Umar threw back the lid of the chest, showing an empty interior with room for a great deal more than their bundles. "There!" said Umar, as they set the packages down inside. He closed the chest, took a step backwards, in which Jami joined him, and murmured a few words, describing interlocking circles in the air with both hands as he did so. He stopped speaking and gesturing. Both men eyed the chest. For a long moment nothing happened; and then, first the outlines, then the body of the chest began to grow indistinct, as if it was becoming insubstantial before their eyes. Slowly it thinned, until finally it was gone, vanished completely. Umar reached forward and waved his right hand through the space it had occupied. His hand met no more resistance than that provided by the empty air itself.

Umar frowned.

"That spell works more slowly lately," he said. "Did you mark that, Jami? Just this last week the chest has been taking longer and longer to disappear."

"You're right," said Jami.

Umar combed the gray hairs of his short beard with his fingers, worriedly.

"It should not be so," he said. "And the mage I bought the spell from is gone this eight months now with a caravan into Persia."

Jami thought for a moment.

"You know the coffeehouse of Tahmasp al-Farsi," he said. "I've been meeting a friend of mine—Lukas de Finistere—there, now and then, about this time of day; and lately there's been someone there who is newly come to town. They say he's a magician, and he's certainly Persian. Mir-something . . . Mir Akbar, I think his name is."

"Ah," said Umar thoughtfully. "He would want a large fee, of course . . ."

"Who could you find who wouldn't?" said Jami. "Shall I see if he comes there this evening? It's about the hour now for him to arrive."

"Yes, yes," said Umar, crossly. "Of course, I'd deny no one a fair price for magic done for me; and if it's needed— yes, seek him out and tell him my problem."

"I'll go now," said Jami.

"After you help me put up my shutters."

"Of course."

Jami grinned at the dapper little man.

With Umar's words still in the back of his mind, he helped the other secure the shop, then stepped into the bazaar street and turned left, in the direction the desert dwellers had gone.

He did not, however, go directly to the coffeehouse, but hurried along until he reached the gates to the outer courtyard of Sulayman Tufeek, a kinsman to more than one desert chieftain and for that reason the man to see if you had goods to send over the caravan routes. As Jami reached the gates of Sulayman Tufeek's courtyard, they were just swinging closed, although it was not yet evening.

He watched from a distance without approaching the gate himself. Within him, the rage, the hollow madness he had felt at the sight of the horsemen and particularly at the sight of Sheik al-Birain, himself, woke once more.

He turned and began to walk a circuit of the house. On three sides the courtyard wall set up the boundary of Sulayman Tufeek's property. But on the fourth, that side that fronted the Street of Tears, the courtyard wall ran only halfway, back to where it reached the front of the house; and from there on that side was the tall, blank side of the house itself, unclimbable. However, in the street and near the point at which courtyard wall met house wall, there was a solitary sycamore fig tree. It stood too far from the wall to be of any use as a means of entry—which was probably why it was allowed to survive uncut. But the shade of its thick branches would make a well of darkness in the evening when the last of the light and the thoughts of food and sleep would make guards careless. At that time an active man with a rope and grapnel could go up the wall by the house and wait hidden in the shade on the lower roof until darkness fell, after which all the jumble of Sulayman Tufeek's rooftop levels would be open to soft-footed traffic.

Just such a shadow was lying on street, wall and roof at this moment; for by preference the desert dwellers always rode into the city late in the day; and even now the twilight was fading fast about him. But Jami had no grapnel with him; and even if he had, it was not his way—though few of the native inhabitants of 'Ayla would have given this tall, burly barbarian from the Dar al-Harb credit for it—to do things unplanned. He turned away and headed toward the coffeehouse of Tahmasp al-Farsi.

Twenty minutes later, he entered that particular establishment. The premises consisted of a single large room, around three walls of which ran a carpeted platform on which the guests sat cross-legged on cushions—Jami's legs ached at the sight of them. After years in Arabia, his legs still went to sleep if he had to sit that way for any length of time. These people, used to the position since childhood, found it merely comfortable.

"Ah, Jami," said Tahmasp al-Farsi, himself, bustling up to him.

The proprietor of the coffeehouse was a short, tubby man in a brown and black striped caftan and white turban.

"Your friend the Firanji—" (for once the Arabic word for Frank, the name they gave all Europeans—even on occasion Jami himself—actually fit, since the man in question had had a French father) "—the Firanji minstrel has already come and gone. He left word he would find you at your own house, later."

"Thank you, Tahmasp al-Farsi," said Jami, politely. "My thanks for passing that message on to me. But in fact I was looking for someone else as well."

His eyes were roaming around the seating platforms as he spoke. "Have you seen the Persian magician just lately come here to 'Ayla? I'd like a word with him on behalf of the Guild of Jewelers—"

He broke off, for his eyes had found a portly figure, taller than the average.

"Ah, I see him now," Jami said, starting across the open central part of the floor toward the stranger.

The Persian magician, Jami thought as he approached the man, made an imposing figure—and knew it. The other was tall enough to carry his extra weight with an air of importance. He was perhaps twenty to thirty pounds overweight and he wore a silk caftan of a bright emerald green trimmed with bands of fine green damask. A sash of forest green girdled his ample waist and carried a silver pencase. Most remarkable about his appearance was his turban. Its white fabric was wound about over some sort of tall red velvet cap, the exposed tip of which stuck up like a thin, sharp spike. The headgear marked him as a Shi'ite Muslim but to Jami's eye gave him an air of authority as if it were a crown. Placed on the floor below the platform on which he sat were the red velvet slippers he, like the other patrons, had taken off and placed handily before sitting down.

On the middle finger of his left hand, he wore a gold ring with a large, square-cut orange stone in it. No, Jami corrected himself, the stone was a ruby. The lamplit interior must have distorted the color. Before the magician was an embossed brass tray bearing two of the small, handleless coffee cups and a plate of roasted melon seeds. The Persian finished the seed he had been nibbling and reached for a cup.

By this time Jami was almost to the man.

"May I join you, Magician?" he said, halting in front of him.

The magician glanced up. He looked directly at Jami, which the latter found disconcerting. In the Arab world it was considered impolite to look directly into someone else's eyes, particularly when strangers were meeting for the first time.

"Sit down. Join me." The magician's voice was a deep, resonant bass, his eyes were black. He made a sweeping gesture of invitation with his left hand to the empty cushion on the other side of the tray before him. In truth, the establishment was only about half full at this hour, so that there was some little distance separating the magician from the other customers that were both behind and before him on the platform.

Jami seated himself.

"The other cup is for you. I was expecting you."

"Expecting me?" Jami looked keenly at the other, as he folded himself up on the opposite cushion. It was not possible; but, he reminded himself, you could never tell what was possible with those who worked in any area of magic— from Hobe, the speyman of his boyhood back home, to whatever kind of the unreal Persian magicians like this one engaged in. Magic was a fact, in this Christian year of our Lord 1359—the Muslim year 735—which non-magicians had to live with.

"Of course," said the magician. He waved the hand on which the ring now glinted as black as some secret recess in the center of the earth. "You may tell Umar al-Hafiz that the spell on his strongbox, the one that sends it with its contents for safety to the home of the Djinn, will work promptly from now on. My fee will be one of his emeralds, which I have already selected. I will come to the shop tomorrow to pick it up."

"So, the sick spell is already cured?" Jami grinned wolfishly. "That was fast."

"A small matter," said the magician, "—to one of my attainments, that is. It was a weak magician who sold your jeweler friend the spell in the first place, and such spells can only be as strong as those who cast them. Also, any such spell will decay after its strength runs out. Luckily for Umar al-Hafiz, my strength as a magician is great indeed. I have remade the spell so that it will not decay until the hour of his death, at which time his heirs will need access to it."

"It seems as if I hardly needed to come at all," said

Jami. "If you knew my errand and could do your work from a distance."

"Not only do the hungry seek food, food seeks the hungry," said the magician unctuously. "You were not to know that I know the thoughts of sultans and slaves alike—and even of a licensed infidel visitor in the Dar al-Islam like yourself, Jami Ibn Walter al-Ilarethi al-Firanj—that is to say—al-Scoci, rather than al-Firanj."

Jami sat very still; but within he was jarred as if by a physical blow. He had not thought there was anyone here on this southern side of the Mediterranean who had even heard of the small kingdoms of Scotland, of which one had been—and with the Lord's help, still was—his father's.

"Few people have heard of my homeland," he said at last, slowly.

"True enough," said the magician, folding his plump hands together. "Doings in the barbarous and unbelieving Dar al-Harb hold little interest to most of those in our blessed House of Islam. But I am more than most. I know not only your proper name and place, but that you were a prince and brave fighter in your own land before you came among us. You speak, Jami al-Scoci, to a full adept of the Inner Science, Mir Akbar ibn Ja'far al-Surawardi al-Shiraz; but you may address me simply as Mir Akbar. Such adepts as myself are few, but we form a brotherhood that is sworn to simplicity and humbleness; and do not, like lesser workers with the Art, pride ourselves or puff ourselves up about our abilities."

"I see," said Jami.

His reply was almost automatic. His mind was suddenly busy with the thought that perhaps somehow the skills of this Mir Akbar could be put to use to aid him in the revenge he had waited so long to wreak. He reached out and drank unseeingly from the cup in front of him; and the thickly sweet taste of the coffee brought back the memory of sitting opposite Sheik al-Birain in the other's tent as they spoke of an attack Jami would lead for the sheik on one of the heavily armed, but rich, caravans that passed through al-Birain's territory.

For a second, also, the lovely, brown face of Sati came back to him. Not as he had last seen the small girl from Hindi, dead on the midden heap of al-Birain's camp, but as he had known her in life—smiling at him in spite of the persecutions of the Muslim women of the camp. He pushed that image from him. He had been thinking, he reminded himself, of some way the magician's powers might help him to deal with al-Birain now that the sheik had finally decided to visit 'Ayla . . .

"You are interested in my ring?" The voice of Mir Akbar roused Jami to the awareness that he had been mindlessly staring at the point of light that was the ring of changing colors on the magician's hand, now extended toward him so that it was held close under his eyes.

It was, he now saw, a rock crystal ring, its top cut in the shape of its owner's seal. He had seen many like it in Umar's shop. Now, however, its color had become a rich green and, close as it was, he was able to read the Arabic letters of the inscription on it. They spelled out *kulluhu sirr*, which translated to "they are all hidden." He had heard of that phrase somewhere as an anagram of the occult arts of Islam.

"I see you can read," said the voice of Mir Akbar in his ear. "A ring like this, varying only with the seal of him who owns it, is worn only by a Master of Inner Science. I, of course, am not only that. I have also scaled the Emerald Rock on the peak of the Cosmic Mountain; and beheld both the Midnight Sun and the Black Noontide."

"Wondrous!" said Jami, recovering and straightening swiftly from his examination of the ring.

Mir Akbar beamed.

"Well, no doubt," he said. "But for one like myself . . ."

He waved his ringed hand lightly in the air.

"Indeed, you are an observant man, Jami al-Scoci," he went on. "Not that that surprises me. Calculations I made from the letters of your real name indicate very good fortune for those helping you in any way. I told Sheik al-Birain so, not half an hour past—"

"Al-Birain?" Jami's interruption was unexpectedly sharp. Mir Akbar frowned.

"Indeed. The desert sheik that just today rode into town. As it happened, he had heard of my presence here and asked me to wait on him earlier today, in his camp outside these walls as soon as it was set up and before he rode in to visit, as he does now, at the home of Sulayman Tufeek."

"He already knows me," said Jami, tightly.

"So I was aware, even before he spoke," said Mir Akbar. "My art also let me see at that time that you would come seeking me here, so that I have arranged to be here where you could find me. Since you carry good fortune to those who help you, I will be such a one. You may ask me three questions. I do not say how I will answer, if at all, to any of them; but the man I read you to be will find in this opportunity I offer much of use to him. Ask, then."

Jami's mind raced. He had thought no further than the fact that al-Birain was here in town, which to Jami was now home territory. There had been no time to plan the means by which he might make the sheik pay at last for what his malice had caused him to order done to Sati.

Jami had heard vaguely of occult calculations that could be made from the letters of a person's names but had paid little attention to what had been said then. Still, if this Mir Akbar was willing to be at all forthcoming in his answers, valuable information might be gained. What Jami's heart wanted most was the chance to rob al-Birain in proportion as the sheik had robbed Sati of life and Jami, himself, of Sati. Killing the sheik was not practical. Al-Birain's whole tribe would be out for Jami's life if it ever became known he was the killer; and that fact would be hard to hide, since there would be no reward in doing whatever he was about to do to al-Birain unless at least al-Birain knew who had done it—and it would be difficult to fulfill that requirement and keep Jami's hand in the sheik's death hidden from those who would automatically avenge him.

But if Jami could just frustrate al-Birain in what the other wanted most, preferably of something he wanted almost as much or more than life itself . . .

"Very well," said Jami, "and I thank you for the offer, Mir Akbar. Tell me, with your amazing wisdom and insight, what is it al-Birain wants, more than anything else?"

Mir Akbar laughed silently, his belly jiggling his sash up and down.

"It doesn't take a magician to tell you that," he answered. "Any astute man who knows the Dar al-Islam as a whole can tell you—though of course I can tell you more, being able to look into the minds of men. What al-Birain wishes is what he has wished for, for a long time—to make himself Sharif of Mecca and control the holy places."

Jami sat for a moment, chagrined. This was not the information he wanted. He himself, as first a slave, then a free leader of warriors under the sheik, had come to understand as much about al-Birain. What he needed was information he could not otherwise discover, information useful here and now.

"Let me put that another way," he said, "what does al-Birain seek here in 'Ayla, on this visit?"

"Two!" Mir Akbar held up two fingers. "Two questions gone, Jami al-Scoci. Now you have asked information that only such as I could give you. The desert sheik has come to 'Ayla in search of one thing only, one thing he greatly desires to help him in becoming Sharif and to satisfy his own pride of self. That thing is at this moment the most valuable thing in 'Ayla, and al-Birain does not yet have it in his possession."

He stopped speaking and smiled wickedly at Jami.

"You haven't told me what that thing is," Jami said.

"Nor will I," said Mir Akbar, "unless you make it your third question to me."

"That's hardly fair," said Jami. "It seems to me that my last question required you to tell me what it was."

"Did I not say I did not promise even to answer?" countered Mir Akbar. "It's up to you to ask if you want to learn."

Jami shrugged.

"Very well," he said. "What is this thing; and why is it so valuable to al-Birain?"

"A double question." Mir Akbar shook a finger at Jami. "But out of the goodness of my soul I will answer both parts anyway. If you should go to the House of the Flowery Brotherhood in this city; and if you could pass all their guards to a small room hidden in the walls behind where the magic automatons play their music so that those of the Brotherhood may dance themselves into what they conceive to be a holy state of transport—fools that they are, for the magic that makes the automatons play better even than men inspired robs these worshipers of strength each time they dance—but that is neither here nor there."

He paused to sip from his small cup of sweet coffee.

"If," he went on, "you could so pass to the room I mention, entering the passageways behind the music platform and always keeping to the left as you go, you would encounter great danger, of course, but you also might come at last to the chamber that holds what the Brotherhood wishes to sell to al-Birain for riches that have given even him pause at the price—the White Flower of Passion."

"The White Flower of Passion?" Jami stared at him. "And that is—what?"

"Not what, Jami al-Scoci," said Mir Akbar, wiping his lips. "Who. Though in truth she is neither woman nor thing, but something of both; a work of magic beyond the imagination of all but the greatest of us in the Inner Science.

Have you never heard of her? There are desert tribes that think of her as a talisman, the possession of which means that her owner may successfully achieve anything he desires—certainly to be Sharif of Mecca if he wishes; and it is the allegiance of those tribes that al-Birain needs to further that ambition. Also—it is said that possession of the White Flower, who is lovely beyond any man's dreams, confers on that man a potency with women such as has never been seen in any individual otherwise. The workers of Ebal obtained her. The Brotherhood of the Flower got her from their Mother House in Persia, who obtained her from where and how even I do not know. They had hoped to use her to gain converts; but she has been little use in that effort. Which is not to be surprised at—magic and religion always work badly together, for reasons beyond the understanding of anyone less than a Master of the Inner Science.''

''What is she—it—then?''

''Ah, you may well ask. She began existence as a very rare flower—but there are correspondencies between flowers and women, which again are not understood by the common minds—a rare flower, one of a kind that bloomed only once in a thousand years. The flower she was bloomed; and that bloom was made into a woman by one who was a greater magician even than myself—a magician so great I'll not even speak his name now, though he's been dead more than four hundred years. Most of the time, she sleeps. But when she wakes, no man can resist her.''

Mir Akbar's belly shook with silent laughter, again.

''Al-Birain,'' he said, ''grows old in spite of his ambition, and finds himself wearying more quickly than he used to in the arms of his women. In addition to what the White Flower will do for him in gaining the allegiance of the desert tribes I spoke of, he thinks the White Flower can make him young again. And so she can—and that is his personal reason for wanting her.''

"And," said Jami, "this flower-woman is in the House of the Brotherhood of the Flower, so you say."

"So I tell you. There is no doubt she is there. High as her price is, al-Birain could, of course, pay it, with the loot of a hundred caravans in his coffers. But he is of the desert and used to taking what he wants, rather than buying it; though as a good Sufi Muslim, his word—once given—is as carved in rock."

"Interesting," said Jami, thoughtfully. "Yes, I know his word is good. His *word*—" Jami emphasized his last utterance "—was good, even to me, even as a slave and infidel."

"Do you not want to know more about the Flower of Passion?" There was a note of something very close to malicious humor in Mir Akbar's voice. "I will tell you more. The White Flower sleeps except when she's needed. She wakes only when the Veil of Time is wrapped around her. Once wakened, she'll stay awake until the man she's with falls asleep. It's a mistake to wake her lightly. She has only one purpose with a man, and no one can resist that purpose, no matter what else might be threatening at the moment."

"Is that so?" said Jami.

"It is so. What complicates matters is the fact that the Veil of Time has many appearances. It can look like any piece of cloth, old or new, ragged or whole, clean or dirty."

"I see," said Jami. "So how would one recognize this Veil of Time, when one sees it?"

Their eyes held each other across the coffee cups, dark brown locked in gaze with bright blue.

"It will have the warmth of living flesh, when you touch it," said Mir Akbar, almost in a whisper. "And now, Jami al-Scoci, you have had answers enough in return for whatever good fortune you can bring one who befriends you. I will tell you no more."

Jami nodded.

"Thank you for what you have already told me, Mir Akbar," Jami said, rising. "And I will carry to Umar al-Hafiz the welcome news you gave me about the spell on his strongbox now being repaired."

"Don't forget to tell him I will be in tomorrow to pick up the emerald he owes me as payment," said the magician.

Jami went out.

The sunset had died while he was inside. Above, the sky still held some light to the west; and to the east, a few stars were beginning to be seen. But the streets were already dark. He turned toward home.

When he came at last to the small house he rented from Umar, the upper of its two storeys was bright with lights against the now full dark of the evening. He stretched his long right arm through the opening between the last two of the vertical iron bars reinforcing the courtyard gatedoor, to lift the heavy latch bar with the one powerful fingertip that could reach it in that position—his own version of a pick-proof lock—and let himself in. As he silently approached the outside stairs to the second floor loggia, he heard Lukas de Finistere playing on some stringed instrument and singing. Of course, Butterfly and Light-of-Pearl would have talked the minstrel into entertaining them. He was someone they could listen to for hours; not only with the pleasure usually felt by his audiences, but with the appreciation of fellow professionals. Jami cocked an ear to the words Lukas was singing in his rich baritone.

> *I love a maid, I love a ghost,*
> *And the two are not the same . . .*

They were lines from the *Song of Tyfel*, the half-man who lives at once in both the real and the unreal worlds.

Jami paused in the dark of the garden. The damp breath of the fountain cooled his face. Between the light coming from the bedroom windows behind them and the lampstand they had brought out onto the loggia, his friends were clearly visible. A turquoise linen caftan and orange velvet cap set off Lukas' olive skin and gleaming black hair. Butterfly and Light-of-Pearl were clad in open-fronted gowns of gaudy pink and gold printed cotton over narrow dark-green trousers. Their brass jewelry glinted as bright as gold.

The girls perched—there was no other word for it, they were so small and light—on two separate cushions, listening, caught up in the song. Even their fans were still as they watched the minstrel strum his crook-necked lute. It was strange that they, so tiny and beautiful, should always prefer the most grim and bloodthirsty of the songs in Lukas' repertoire.

Jami stood where he was, waiting. The rich scent of damask roses wafted around him. To go up now would interrupt the song, which was almost over, anyway; and, in truth, there was a pleasure for him in standing like this, invisible to them, watching the closest thing to a family he had here in 'Ayla.

It was strange, he thought, watching, the way life had drawn the four of them together. Possibly less strange insofar as he and Lukas were concerned, for both were misfits— Jami a prince exiled from his Highland home, and the minstrel a crusader's son by a Levantine woman. But blue eyes called to blue. They had both recognized the other as having an inner self which the world at large seldom suspected; and they both shared a hidden ear for a trumpet call that passed unheard by most men and women.

But in the case of Butterfly and Light-of-Pearl, it had been sheer chance that had led Jami to them. He had only stepped into the booth of a dancing master on a moment's whim to watch a performance. But that visit had ended with him picking up the dancing master in both hands. The only reason he had set that cold and greasy man back down alive was because of that still place in the back of his mind that never abandoned him. It had pointed out just in time that while it was one thing for him to take the two young girls away from such an owner, it was another thing to keep them, without a bill of sale that showed they were rightfully his. So the dancing master had written the invoice to Jami's dictation, and ended by losing half the price Jami was ready to pay him—and almost his life for a second time—by mistakenly assuming that the infidel could not read.

But finally, with the bill of sale tucked in his sash and carrying one of the girls on each arm like children, Jami had brought them home. They had been so drilled, almost from birth, that they had become like little automatons, whose only concept of life was to be of service to some master. But gradually, as the days passed, he watched the individuality kindle in their eyes and spread out through their small bodies, as they became persons for the first time in their existence.

They had been sold as twins to the dancing master when they were young children. But as they grew up it became obvious that twins they were not—and that may have been one of the reasons for the dancing master's continuing cruelty and anger toward them—though they were remarkably alike. It was only when you looked closely enough to see the slight mongoloid fold above the eyes of Light-of-Pearl that the differences between them became obvious. Otherwise, they were both dark-haired, and brown-eyed, with heart-shaped faces and beautiful, slim and incredibly strong small bodies, with muscles that were the product of their dance training. Legally they were accounted Nestorian Christians, and now belonged to Jami as slaves—but they had no idea of their own ages or anything about their own history. Jami guessed them to be somewhere between fourteen and seventeen years of age.

Once they had come to life as people, he had awakened one day to discover that they owned him—not he, them, but the other way around. It was an unexpected development, but not an unhappy one; and it had made things even better when it turned out that Lukas had a kindness for them, too.

In many ways, I'm a lucky man, thought Jami. For a moment he forgot everything but the warmth of the present moment that enclosed him; and then, like a snake in a garden, a certain memory stirred hungrily in him once more. He thought of al-Birain, went up the stairs and entered the loggia.

Lukas broke off the *Song of Tyfel* at his appearance. The two girls jumped to their feet and came to him. Still seated on a pile of cushions, the minstrel struck a different chord and began another song in Norman French.

> *Far to the north, in the berg-country,*
> *Where walks the Broken Bear—*

It was *The Death of the Brothers*, the rousing old ballad he and Jami had put to use as a drinking song. It had become a custom between them that it should be sung at least once on any of the occasions when they drank together; and, in fact, Butterfly was already on her way now downstairs to the cupboard to fetch another bottle and wine-cup. Pearl had already gone into the master bedroom to bring out an ewer and basin that Jami would use to wash up.

As they settled down to their drinks, Jami grinned at his friend.

"What brings you here? I heard you were looking for me. Tahmasp at the coffeehouse said so."

"How'd you like to get away from 'Ayla for a while?" Lukas answered.

"Get away?"

"Out on the Red Sea," nodded the other. "It seems I've won a small ship in a late dice game with some shipowners down by the docks, last night—and it struck me, now that the hot season is upon us, that it'd do none of us any harm to find a place away from these dusty streets and baking rooftops. With this boat we could go for a sail up the coast to the Gulf of Suez, or else all the way down to the Yemen; then if we find a pleasant spot away from the wind and all, we can simply anchor for a few days and get the taste of town out of our throats. I broached the idea to my own lady this morning and she liked it. I told her I wanted to invite you, Light-of-Pearl and Butterfly, to make up the party.''

"And she agreed?" Jami stared at his friend. "I thought she didn't approve of me."

"Nonsense," said Lukas, drinking deeply. "She thinks you're a good influence on me."

Jami stared at him.

"Zulayka Ten Dinars thinks that?"

"Zulayka?" Lukas frowned. "No, no, Shirin's the lady I love."

"When did it become Shirin?"

"Oh, sometime since. Zulayka never did understand how a minstrel has to be continually on the move. Besides, you should see Shirin. To see her is to be enchanted by her. And such generosity, too." His fingertips brushed new gold earrings. "But now, how about this cruise in my new boat?"

Jami opened his mouth and saw Butterfly and Light-of-Pearl watching him, eagerly. They would like a holiday like the one Lukas was proposing—and God knew they deserved some such enjoyment. But then, like a deep-seated throbbing, the hollowness that was the madness where al-Birain was concerned woke once more within him.

"Let me think about it," he said. "Give me a night or so to sleep on it . . ."

"All right," said his friend. "Take a night and a day if you like. But let me know the day after tomorrow. Shirin's eager to leave; and I must say, so am I."

They drank and talked and sang. Time went by. Butterfly and Light-of-Pearl disappeared into the bedroom, leaving the two men alone together.

"Do you know the place of Sulayman Tufeek very well?" Jami asked the minstrel.

"I've been invited there twice," Lukas nodded. "Just as far as the rooms of the main floor and his garden—marvelous place. And I speak as one who's been chased out of the loveliest gardens—and other rooms—from Damascus to al-Qahira."

"You heard that al-Birain just rode into town?"

"The Sheik of the Two Wells?" The minstrel nodded again. "I heard the news this afternoon, from a Persian magician, just as I was leaving al-Farsi's to come here. That's a man to stay clear of."

"The magician?" said Jami, and his eyes became thoughtful. "Perhaps you're right."

"Not the magician," said Lukas. "The man is a windbag."

"Or a very clever man pretending to be a windbag," answered Jami. "If he is what he claims he's at least a man with some wisdom; and the wiser the person the less likely to show you his true face without good reason."

"No, no. Forget the magician," said Lukas. "It was al-Birain I was speaking of—the desert sheik it would be wise to stay clear of."

"Come now," Jami looked up from his cup. "No one's too dangerous when the prize is worth it."

Lukas shook his head once more.

"These desert men aren't civilized. They're like wild animals. You never know when they'll turn and bite you. And if al-Birain weren't dangerous enough, Jami, there's that chief man of his, Ghaseem—the one they call Abu-al-Sikeen, the Father of Knives. Stay clear of them both, old friend."

Jami grunted wordlessly, drinking.

Lukas' eyes narrowed, gazing at Jami over his winecup.

"Why?" he said, quietly, "what is there between you and this sheik?"

"Who said there was anything between us?" answered Jami and drank deeply again.

"I've seen that look on your face before—but only a few times before," said Lukas. "There's something more here than just a passing interest in a visitor to 'Ayla or the possibility of some gain to you where this man is concerned."

Jami sighed and lowered the cup. He glanced about to make sure neither of the girls was entering the room with something more for them in the way of food or drink. He lowered his voice.

"I was once his slave."

"His slave!" Lukas stared at him. "I can see why you might have cause not to love him."

Jami shook his head.

"For a slave, the life wasn't bad," he said. "I'd been the chief guard on a caravan al-Birain's tribe attacked. I was wounded and they left me for dead; then I came to, hours later, half empty of blood, out of my wits, and hunting the enemy—any enemy. I got as far as al-Birain's tent and almost to his feet before I fell from weakness, so little they were expecting me. Al-Birain was impressed."

"So he took you as a slave warrior for his own use?" said Lukas.

Jami nodded, drinking deeply again—this time not to hide the expression on his face but because he felt the need of wine, remembering the ending of the story.

"And—?" Lukas urged him on. "Tell me the rest of it—unless it's something you'd rather tell no one."

"Of all men in Islam, I'll tell you—but only you," said Jami. "It's briefly enough told, anyway. I pleased him. I came to lead his fighters. He freed me by way of reward and gave me a slave of my own. Her name was—"

"Was?" prompted Lukas, for Jami's voice had thickened and stopped.

"Was Sati," said Jami.

"I see." Lukas' eyes closely watched his friend. "And you came to love her, this slave named Sati?"

"You're perspicacious," said Jami, drinking.

"Who," said Lukas, spreading his hands expressively, "knows more of love than I? Possibly somewhere there may be a man or two who knows as much; but who knows more? You loved her, then?"

"She . . . she wasn't much taller than either of the girls here." The words came from Jami with a rush, now that he had opened his lips on this secret at last. "But she was slim. Her bones were like the bones of a bird, and her face was brown, her hair was black. She was too small and light to do the tasks they put her to about the camp—she'd been captured from one of the caravans I had led the taking of. Her eyes were brown and large and beautiful. She was a gentle creature, in God's eyes—for all she never knew God and prayed to idols all her life."

"And al-Birain gave her to you by way of reward?"

"At the same time he freed me," said Jami. "Now that I was a free man, he said, I needed servants of my own. She was all those servants rolled into one. It didn't help her with the bedouiyyat—the women of the camp. They thought of a thousand cruel and spiteful things to do to her because she was a pagan. And she had to be with them all the time except when I was in camp and free to spend time with her. I couldn't protect her from them . . . only at night, when I held her in my arms. And she used to tell me . . ."

He broke off again, his throat closing at the memory.

"She used to tell me it was worth it—our nights together."

"Ah," said Lukas, "she loved you, too."

"Yes."

Jami drank. "You've got a head for drink like the solid oak these Muslims know nothing about," said Lukas. When Jami had begun to recall his days with al-Birain, they had slipped out of Arabic into Norman French; nonetheless, Lukas lowered his voice as he made his reference to

"Muslims." "Still, suppose you drink a little slower—at least until you've told me all of this."

"In God's name! Who are you to tell me how I should drink?" said Jami harshly, pouring yet more wine down his throat. "How do you know how I feel?"

"I know what it is to love—and to hate," said Lukas, softly. "Drink as you wish, then. We will not quarrel tonight, brother-at-arms."

Jami drank. The wine seemed to do nothing for him but feed the savageness in him. He woke to the fact that Lukas was once more speaking to him. "How did al-Birain give you cause to hate him so, then?" Lukas was asking.

Jami took a deep breath.

"Not lightly. My life working and fighting for him was good—I said that, didn't I? But Sati suffered so, I made up my mind to take her away from the tribe. For that, I had to wait until I had the chance to do something which would make al-Birain let me choose my own reward. He was never ungenerous and his word was always good."

"So people say," murmured Lukas.

"It's true enough—in its own way," said Jami. "When the chance came and I named what I wanted, it was something he didn't expect and didn't like; but he'd set me free to choose what I wished. I told him I was growing slower as a fighter, that I'd grown weary of battle. I wanted to settle down in some town and make a peaceful life there. What could he say? He had made me a free man. There was nothing he could do but let me go—unless he wanted to violate that word he was so proud of keeping."

Jami lifted his wine cup again to his lips, but this time the wine tasted strangely sour and unwelcome. He set it down again after having only wet his lips.

"He said how sad he was to lose me; but he promised I should go, with his blessing and with gifts. He only asked that I do one more task for him before I left. It was a small thing, a raid after some horses stolen from us by the Qutayba tribe—''

The glass winecup cracked in Jami's grasp. He let go of it just before the razor-edged shards sliced the flesh of his hand, and they fell to the carpet. Jami stared down at the puddled remnants of red wine soaking into the red threads of the carpet, dully.

''When I got back,'' he said, after a long moment, ''I did not see Sati as I rode into camp, although she was always out waiting for me. Fool that I was, I only thought that she had been put to some job that kept her from being there. I went on to al-Birain to report the horses recaptured, together with arms and other loot from the Qutayba fighters guarding them. He welcomed me, he gave me tea, he told me again how sorry he was to see me leave him—and he gave me gifts. Money, clothes, horses—and, last but not least, he gave me Jihan.''

''Who was Jihan?''

''Jihan?'' Jami pulled himself back from the memory with an effort. ''She was a beauty, as these Bedouin see beauty; the pick of a recent caravan we'd overrun, and al-Birain's special pet until then. 'To show how much I love you,' he told me, 'to show all men how much you are beloved by the Sheik of the Two Wells, I give you what is closest to my own heart, this gem of beauty . . .' And he smiled at me. 'It is not meet,' he said, 'that one so loved of his sheik should go into exile in the cities served only by an ugly brown woman. I have given you Jihan, therefore, that all may realize you were a man of consequence as my leader in battle.' ''

Jami reached for the carafe of wine and drank from its neck.

''It was then, for the first time, I began to be afraid. I remembered how I hadn't seen Sati on my way to his tent. I protested—politely, of course. I told him the gift was too much for me. He waved everything I said aside, as if I was only being modest; and I played my last card. I quoted the old saying about two women under one roof, that it was best to have either only one, or the four wives that their Prophet Mohammed allows.''

Jami stared at the carafe.

"It was then that he told me—and for the first time I realized—suddenly—that this was his way of paying me off for daring to leave him at my own wish, rather than his. I protested. I said he was being too generous, because I smelled a trap. But he only acted as if I was being properly modest and, at last, I ran out of words—''

Jami beat his fist on his knee in fury and remorse.

'' 'True,' he said, 'but one woman and an infidel should not do badly. Two, now, would indeed have brought trouble under your roof. Therefore I have ridded you of that all but useless slave I gave you earlier. I've ordered her throat cut.' ''

Jami paused for the space of several long breaths.

"He was watching me as he said that. He was waiting to see what I would do when he told me. But I had seen it coming, and something like steel had taken over in me. I was ready for him; and I smiled back at him.

'' 'My sheik thinks of everything,' I said. 'Great is your wisdom, al-Birain.' But I did not fool him.''

"Are you sure?" asked Lukas.

"I'm sure," Jami said. "He knew, they all there knew, how I had felt about Sati. And he knew me. I come from a cold, hard land, where we can wait for the moment to pay back an injury. He knew me well enough to know that much about me, as well. It would be beneath him to fear me, so he's let me live and prosper here in 'Ayla these past years. But he knows—he knows how I feel and how I wait for the moment that'll one day come.''

He stopped speaking. This time Lukas was silent. The minstrel drank thoughtfully.

"I saw her on my way out of camp," Jami said. "I saw

her as I rode out with my horses, my gifts—and Jihan. I passed by the midden heap where they had flung her body—they were to move camp in a day, in any case—and I could not even stop my horse for a moment or get down from it to hold her for one last time in my arms, before I left her to the vultures that were already circling above. He must have waited to kill her until word came that I'd been sighted riding back toward the camp, so that I'd be forced to see her for that last time almost as if she was still alive.''

"And now," said Lukas, "you plan to do something to pay him back, now that you have him here in 'Ayla.''

"Wouldn't you?" said Jami.

Lukas sighed.

"God be my guard," he said heavily. "I would. But I could still wish you'd put all this from you and come away as I suggested in my new boat.''

"Later," said Jami. "After.''

"If there is an after," said Lukas. "Only remember, Jami, there are those who care for you and would not be happy to see you butchered and made into small pieces by desert blades.''

Jami nodded thoughtfully—not so much as one who agreed, than as one who took the matter under advisement.

They continued to drink and talk the evening away, until the moon was high in the sky, and Lukas was due to meet his lady-love. Jami saw him out through the front gate and barred it again behind him. Butterfly and Light-of-Pearl were already asleep. He went, not in through the door to his bedroom, but directly to the ground-floor storage room and unlocked its door.

In a corner he found what he was looking for, a length of rope strong enough to hold the weight of a man like himself, with a three-pronged grapnel at its end. He uncoiled and carefully recoiled the rope; and carried it, with its attached grapnel, to just inside the ground-floor door. Then he went out and locked the door again behind himself.

Having done this, he went back upstairs and to bed. As he had suspected, Butterfly and Light-of-Pearl were deeply asleep. Moonlight through the lattice windows cast a grid of shadows across their still forms. He threw himself down on the mattress, feeling again the bite of memory and the bitter loneliness that seemed to grow out of it. He raised himself on one elbow, half-tempted to wake the girls for company, then thought better of it. It was only a foreboding born of the dark hours, he told himself, that had made him suddenly aware of the need to feel their living bodies close beside him, despite the heat.

He woke sometime in the morning to a sound of hammering on the courtyard gate and a voice shouting his name. Growling, he sat up on the edge of the bed and rammed his legs into his trousers. He stepped out of the upstairs entrance door to see the girls in the courtyard already, at the gate but not touching it, staring up at him for directions.

He looked down past them from the advantage of his higher position, and saw three desert men in the street.

"Who're you?" he shouted down to them. "What do you want?"

The largest of the three lifted his face to answer. Jami saw a long, heavy-boned visage with a savage beak of a nose.

"I am Ghaseem!" he called back. "Ghaseem, whom some call Abu-al-Sikeen! Are you Jami the Infidel?"

"Would you be knocking at my gate if you didn't know who I was?" Jami yelled back. He was still only half-awake, and his tone was acid. "I asked you what you wanted."

"The great Sheik al-Birain wishes you to come talk to him, man!" called the one who had identified himself as Abu-al-Sikeen. "Come! We'll take you to him."

"I'll be there in an hour—two hours," said Jami.

"The Sheik al-Birain tells you to come now."

"Two hours or not at all. Now, clear out of here," said

Jami; "and tell the sheik I'm coming. I'll see him at the house of Sulayman Tufeek, two hours from now."

Even across the distance that separated them, his eye was caught by the way Abu-al-Sikeen grinned up at him, savagely.

"May you enjoy life for as long as you live it, man!" shouted the other, and led his two companions off.

Jami went back upstairs and finished dressing. He came down to eat the breakfast of figs and yogurt and flatbread, which by that time was ready and waiting for him on a table in the shade of the first floor portico. He had to face the gaze of two pairs of brown eyes drilling into him.

"Oh, Pearl," he said. "Will you go to Umar as soon as breakfast is over; and tell him I've spoken to the Persian magician, who has already cured the spell on the strongbox and will be in for his payment today. Also tell him I won't see him for a day or two. I've a little piece of business of my own to take care of."

Umar would not object. The little jeweler knew that the retainer Umar's brotherhood paid Jami for his occasional guarding duties was not enough alone to support him. It was understood between Umar and himself that he would supplement that income with other jobs from time to time. But Jami noticed that although Pearl had nodded, she and Butterfly were continuing to watch him relentlessly.

"It's nothing!" he told them, gruffly. "Just a small matter of business, I tell you! Let me eat in peace."

They stood quietly, but the eyes continued to watch him.

Free of the house and their regard at last, he went directly to the establishment of Sulayman Tufeek. The gates of its courtyard were open now, but a pocket guard of half a dozen desert warriors, with curved swords hanging scabbarded from their waist sashes, lounged just within; and when Jami would have entered, they barred his way.

"I'm Jami the Infidel," he said. "Your sheik wants to see me."

They said nothing. Neither did they stand aside. He

throttled down the quick anger—the too-quick anger, fanned in the day's dry wind—that rose inside him.

"Get me that chief man of your sheik—what's his name—Abu-al-Sikeen," he said. "He knows why I'm here!"

They conferred for a moment, then one of them went toward the house. Jami waited.

After several minutes, two figures came out into the courtyard. One walked like the guard that had just gone in, the other was a much larger man, and the outline of the large, hawk-like nose was barely visible in the shadow of his headcloth. The bigger man had a familiar grin that became visible as he got close to Jami.

"God has brought you, man!" he said, ironically. "Come with me. But first give me that sword you wear."

Jami drew his sword and passed it over, then followed the hooded man into the house. Once inside, they took a left turn and went through several small rooms paneled in gleaming tile to emerge into a large reception hall. For once Lukas had not exaggerated. This was the grandest room Jami had yet seen in the Islamic world.

From its high ceiling of carved and gilded beams hung oil lamps of enameled glass suspended to an arm's length above head height by brass chains. Tall arched windows filled with delicate latticework overlooked an inner garden courtyard beyond and swept down to padded benches along the side walls. The blue and white tiled floor was spread with bright floral rugs and cushions.

The room was full of desert tribesmen, a few seated cross-legged on the floor, others standing in small groups and talking softly. Serving boys moved among them bearing silver trays heaped with marzipan. The rosewater another lad was sprinkling from an iridescent bottle only made the reek of their wool-robed bodies seem worse to Jami's nose, now long accustomed to city, rather than country smells.

With the appearance of Abu-al-Sikeen and himself, the crowd parted slightly, enough so that Jami was able to see at the far end of the room a carpeted platform heaped with a multitude of pillows. It made a throne of sorts for two very dissimilar individuals. One was a rainbow-draped bulk of a merchant. Silken sleeves rippled, rings flashed on this man's gesturing hands. But what held Jami's eyes was the other occupant of the platform—Sheik al-Birain himself, his own garments simply but brilliantly white against the dark cabinetry behind both men. The sheik's parrot, now unhooded and fastened with a fine gold chain to a perch beside the platform, stared at Jami as he approached.

"Fool!" it shrieked, suddenly and raucously. "Fool! Fool!"

Jami had been expecting the sudden shove from behind; so that when it came, he swayed away from it and Abu-al-Sikeen almost stumbled to the ground with his missed effort. He recovered himself and his eyes burned above his fierce grin at Jami.

"Kneel to the sheik!" he said, under his breath. "Kneel, man!"

"I am a free man and a king's son," answered Jami, clearly. "I do not kneel."

His voice carried through the room. Conversation ceased. Neither Sulayman Tufeek, nor al-Birain had looked at Jami until this moment, even when the parrot had cried out. But now both looked.

"Infidel, you're facing the great Sheik al-Birain—" began Sulayman Tufeek. His voice stopped as al-Birain beside him held up one long-fingered hand.

In the patterned light from the tall, latticed windows striking directly down upon him, the narrow, lined, brown face of the Sheik of the Two Wells was clearly visible; and Jami read no expression in it at all.

"I'll talk alone to this man," al-Birain said.

Sulayman Tufeek got to his feet, bowed, stepped down from the platform and left. Everyone else in the room was now leaving, except for five armed tribesmen who stood by the platform. When the others were all gone, al-Birain spoke again, still looking at Jami but not addressing him.

"My sword," he said.

One of the guards left the room. He came back a moment later, carrying a great, two-handed sword whose blade was split halfway up its center like the tail of some steel fish. Al-Birain took it and balanced it across his knees. Jami stared at it. It looked too odd, too ornate, with its gold inlay and bejeweled hilt, too long and heavy, to be an effective fighting tool, but there was something about it that made his hands yearn to hold and swing it.

"You have never seen this before, Infidel," said al-Birain. "This is the sword of my ancestors." He ran his right hand along the length of the chased blade. "It was won in battle against false Believers and has been carried through many generations. Each owner of it has had it inscribed with his own words. It is not magic, but has great strength from the lives of those who've carried it."

His dark eyes went to the sword, then moved upward from the blade to meet Jami's.

"Do you understand?" he asked.

Jami bent swiftly and when he came up again there seemed to be a small piece missing from his right boot. In his hand was a short, broad-bladed black knife with a hilt of the same texture and color as the dark cloth of the boot-top. The sworded guards swayed toward him with one accord, but al-Birain held up his hand and they stopped.

"Children," said the sheik, calmly, looking around at them, "what can harm me when the Grandfather of Swords is in my hands?"

"The knife in my hands," said Jami, "is the knife of my ancestors, passed down from father to son longer than anyone can remember. Like your sword, it has great strength, which I can feel when I hold it like this. I can also feel the strength in the sword you hold. As you say, it's not magic but the courage of the men who've used them, stained into the blades over many lifetimes.''

The sheik nodded.

"We understand each other,'' he said, ''and since such weapons as these with great life in them are in our hands, perhaps we can speak openly to each other. I've learned that there's something I want, something I have a right to, here in 'Ayla, and a certain magician's told me that perhaps you're the man to help me to it.''

Jami looked into the expressionless face above the neatly trimmed beard.

"Would the magician have been Mir Akbar?''

"Since the Grandfather of Swords is in my hands,'' said al-Birain, ''I'll answer you plainly. It was Mir Akbar. He told me about you yesterday morning, not knowing I knew you, when I had him come to advise me on a matter. He said that for my present need only you could be sure to fulfill it. He seemed wise.''

"I believe him wise,'' said Jami.

"I, too, otherwise I would not have consulted him,'' said al-Birain. ''As I've told you, there's something I want. If you'll fetch it for me, I'll reward you in proportion to the task.''

"It's regrettable, but I've tasks already here in 'Ayla that leave me no time for other work,'' said Jami.

"This is no ordinary work,'' said al-Birain. ''There's a woman who belongs to me, a woman I want you to bring back to me from those who hold her.''

There was a moment of silence in the large room. The sunlight from the tall windows struck down on them all, glinting on the great double blade of the Grandfather of Swords, on the knife in Jami's hand, on the sword hilts protruding from the blue velvet scabbards of the guards and their dark eyes above the hilts, watching and listening closely.

Jami slowly stooped to put the knife back into his boot

and straightened up again. He looked deliberately right and left at the guards.

The right hand of the sheik lifted from the double blade with its inscriptions in Arabic and waved the guards back. As they retreated, he beckoned to Jami. Jami stepped forward until their two faces were only inches apart; and al-Birain spoke, lowering his voice so that the guards could not hear.

"Can't what stands between us be put aside?" he asked in a voice barely more than a whisper. "So that you can serve me one more time as you served me still in the desert, after I freed you?"

Jami answered as softly.

"The God of the peoples of the Book knows what stands between thee and me," he said. "He does not forget—no more do I."

Al-Birain nodded slightly.

"Then you'll not do this thing for me?"

"I didn't say that," Jami replied. "I'll do it, but only under certain conditions and for a special price."

"And what would that be?" The sheik's eyes were steady on Jami. "There's a limit to the gold and silver anyone owns, but within those limits, I'll pay any reasonable price."

"No gold. No silver," said Jami. "My fee is to be your protection in any place where you would ordinarily extend it, whenever I or mine are there—and I want you to swear that on the souls of your sons."

There was a little, almost unhearable inbreath from the lean face above the neatly trimmed gray beard. Al-Birain's eyes changed.

"A Sheik of the Two Wells does not swear on the souls of his sons," he said.

"This one will have to," said Jami, still under his breath, but grimly, "or I'm not for hire."

Al-Birain sat. No one in the room moved or spoke. The

heartbeats in Jami's chest counted the seconds as they passed. Finally, al-Birain stirred a little and spoke.

"Then I'll swear on the souls of my sons that once you have brought me this woman and all else that belongs to her, then you and yours shall have the protection of me and mine when you and they are in any place where my power runs."

"It is sworn?" said Jami, for he had bargained with desert people before this.

"It is sworn now," said al-Birain.

Jami took a breath in his turn.

"Then tell me what you want me to get for you," he said, "and where I'll find it."

"Do you know the dwelling place of the Flowery Brotherhood?"

"Yes," said Jami. "It's to the west of this house, in this same quarter of the city."

"Yes," said al-Birain. "They only came to 'Ayla a few years ago, but they have attracted powerful supporters. Their influence grows."

"So I've heard," said Jami.

Al-Birain's gaze was on the windows, going past Jami.

"They have a dream," he said, "of bringing their message to all True Believers in God. As part of that dream, in their *khaniqah* here they've hidden a woman who belongs to me. You'll find her in a secret room behind the great hall where their public services are held. She'll be under a spell, asleep. Don't try to wake her. Bring her to me as she is."

Jami stood for a moment, as if in thought.

"You say this woman is yours, and I've no reason not to believe you," he said. "But even if she is, the laws here won't forgive me for going illegally onto another's property to get her back, even if once you've got her back they let you keep her. The only thing that could save me if they hear of this, would be if it turned out I had some right to go in after her."

"But you have," said al-Birain. "The ancient laws of our tribe say, 'where I sit, there I establish my house.' I sit here now in this walled quarter, therefore this quarter is my house. If I send you into a room in my house to bring me my property that is there, the responsibility for that doing is mine alone, not yours."

"Yes," said Jami, "but will you bear that responsibility if I'm arrested and brought into a court of law for doing this for you?"

Al-Birain stared with unmoving eyes at him.

"I will bear it before any court of law. You will be guiltless."

"I see," said Jami. "And will you swear that on the souls of your sons?"

"It is sworn," said the sheik. "Here is my house and all things done by my order in it are my responsibility."

"All right," said Jami. "Then I'll get her for you. Can you give me a map of the temple to show me where the secret room is?"

"The Father of Knives will give you one," said al-Birain. "Also, be sure not to wrap her in the cloth you'll find there with her, lest the spell escape; otherwise we won't be able to wake her. You will know it from all other cloths by the fact that it will be warm—as warm as living flesh to the touch. It and she must be examined by a magician like your Mir Akbar before we can wake her safely. Bring it and her to me; and what I've sworn will be so. How soon can you get her for me?"

"As soon as I can," said Jami. "The time it'll take is going to be the time it takes to do it, in the way I choose to do it. A day. Perhaps several days."

"Whether you have her or not, come back to me in three days."

"In three days, then," said Jami.

He went out, escorted back to the gate by Abu-al-Sikeen. Out of the corner of his eyes, he studied the large desert dweller, noting several slits in the cloth of the other's robe that seemed to have no purpose, unless they were there to allow him access to knives concealed within. At the gate, Abu-al-Sikeen handed him a map of the interior of the Brethren's compound.

"God attend your success, man," the sheik's lieutenant said. Jami looked into the headcloth-shadowed face of the other to read the expression there; but this time Abu-al-Sikeen seemed simply and wholeheartedly to mean what he was saying.

Jami went back toward his own place. Time had gone by since he had left it this morning, and it was nearly noon. A short morning—but then he had slept later than usual after drinking the evening away with Lukas. As he came up the stairs, he heard the sounds that meant Light-of-Pearl was throwing things about in the kitchen. Because of their early stage training, both girls could throw even small and simple objects with a force and accuracy that was literally deadly. A few pots and pans bounced off the kitchen wall harmed nothing. But they testified to a major upset.

"What's Pearl's trouble?" Jami asked Butterfly, who was sitting, embroidering the hem of a scarf she was making for herself, in the portico outside the kitchen.

"She's angry with Mir Akbar," said Butterfly, sadly, "and it's my fault."

Translated in the light of Jami's experience, this meant that Light-of-Pearl was incensed over something that the Persian sorcerer had done to Butterfly. The two girls had had no one but each other to cling to for so long that they were inseparably paired on any emotional situation that involved either one of them.

But it was typical that Light-of-Pearl should be the one throwing kitchen utensils. She was the tougher of the two and grimly protective of Butterfly.

"What was it Mir Akbar did to you?" Jami asked Butterfly, now. "And when?"

"He stopped by here while you were gone," said Butterfly, shyly.

"But what did he do?"

"Oh, nothing—really."

"Pearl!" roared Jami; and Light-of-Pearl emerged from the kitchen primed and ready for action. "What happened when Mir Akbar came by this morning?"

"He said he wanted to see you. You told us yesterday he was one of the people we could let in, in the daytime."

"I did?" said Jami, who for the life of him could not remember doing any such thing. He chilled at the thought that the magician might have put a spell on him as they talked at the coffeehouse, to make him tell Butterfly and Light-of-Pearl such a thing without later remembering he had done so.

"Well, from now on, don't," Jami said. "When yesterday did I tell you this?"

"You said it last night, after Lukas left. So we let the magician in."

"And he left after just a little bit," put in Butterfly.

"Then what's wrong?" Jami demanded.

"Nothing!" said Light-of-Pearl. She went back into the kitchen and began throwing pans again.

"Will you tell me what happened?" Jami said to Butterfly.

"He just admired our flowers, that's all," answered Butterfly.

Both girls loved flowers, and the courtyard was surrounded by two armies of them, half cultivated by Butterfly and half by Light-of-Pearl, including everything that could conceivably be brought to blossom in 'Ayla.

"And he took some!" shouted Light-of-Pearl from the kitchen. "Just helped himself, after he'd said he was going to leave and after I'd left him there alone with Butterfly. Without even asking her, he just waded in and started picking!"

"And you didn't tell him not to?" said Jami to Butterfly. He sighed. "No, you wouldn't. But is it all that important—a few flowers?"

"It isn't. Really it isn't," said Butterfly, "and he meant well. He'd been interested in which flowers we liked best and those were the ones he picked: a pink rose from Pearl's bush, a yellow one from mine."

"Well, then?" Jami appealed to the open door to the kitchen.

"Maybe they weren't just any flowers!" Light-of-Pearl's voice flew back. "Maybe they were the best blossoms there—like 'Fly's largest rose. Maybe she had some plans of her own for it—how did he know? But did he ask? Did he try to pick them when I was there? Oh, no! He knew better than that!"

"Was there something special about the rose?" asked Jami, still following the light of his personal experience with previous situations.

"Ask her!" shouted Light-of-Pearl.

"Was there?" Jami said to Butterfly. "Well, was there?"

Butterfly began to cry, while trying hard not to. Her face got very tight and she held her mouth fiercely closed, but tears began to leak from her eyes.

"Yes, there was!" snarled Light-of-Pearl, appearing once more from the kitchen. "You weren't supposed to know. It was something for your birthday—now it's spoiled. She spent weeks trying to get a rose to bloom that big!"

Butterfly ran from the room.

Jami sat down heavily on a cushioned window ledge.

"All right," he said. "I'll go and talk to Mir Akbar."

"Talk!" cried Light-of-Pearl. "Why don't you let me go see him? Watch me talk to him!"

"No, you won't," said Jami, hastily. "Leave him alone, Pearl. Do you hear me? He must not have realized that the flowers were that important to you; and I'm sure I can get him to put the ones he took back on their stems and get them growing again by some magic or other—''

"It won't be the same thing," said Light-of-Pearl, "not to 'Fly. She was going to get up very early the morning of your birthday and pick the flowers at the last minute. It wouldn't be the same thing now that Akbar's handled it with his fat, greasy hands."

"Hell!" said Jami. "I'm sorry. Look, maybe I can think of something to make Butterfly feel better. But you leave Mir Akbar alone! You can't just throw a rock at him the way you might anyone else and get away with it. He's a magician and what he can do scares anyone."

"He doesn't scare me!"

"Well, he ought to. Anyway, you stay clear, and let me deal with him. I'll go talk to Butterfly."

He went into the back part of the house and found Butterfly curled up in the center of the big bed. He lay down next to her and put his arm around her; but for quite some time she did not respond. But finally she turned about and crept into his arms. He stayed with her until she fell asleep, then left.

Coming back into the main part of the living quarters, he found Light-of-Pearl, the tough one, crying quietly to herself in the kitchen. Sighing, he picked her up and took her with him to one of the big chairs in the main room; and sat there with her until she felt better. Little by little, the full story came out of her. The two of them had got it into their heads that Jami lived too much with violence and danger—a sense of guilt stirred in him as he heard that—and for his birthday they had made intricate plans for a day which should be all happiness and love. It was to begin with his being gently wakened to music and flowers; and it was this important first part of their plans that Mir Akbar had trampled roughshod across by helping himself to their choicest blossoms.

". . . after first asking us to find out just which ones they were!'' said Light-of-Pearl. "And now, there's no surprise to it. You know all about it.''

"I'll talk to him and see if he can't fix what he did,'' Jami said again. "And maybe we can come up with something else that'll work just as well as what you had planned. And meanwhile, how about this boat trip Lukas was talking about? Wouldn't the two of you like that?''

"Then you'll go?" Light-of-Pearl sat up straight on his lap. "You'll tell Lukas and we can go tomorrow?''

"Well, maybe not tomorrow . . .''

"Oh.''

"I've got something I've got to finish up—something I've got to do with this Sheik al-Birain that just came into town yesterday. But it can't take more than a day or two at most; and then we'll go. It's a promise.''

"You did say it now," said Light-of-Pearl. "That it was a promise.''

"It is. Now, get off and I'll go see about it. The sooner I get to it, the sooner it'll be done.''

Light-of-Pearl slid off him and stood up.

"You'll be back for dinner?''

"If I'm not back by sunset, don't wait for me," said Jami. "But I think so.''

He went out.

However, he did not get back for dinner. Half an hour before that time, he was entering the large double gates to the courtyard of the *khaniqah* of the Flowery Brethren, swathed in a desert dweller's robe and headcloth. It was the time of the sunset service called the Remembrance of God; and he had deliberately picked a moment in which the only others also passing through the compound were latecomers who would not be curious about a sight-seeing Bedouin. The *khaniqah* was not a mosque, which a Christian like himself might risk entering only on pain of possible capital punishment; but he had no wish to have himself identified by some other sight-seer from the regular populace of 'Ayla who might know and therefore recognize Jami al-Firanj.

His estimation of the situation had been correct. None of the other late-comers paid him any attention, but hurried, as he was pretending to hurry, on through the open doorway of the large domed hall where the service was already taking place. Once within, he found himself under the domed roof in a single large room which continued until it came up against a further wall of the building that housed the *khaniqah*'s more private quarters. It would be beyond that wall that he would have to search for the Flower of Passion— but he would be wise to make his move from this hall into that further section of the *khaniqah* quietly, and without haste that might attract attention. Better to wait until the dancing was at its height.

Those who were to dance were just entering now. Within the dome, two tiers of spectator galleries all but surrounded the dancing circle. Veiled women and small children filled the upper level, with men in the lower. Behind and all around them the upcurving walls of the dome were resplendent with interlaced, decorative calligraphy that suggested the shapes of flowers. Jami could read normal Arabic script, but not this; and, after a moment of trying to do so, he looked away. Strangely, it hurt his eyes to stare at it too long.

Dividing the two tiers of galleries was a decorated niche holding a platform on which stood a small group of men surrounding one in particular who had a long white beard. This bearded one would be the Pir, head of the religious community. Directly opposite him across the dancing circle was a dais extending forward from the back wall, its front guarded by a carved wooden railing and a painted wooden backdrop between that railing and the wall. In between railing and backdrop, four musician-figures made of brass sat cross-legged, playing respectively a tamborine, two different varieties of flute and a sort of lyre. They were dressed in actual clothes and wore fake beards. Hard enameled eyes glared down at the dancing circle as they played.

The dancers were just trooping in as Jami unobtrusively pushed himself among the semi-circle of men standing in the open space that remained between the galleries and the back wall bearing the dais with the automaton musicians. The dancers moved through a space opened for them as this crowd parted. Then they circled the floor three times, salaaming to the Pir as they passed him. After this, they threw off their blue Sufi coats, revealing white robes with sleeves so long they draped over and obscured their wearer's hands. They began to dance and whirl about to the music of the automatons. The pace increased, the ecstasy built and began to communicate itself to those standing and watching.

Jami felt it also; and his nerves, tight always when he was engaged in a venture like this, tightened even more. There was a sort of exhilaration that took him at moments of risk in any case—it had been that way ever since he had been a boy—something that tempted him to take chances he would not take ordinarily. Grown now, he was aware of the danger of this feeling; and the dancing and music were reinforcing it.

Quietly, he began to work his way bit by bit back through the crowd without drawing attention to his movement, and after a few moments he stood outside the crowd, in the shadow between the two stands. He slipped back even further, then began to drift along the outskirts of the crowd toward the back wall.

He reached it at last and his fingertips touching it felt through the tiles of its surface a vibration that rose and fell with the cadence of the music that the automatons were making. Around and within the dancing circle, the sighs and moans of the worshipers were rising to a babble of voices, crying out. He was now close to the side and back of the dais that held the musicians, itself.

There was space behind the dais and the backdrop. Ma-

chinery moved there, reaching arms through the lower part
of the backdrop to power the automatons. He moved along a
narrow space between the machinery and the wall; and
found, as the map given him by the Father of Knives had
shown, a small doorway set in the very wall itself.

He turned in through it and found himself in a tunnel-like
passage, its walls of plain, undressed stone and without the
elaborate tilework that had decorated the great hall. It bent,
apparently to his left, for the faint glow of a further light
showed around a curve perhaps thirty paces ahead. Jami felt
disappointment. Thirty paces was farther back than the wall
behind the automatons could be thick. Plainly this passage
would carry him beyond the secret room al-Birain had
mentioned. He went ahead, however, and around the further
bend in the tunnel came upon a cross-passage with a single
torch in a wallholder, lighting the intersection.

He half-closed his eyes, picturing where he must stand
now in relation to the hall he had left behind him. Placing
himself, he turned left down the intersecting corridor, listened a moment, heard nothing, and went in that direction.

He continued along the corridor, then turned left again on
a second intersecting way. He went on around two more
turns in this last tunnel—and abruptly stopped.

He had been growing more and more tense as he continued through these corridors without encountering a single
guard, or even one of the *khaniqah*'s inmates. The way he
followed was a suspiciously open one, if indeed it led to a
room where the Flower of Passion slept; and ways that were
open when they should not be so, in Jami's experience,
were almost always deliberately designed to lull an intruder
into carelessness. He stopped once more to listen.

He heard nothing.

He licked one finger, wet his nose and sniffed. After
more than a year in the smoke and stinks of 'Ayla, his sense
of smell had lost much of its normal acuteness. But the
exhilaration in him had the effect of heightening all his

physical senses, and perhaps some beyond the physical, for in this state his mind also raced and burned with a speed and clarity that came only at such times. Certainly, in this moment he might scent things that the ordinary city dweller would never notice. Now, as he sniffed, he smelled something that lifted the hairs on the back of his neck; though why it should do so, or what it was he scented, he could not tell. Whatever it was, his body recognized it enough to fear it instinctively. He continued, more slowly and cautiously; and came finally around one more bend in the passage to see an end to it, and light beyond that indicated a larger, open space into which the passage finally gave.

He moved up to the edge of the opening, keeping flat against the wall. The odor was plain now, a rank animal smell with something ugly and bitter about it. Softly, he withdrew his sword from its scabbard, hidden beneath his desert robe, and held it vertically up to flank the edge of the opening, so that it faced into the room.

He glanced down, using the highly polished blade like a crude mirror to look around the corner. In the bright metal he saw reflected something dark that—as far as he could judge—looked no larger than a medium-sized dog. As he watched its blurred shape, it moved.

He heard the rattle of a chain on stone and caught a glimpse in the sword-mirror of a golden, animal-like body flecked with silver, in a small room—barely a widening of the corridor lit by a torch in a wall bracket. Then he lost the image. He searched for it and found it again. The creature was facing away from him and would have looked something like a leopard in crouched position, ready to spring, if it had not been for the facts that the body seemed permanently formed into the crouching position, its muscles were bulky and enormous by comparison with a leopard's and it had a huge head with a massive mouth showing a glimpse of great canine teeth. Oddest of all, a white beard swept down and back from its lower jaw.

He had seen—in Europe before he had come to this land where the making of images was a religious crime—a drawing of a creature called a *sanaja*, made by a man who claimed to have journeyed to a mountainous eastern land called Tibet or Thibet, and seen the dead body of one there. The *sanaja* was supposed to be magic, in that like the basilisk, its glance could kill.

Jami squinted at the reflection in the blade, trying to figure out whether the creature—if it was a *sanaja*—was facing toward or away from him.

There was the sound of the chain being dragged on stone again as once more the creature changed position, and now Jami saw it in relation to the corner of the passageway behind which he stood.

For the moment, it was facing away.

Jami gripped the sword and stepped out to look around the corner directly. The creature was indeed facing away from him; and, as he had suspected, it was a *sanaja*.

This present moment might not come again. It was facing away from him and the room was small. He lifted his sword in both hands, took one long and silent step within, closed his eyes as the creature whirled to face him, and struck downwards in the direction he had already chosen.

It was one of the hardest blows he had ever made. The shock of the blade's hitting threatened to tear his arms loose from his shoulders. There was a thump, a rustle, and silence.

Cautiously, he opened his eyes a crack—and caught sight of golden, silver-spotted fur motionless against the dark stone floor. He opened his eyes a little wider; and saw in one quick glance, before averting his gaze again, that the *sanaja* was dead. It had to be dead for it lay facing away from him and was almost cut in two. He had struck farther back from the head than he had aimed, almost into the shoulder area; but he had shorn through the spine and most of the body, just the same.

Even dead now, the creature might have the power to kill

him or turn him to stone. Avoiding all direct sight of its now blankly staring eyes, he stepped around the body to the further wall, in which there was a heavy, wooden door bound with straps of black iron.

The door, when he tried it, was locked. But the large keyhole showed the lock to be not one of the most sophisticated of its kind. He reached in through a slit in his robe to the belt beneath it, for a small, toothpick-bladed dagger, and inserted its tip into the keyhole. Only a couple of minutes' work were needed for him to lift the tumblers. The door opened and he put the dagger away again. It was typical of the Brethren, he thought, that having set the *sanaja* in guard position, they had thought there was little need of further protection for this treasure of theirs.

He went in.

The room into which he stepped was hardly more than a cubicle. Three long paces each way would have measured its length and width. Its floor and walls were of the same undressed stone as the passageway he had just come through; and it was furnished with only a tabouret, or small table, holding what looked like an ivory cosmetic box sitting on some sort of gray dustcover flung carelessly over the tabouret, a thin mattress lying on the bare stone floor, and a large white candle in a candle-holder, set also on the floor. On the mattress itself lay what seemed to be a woman of less than twenty years of age, with long blond hair and dressed in a loose, white, ankle-length gown, uncovered and asleep.

The candle had the thickness of a woman's arm; and it burned apparently under the spell of some religious or other power, since it seemed not to have burned away any of its substance although the room's air had a musty smell as if it had not been opened in some time. The air, in fact, was not only musty, but cold; but the uncovered shape on the bed seemed to slumber in perfect comfort.

There was also something cold about the whole arrangement of the room—as if the figure on the bed was not that of a living creature, but simply some inanimate item to be carefully stored, for value's sake, but not responded to in any human way. Jami stepped to the side of the bed and looked down. The Flower of Passion was indeed beautiful. Jami had never seen anything like her. At the same time, sleeping as she was, she did not raise any response in him beyond what might have been evoked by a remarkable stone sculpture with her form. On impulse, he reached down and touched her face; and it was of the same temperature as the rest of the room.

He looked beneath her and saw that directly under her was a richly red bedcover. He reached down and took a fold of it between thumb and forefinger—but it felt like any other stuff of the same weight and texture. Beneath it lay two more cloths, the next one cream-colored and the bottom one midnight blue; but they, too, felt like normal cloth. He looked around the room and at first saw no other fabric until he realized he was looking right at the dustcover over the tabouret. Reaching out, he touched its thin grayness and his fingertips felt—not cloth, but the warmth of human flesh. He breathed out in satisfaction. Reaching in through a slit in his robe, he removed from around his waist another, smaller robe and hood like the one he himself was wearing. After thinking for a moment, he wrapped the gray cloth about his waist where he had carried the extra clothes.

The Flower of Passion continued to slumber undisturbed while he was doing this. It was strange to handle such a cold figure as if it was living—but when he checked the pulse in her throat, he felt a slow, steady heartbeat.

He put on her the extra hooded robe he had brought, covering her face carefully with the veil; and, after a moment's thought, he wrapped her in the red bedspread.

His original plan where al-Birain was concerned had been of the sketchiest—merely to frustrate the sheik in whatever the other wanted most. That, and to survive the doing of it.

He had for some time had in mind the service price he named for himself to al-Birain, protection for him and any belonging to him—since that was a first step in any revenge. Effectively, it stopped the sheik himself from taking a counter-revenge once he discovered what Jami had done to him—whatever that might turn out to be. But what it should turn out to be had been left in Jami's mind to be worked out later. He had planned only to take advantage of whatever chances should come up to frustrate al-Birain, trusting that such chances would come, or could be made to come.

Now, for the first time, the glimmer of a possibility had kindled itself in his mind. If he could deliver the Flower but somehow withhold the cloth that would wake her, he would have achieved what his soul longed to do. It might be that al-Birain would be swift enough to discover that the red bedspread was not the cloth he needed—but with luck not swift enough to do so until Jami was out of reach or in a position to remind the sheik of his oath on the souls of his sons. Certainly, the red bedspread looked more likely to be an important piece of fabric than the gray rag now around Jami's waist.

Picking up the Flower of Passion, he carried her out past the dead body of the *sanaja*, being careful not only to avert his own gaze but to hold her so that her face was shielded from the dead creature by Jami's body as they went past the dead destroyer. It might be that she, being of plant and magical origin, was immune to any remnant of the *sanaja*'s power to slay, but there was no point in taking chances. He started back down the passageways by which he had come.

His memory for routes like this was unthinking, a result of one part of his early training in which the older warriors of his homeland had made a half-serious game of trying to lose the young ones on hunting trips and cattle raids. What concerned him at the moment was not the finding of his way back to the main hall of worship, but the necessity of passing through the hall and that part of the temple between the hall and the street, without being stopped and questioned by some of the Brotherhood. The service had been close to its climax when he had left the hall. It would be over, or almost over, now, most of the worshipers would have left; and it was always just short of safety that the greatest danger lurked.

But, once more, he met no one in the corridors he went through; and this made him strain his eyes and ears all the more for any warnings of other human traffic. Granted that the *khaniqah*'s people had felt fully safe with the *sanaja* on guard, he was second by second more in violation of the odds that dictated he must run into someone from among the many people who must live and work in this place.

He was on the last twenty steps of the first leg of the passage into the wall when the dimly illuminated circle of the opening at the entrance to the hall was occulted by a figure wearing a beggarly patched blue coat like the one al-Muqla had been wearing. At the same time he heard the noisy sound of leather slippers on the stone floor of the passageway. A second later that sound had stopped and the dark shape before him had become still.

"*Ya sayyedi*—oh, my lord!" called Jami. "My lord, help me!"

He hurried toward the dark shape blocking the passageway before him and it backed away from him, out into the hall and the dim light provided there by the ceiling lamps lighting its vast space. The service, Jami saw, was apparently over, for the hall was now empty. Emerging into that light, just behind whoever it was he had just encountered, Jami saw that he was facing a man in his mid-forties, tending to fat and with a pouting, angry, and possibly frightened expression on his round face.

"What are you doing here?" snapped this individual.

"My lord—we need help, my sister and I. I've been looking everywhere—"

"What's the matter with you? You aren't supposed to be back here in the private quarters. Don't you know that?"

The other, Jami judged by the color and patching of his clothes, was not likely to be one of those in high authority within the *khaniqah* itself, but probably of about the same rank as al-Muqla. Jami continued to babble.

"But my lord, I—"

"Silence! There are no exceptions! You're in trouble now, my friend. Now, I'll have to call the guards."

"Yes, yes, call the guards or anyone you have to call, my lord," said Jami. "For me it doesn't matter, but my sister is dying. Please—please help her!"

He took a step forward toward the fat man.

"Feel how cold she is—"

The other recoiled.

"What's wrong with her? What're you two doing here?"

"Looking for the Pir, the holy Friend of God, to help us."

Jami took another step forward, and again the other backed up, his eyes on the still figure in Jami's arms.

"Help you? Why? What's wrong with her, I say? Stand still, there!"

"They call it the plague. It came to our village two months ago. People got sores all over . . . they had terrible pains, day after day. Finally they were worn out, and died. Everyone died. My sister's the last—"

Jami took another step forward, half-holding out the Flower, as if he would lay her in the arms of the other man. The other skittered backwards, covering his mouth with his hand and pressing himself against the wall of the passageway, pointing past himself, toward the hall.

"Don't touch me! Go that way! Do you hear me? No one can do anything for you—well, not now anyway. You'll have to go. Come back tomorrow! Come back tomorrow and our glorious Pir will save your sister, but not now! Do you hear me? Go!"

He jabbed his finger furiously at the front of the hall; and Jami let himself be herded to the hall entrance and out into the street. The minute he was outside, he heard the heavy-bodied Brother behind him shouting for the guards who apparently should have been on duty at the entrance; and a moment later, the heavy double doors to the courtyard banged shut together.

Turning, Jami loped off down the crooked, twisting street, until darkness and a turn in its route hid him from the temple. Then he sank down in a patch of deeper shadow, panting and still holding the Flower, who continued to sleep serenely.

It took him some minutes to catch his breath. The Flower might be a vision of loveliness, but her weight over a distance could become more than was comfortable to carry at a run. When he had his breath back, he got up and began the slow process of bearing her the rest of the way home.

When he got to his house, it was alight above-stairs, but dark below. He called the girls down to light a lamp and carried the Flower into the reception room, fending off the questions of Butterfly and Light-of-Pearl as he laid his sleeping burden on the cushions at one side of the room. It was plain they had been worried about him and were full of unasked questions about the Flower. He cut them off before they could start.

"She belongs to Sheik al-Birain," he told the two, shortly, "and I'm taking her directly to him. But first, I've got something I want you to keep for me."

He reached in under his robe, unwound the gray cloth he had placed around his waist and handed it to Light-of-Pearl.

"Put it someplace safe," he said. "Butterfly, will you go next door and borrow Ibrahim al-Haddad's donkey and cart?"

"Who is she?" said Light-of-Pearl, staring at the Flower.

"Just someone belonging to the Sheik al-Birain, I told

you!'' he answered, impatiently, ''and I've got to get her
back to him safely.''

In silence, Light-of-Pearl took the gray cloth into the rear
part of the house and a few moments later, Butterfly led the
donkey and cart of their neighbor, the blacksmith, out into
the street before their gate. Jami carried the Flower down,
still wrapped in the red bedcover, and put her in the cart.
Then he climbed up on the seat of the wagon and looked at
Butterfly and Light-of-Pearl, standing in the dark street,
watching him.

He was conscious of a need to say something to them;
and at the same time he did not know why. There was an
uncomfortable feeling in him. It was as if this house of his
was as much theirs as his; and he had violated their share in
it by bringing the Flower here, or even engaging in stealing
her in the first place. He tried to put his thoughts in order,
but they would not be marshalled.

''Don't let anyone in,'' he growled at them, finally, ''and
that particularly includes Mir Akbar!''

''All you have to do is tell us,'' said Light-of-Pearl; but
her eyes were worried. ''You're just going to deliver her to
that sheik? Is there going to be trouble?''

''He'll probably fall on my neck and bless me—in his
desert style,'' said Jami. He flapped the reins against the
small donkey's back. ''Get up.''

The donkey got up and they creaked off up the dark
street. Behind him, Jami heard the gate shut and the bar
thud home into position.

When he got to the house of Sulayman Tufeek, lights
shone from the windows there, also, and there were more
than a few people coming and going in the courtyard. But
the gate was locked, and he had to call for someone to open
it.

''It's you, man,'' said the Father of Knives, appearing
out of the dimness among the robed figures on the other side
of the still-closed gate. He spoke sharply to several of the

robed men standing about and these moved to swing the gates wide. Jami drove in.

He walked around behind the cart and took up the Flower, still wrapped and slumbering, from the bed of the wagon. Abu-al-Sikeen led the way into the building, and to the audience hall, where he found everything the way it had been when he had last seen it, including the sheik once more in conversation with Sulayman Tufeek, among the cushions on the platform.

This time, however, he did not have to raise his voice before the room was cleared about him. In the moment in which he followed Abu-al-Sikeen through the door of the room, Sulayman Tufeek got to his feet, bowed to al-Birain and came toward the entrance to the room; and all the others there, except the guards about the sheik, also filed out. By the time Jami reached the front edge of the platform and laid the Flower down on it, there was no one else present but the sheik and the guards, Abu-al-Sikeen, and himself.

The dark eyes of al-Birain went to the red-swathed figure at his feet. He took a slow, deep breath, his wide chest spreading under his snowy robe as he gazed down at the Flower. For a long moment, Jami thought that he and everyone else in the room had been forgotten by the sheik; and a touch of alarm moved in him. Once more his senses were keyed to a fever pitch and the exhilaration was filling him, warning him of some possible danger here.

"O Sheik," he said. "You're satisfied?"

Al-Birain did not start. But he lifted his head as someone might who had just been roused from a deep dream. He looked at Jami, but Jami had the feeling that the other hardly saw him.

"Yes," al-Birain said, after a moment. "I'm satisfied. Go—and I'll send you a small present as a token of my appreciation, over and above our bargain, in the next day or so."

Jami nodded. He turned away toward the entrance, Abu-al-

Sikeen falling into step beside him as he left. At the door Jami glanced back and saw that the sheik had gone back to gazing at the Flower. He sat motionless upon his cushions on the platform; and all about him, his guards also stood motionless as statues.

"Sleep well, man," said Abu-al-Sikeen, as he let Jami out into the darkness of the street. Jami tried to see the expression on the face within the other's headcloth, as best he might, but the dimness of the light defeated him. They were almost exactly the same height.

"Sleep well, yourself," Jami said, and went.

Sometime in the night he was roused by sounds outside his house—a shouting of voices, and a thud like that of a battering ram against a castle door. He rolled out of bed, pulling on his already-belted trousers, aware that Butterfly and Light-of-Pearl were also up and moving swiftly with him, and came to the front of his house.

The noise was from the street in front of the house and it rang much louder here than it had in the bedroom. It was his name that was being shouted. He avoided the door, but moved to the window beside it and peered out between the slats of the shutter. In the street, beating on his gate with a baulk of timber, were a dozen of the desert men, among them the larger figure of Abu-al-Sikeen.

Jami grinned wolfishly. Suddenly he was wide awake and keyed to the limit. That gate had posts two feet wide sunk half again his own height into the ground; and the gatedoor itself was not only four inches thick, but on its inward side heavily reinforced with metal, although to the eye it looked like any ordinary wooden courtyard entrance. He ran his eye over the men below. They all wore curved swords, but none appeared to be carrying either bows or slings.

He stepped to the wall and took down his targe, a round, heavy shield. He slung it over his back, lifted his crescent-bladed axe from the wall pegs and hooked it to his belt. Men who would face a sword would sometimes not face an axe. Then he hung a quiver full of arrows to the other side of his belt; and taking up the deeply curved bow from the corner, strung it, nocking an arrow loosely to its ready string.

"Open the door," he said to Light-of-Pearl.

She did. He stepped through onto the landing at the top of the stairs and stood, looking down at those below.

They had brought torches, and the street was lurid with flickering yellow light. That light illuminated the landing where he stood and showed him clearly to them. Their voices died. The baulk of timber ceased being hammered against the gatedoor. One voice alone reached up to him.

"Man!" it shouted; and it was the voice of the Father of Knives. "You're to come to the Sheik al-Birain—now!"

In one smooth, whipping motion, Jami lifted the bow and pulled the arrow to his ear.

"Down on your faces!" he called. "All of you. Down!"

The desert men hesitated for a second. Undoubtedly they were brave; but the street was now brightly lit for some distance. There was no cover nearby, and a good bowman could half-empty his quiver of arrows before any one of them could hope to get out of sight. At this short range one of the razor-sharp, broad-head arrows could transfix a man.

They dropped. All but one. The largest figure of them all remained on his feet, and his heavy, hooked nose caught the light of the torches, inside his hood.

"Man," he cried, "there's no escaping the will of the great sheik. Come in friendship while you can!"

"I'll come," retorted Jami, "tomorrow—in the daylight."

"Oh, man—"

"And the longer I wait to see you out of sight, the later tomorrow that'll be!" roared Jami, suddenly furious for reasons he hardly understood himself. "Now, get out of here!"

A moment later, the discarded torches shone down on a street in which no living person was visible.

Lukas came the next morning to find out why he had not heard from Jami about the boat trip; and all the explanations about the Flower of Passion and al-Birain, which Jami had spent a couple of hours making to Light-of-Pearl and Butter-fly the night before after the desert men had left, had to be made over again.

"And you've still got the Veil?" Lukas said, when Jami was done. "The Veil that brings this Flower of Passion to life? It was shrewd of you to ask only for his protection as your first price. But what kind of payment are you planning to get from him, now that he realizes how you've tricked him in?"

The hollow feeling came and went for a moment inside Jami.

"Only the protection I've earned with the job," said Jami.

Lukas stared at him and suddenly burst into laughter, then as suddenly sobered again.

"You did all this just to make a fool of the man?" he said. "And now you'll just make a gift of it to him like a sultan to a slave, after showing how you could have robbed him? He can't live with that."

"He'll have to," said Jami. He heard the dry wind moaning in the eaves of his house.

"But, one of these desert sheiks—" Lukas hesitated. "He'll move heaven and earth to get even with you, now."

"How can he?" Jami said. "If the price of the Veil is his oath on the souls of his sons to protect me and mine?"

Lukas burst into laughter again.

"I'll make a song about that!" he said. But there was a faint uneasiness in his voice. Sitting on other chairs, in the room, Butterfly and Light-of-Pearl watched and listened with still faces.

"Anyway," said Lukas after a moment, "you'll be tak-ing the Veil to him this evening, you say? Then let's play safe. We'll all head for the boat and cast off the minute you're done? Agreed?''

"Agreed," Jami nodded.

"Fine. I'll put Shirin on board late this afternoon, then come here and get the rest of you, to show you where the craft lies." Lukas got to his feet. "Much to do in the meantime. I'll see you later."

Jami sat around the house that day sharpening and tending his weapons. The occupation was a familiar way to kill time; and he found that in this present moment it also helped to fill the strange hollowness he felt within him, and shut his mind to the ceaseless whistling of the wind. When twilight began to bleed across the sky, he got the Veil from Light-of-Pearl and wrapped it around his waist under his shirt once more. He left the house, turning up the street in the direction of the establishment of Sulayman Tufeek; and a beggar who had been sitting most of the day in the street just beyond the house got up and limped off ahead of him, so swiftly he was out of sight before Jami reached the first turn in the street.

He came in the red sunset to the gates of the courtyard of Sulayman Tufeek and they were open. Abu-al-Sikeen was waiting there but did not speak to him. The Father of Knives only inclined his head a little, his eyes glittering like the eyes of the parrot on the gold chain of al-Birain, and led the way into the house and into the large room where al-Birain sat.

The room, this time, was empty except for the guards; but al-Birain smiled at Jami in friendly fashion as he came to the edge of the platform.

"Jami the Infidel," he said, "was there some misunderstanding between us?"

"Not that I can think of," said Jami. "You'll remember I brought you the woman whom the Flowery Brethren were holding, as I said I would."

"And the cloth with her?"

Jami frowned.

"That, too," he said. "It was a red cloth, I remember."

"Indeed, you brought me a red cloth," said al-Birain. "But it was the wrong cloth."

"Oh?" said Jami.

"Yes," said al-Birain. "It seems there was another cloth. Did you notice one?"

"Perhaps," Jami said carelessly. "There was a gray rag of sorts I took with me at the last minute, just in case further covering should be needed to keep the red cloth from getting dirty in the streets."

"Ah?" said al-Birain. "And this cloth, you still have it, I suppose?"

"Yes," said Jami. Their eyes met and held.

"Yes." Al-Birain watched him for a second more, then turned to Abu-al-Sikeen. "We do not need you any longer, my child. You may go."

The Father of Knives bowed, and backed off, turned and walked out of the room. As the door closed behind him, al-Birain turned back to Jami.

"This other cloth, this rag," he said, "it seems it would be useful in making a quick understanding of the magic that causes the woman you brought me to sleep. Would you give me that cloth also, my son?"

"Give you the cloth?" said Jami.

"Of course," said al-Birain, "since it was but a minor part of the original bargain, I leave it to you to set a price on it."

"A price?" Jami smiled at him, hearing the wind about Sulayman Tufeek's house. "How could I ask a price for an old rag like that? I'll be glad to give it to you, freely."

There was a dead silence in the room. Al-Birain did not move, and not a muscle of his face changed.

"Ah," he said.

"Perhaps," said Jami, "the honor of the great sheik is such he may not accept a free gift from someone so insignificant as myself. So let the price be included in the oath you swore on the souls of your sons to protect me and mine against all harm.''

Al-Birain still sat motionless, but for a second, a darkness seemed to shutter over his eyes. In that moment Jami had time to notice that the golden chain that had held the parrot lay limp upon the cushions of the platform, and the bird itself was again nowhere in sight. The walls of the now almost empty room seemed to have no echo and the sheik's voice when he spoke seemed to hold them all.

"First," said al-Birain, at last, "in token of our agreement and happiness in this moment, we'll have coffee together; and you can tell me how you made your way into the *khaniqah* and brought the woman safely out again and back to me."

He clapped his hands.

One of the guards turned and left the room.

"What time of day did you go to the *khaniqah*?" asked al-Birain.

"Just in time for the evening service."

Behind Jami, the door opened again, and the guard returned, preceding a man bearing a silver tray with coffeepot and cups upon it. Both Jami and al-Birain fell silent as the tray was set down and the coffee poured into the small, blue, handleless cups. Finished, the servant bowed to al-Birain and left.

"Just in time for the evening service," said Jami again. "I went in with the regular worshippers."

Al-Birain lifted his cup and drank from it. He looked over its rim at Jami, who had not so far touched his cup.

"Drink," said the sheik, "on the souls of my sons, no coffee in this house is other than wholesome for you."

Jami lifted his cup and drank. The clove-flavored oversweetness of it took him by the throat. He set the cup down again and proceeded to tell the story of how he had reached the room where the Flower had been kept, had killed the *sanaja* and brought her out after encountering the member of the Brotherhood.

The telling went slowly, for al-Birain questioned him about details and seemed to enjoy spinning out the tale. As his first cold cup of coffee was taken away and another poured, he recognized that they were engaged in the social ritual which dictated that they drink three cups each of the clove-flavored and cinnamon-flavored coffees. Happily, he was able to get by merely by touching the heavily sugared liquid to his lips.

Finally, however, the last cup of coffee was brought and handled. Jami brought the story to an end and al-Birain sat back on his cushions with a sigh.

"So," he said. His eyes fastened on Jami. "And now, this gray rag that you were to give me. Tell me where it is and I'll send someone to fetch it."

"But have I first your forgiveness, great Sheik?" said Jami. "Your forgiveness, now and in the future if I ever have or shall offend you—according to the oath you swore on the souls of your sons?"

Once again, al-Birain did not move and no muscle of his face changed for a long moment. He seemed to look away through Jami and through the walls of the house alike. Then he looked out one of the room's tall windows at the now nearly gone light of the day. He smiled and his eyes came back to focus on Jami.

"On the souls of my sons," he said, "as of this moment you are now forgiven for anything you have done or may do to offend me. And now—where shall I send someone to find the cloth we talk of?"

"There's no need to send," said Jami. "Having caught a small chill last night, it happens I wrapped that very cloth around me just before I came here."

He reached in between the buttons of his shirt, took hold of the gray cloth and pulled it forth.

"For the great sheik," he said, stepping forward. He

bowed, and laid it on the cushions before al-Birain. "And now, I should be about other business."

"God go with you," said al-Birain, his eyes only on Jami, above the gray cloth that now lay just beyond his knees.

Jami bowed again and backed away, turned, and went toward the door. He looked back and saw al-Birain sitting with his dark eyes burning at him still, across the distance between them.

"And may God grant you enjoyment of the reward you have gained," said al-Birain.

Jami went out.

Once back in the street, he hurried homeward. Sunset had turned to night while al-Birain had kept him in conversation over the coffee cups; and for some reason the dark brought uneasiness to him. He pushed the feeling from him. The thing was over and he had won; but there was still that uncomfortableness in him. The hollowness he had felt earlier kept him company as he strode rapidly through the dark streets. They seemed strangely deserted, this early in the evening, for he could not have spent more than an hour with the sheik; but it occurred to him that others besides Lukas might have thought to leave the city, together with the noise of the wind, behind them.

It would be good to be away, he thought . . . and then, as he came around the bend of his own street that gave him a sight of his house, he saw that the street and courtyard before it was once more lit with torches and filled with a crowd of people—mostly his near neighbors.

He broke into a run.

The crowd parted to let him through and he saw, without stopping, that the gatedoor stood unharmed, but wide open. He went through it and across the courtyard at a run. The front door to the house was also standing open. Within, lamps burned, making the front room bright. Their light shone on a scene of destruction. Crockery was smashed and cushions ripped; and on the mat before the side window lay the still shape of Butterfly, with the wounds of a dozen edged weapons about her.

On her knees, crouched beside the body, was Light-of-Pearl, unmoving, her face in her hands. She at least still lived, for her shoulders moved to show that she breathed. Jami took one step toward her and a green, beaked shape exploded out of the doorway to the kitchen at eye-level, swooping past him with wings outstretched, crying out hoarsely in its parrot's voice before it was past him and out the open front door behind him.

"Fool! Fool! Fool!"

It was gone before he could draw sword and kill it. He took one step toward Light-of-Pearl, then whirled about like a lion at a sound behind him.

Lukas had just stepped through the doorway. He leaned against its frame, panting.

"I went looking for you," he gasped. "They told me they'd seen you headed home from Tufeck's place."

Jami whirled back again, stepped to Light-of-Pearl and lifted her. She came up into his arms, neither hindering nor helping, like a drugged person. Her body was limp, her eyes watched something as if it moved with her, no matter how he turned her.

He sat down on one of the benches against the wall that still had its cushion, cradling her in his arms. But she would not respond. She only lay there, living but still. She had not been touched physically; but something in her seemed still frozen in some past second of horror from which he could not rouse her.

"Bad business, brother," said Lukas, still short of breath in the doorway. "It was the desert men—those of your sheik. I saw that one they call Father of Knives among them."

Jami lifted his eyes from Light-of-Pearl.

"When did it happen?" He did not recognize the sound of his own voice.

"Half an hour ago, no more, the neighbors say," answered Lukas. "Mir Akbar came first to the gate and talked to one of the girls—they think it was Butterfly. She let him in."

"It would be Butterfly," whispered Jami.

"Mir Akbar went inside with her. After a little he came out alone and opened the gate to the desert men who had since come. They were under the command of the Father of Knives. The neighbors heard the smashing of dishes and shouting, and then they went away—as I say, less than half an hour ago. I was coming to get you and I passed the men."

Lukas' voice changed on the last word, though there was no change in his face. For a second he said nothing. Then he went on with his voice as usual.

"—I did not know. I let them go by me."

Jami lifted Light-of-Pearl gently in his arms and brought her head around so that their eyes looked into each other.

"Pearl . . ." he said, softly. "It's Jami. Just Jami. What happened?"

She stared at him for a long moment, as if she did not know him. He thought she would not answer; and then she spoke, but from far off, as if she was very sleepy.

"The sorcerer came. I had already started to undress. Butterfly let him in because he said it was your life that was at stake. When he got inside, he called to me and asked me to check the roof, to make sure no one was trying to climb over from the one next door. I left him with 'Fly. When I came down, the desert men were in the house, and 'Fly was already . . ."

She stopped talking. Her eyes no longer saw him but once more watched something in the same place, no matter how he turned her.

Jami looked at Lukas.

"He arranged for this before you had a chance to give him the Veil," said Lukas, "before his oath bound him to protect you."

"Will you help me?" Jami said, hoarsely.

Lukas pulled his caftan up, over his head, and dropped it on the floor in the doorway. He stood before Jami in long trousers and a short tunic, unarmed.

"Lend me a sword," he said.

They looked at each other for a second. Then Jami stood up, still holding Light-of-Pearl in his arms.

"Look just inside the door of the storage floor, downstairs," he said. "You can get a sword there; and also you'll find a coil of rope with a grapnel on one end, just inside the door. Bring it and we'll talk as we go to Tufeek's."

Lukas nodded and went out of the door and down the stairs ahead of Jami. Jami continued out into the street, carrying Light-of-Pearl; and the neighbors crowded around him as they came out, then backed away as he shook his head without speaking and walked through them, turning up the street. A few yards beyond the crowd, he was joined by Lukas, with the coil of rope on his left arm at the shoulder and the grapnel held in his hand—the hand that was not now holding a long, light saber-like blade.

They walked together.

"On the Street of Tears," said Jami, as they went, "there is a point where the courtyard wall joins the side of the house of Tufeek, and a fig tree there throws a thick shadow, particularly at night; even when the moon is visible—as it hardly is, tonight."

Lukas looked up at the night sky overhead, which was not quite dark, with a thin layer of torn clouds scudding before the dry wind and letting moonlight through here and there for a moment in unpredictable places.

"I'll have to get in to see the sheik," Jami said. He heard his voice as if it was the voice of someone else speaking inside him. "The only way to do that, will be to pretend to bring Light-of-Pearl to him. When I call at the gate for them to let me in and hold their attention in the courtyard, you throw your grapnel at the point where the courtyard wall joins the house, and get up onto the roof. Once you're on the roof, go quietly to the part of it that overhangs the tall windows of Tufeek's audience hall, which is where al-Birain sits. Anchor the grapnel so that the rope can be let down through one of the windows into the hall. When you see one of the windows broken from the inside, swing down, stand on the sill of the broken window and take Light-of-Pearl from me. Get her and yourself away to your boat."

Jami looked sideways at Lukas. In the gloom, as they walked together, Lukas' lean face looked back at him.

"I can come on in and help you, brother," he said.

"Not and get Light-of-Pearl away safely," Jami said softly. "I've lost Butterfly. We can't lose Pearl, too. No, take her straight to your boat."

Lukas walked for a moment of silence.

"I'll wait for you at the boat, then," he said. "It's moored at the outer end of the dock nearest Ibn Hilal's boatyard. You know the place."

"Yes," said Jami. "But don't wait, tied up. Untie and lay off from the dock without lights, four or five boat-lengths, for a quarter of an hour. If I come running, I'll shout to you before I dive off the dock and you can call me to you."

"And if you don't come in a quarter of an hour?"

"As it'll happen," said Jami. "If I'm not there in that time lift anchor and go. There'll be no point waiting."

They walked a little farther in silence.

"It would be better if we both went in together," said Lukas.

"No," said Jami.

Lukas sighed in the darkness.

"Anything but what I've said risks Pearl too much," said Jami.

They did not say any more until they came to within sight of the establishment of Sulayman Tufeek—once again richly lit from most of its windows.

"I'll have words with al-Birain if you miss our boat trip," said Lukas. He stopped, and Jami stopped, for they were almost within reach of the light of the torches just inside the courtyard gate of the house. Lukas turned toward him and reached out to touch the hand Jami could not free from holding Light-of-Pearl in his arms. "Luck, brother. Look for me when you break the window."

"Luck to us both," said Jami. Lukas turned and was gone into darkness.

Jami squatted down with Light-of-Pearl in his arms. In the distant light from the courtyard torches, he could barely make out the features of her face. Her eyes were closed, so that two pools of deep shadow only seemed to lie below the ridge of her eyebrows.

"Pearl," he said softly.

She did not respond.

"Pearl," he said again. "Pearl, you've got to listen to me. It's important. Pearl!"

She opened her eyes and looked through him.

"What is it?" she said. Her voice still sounded sleepy and remote.

"Pearl, you're going to have to help. I need to get into the house of Sulayman Tufeek to al-Birain, who sent those men that came into the house. I'm going to take you up to the gate and tell them—do you hear what I'm saying, Pearl?"

"Yes," she said. The word was so faint it was almost a sigh.

"I'm going to tell them that I'm going to give you to al-Birain to buy his friendship back. But when we get into the room with him, I'll signal Lukas, and he'll come and get you. Do you understand?''

"Yes," she said, faintly, again.

"You have to be ready to run and jump—to climb if you have to—to get to Lukas, when I tell you to go. Can you do that, do you think?''

"I can do it."

"All right. Pearl . . ." For a moment he held her small body close to him, "I swear you'll be safe. No one will touch you. Do you believe me?''

"I believe you."

"Yes . . ." he said, in a long outrush of breath. His throat ached.

He stood up again, holding her, and began to walk, forward to the gate. When he reached it, he stopped. He could see the dark outlines of guards standing together by the horses, but they did not come to the gate at the sight of him there, holding Light-of-Pearl.

"Abu-al-Sikeen!" he shouted. "Abu-al-Sikeen, it's Jami the Infidel. I want a word with you. Father of Knives!''

One of the shadows detached itself from the group and went into the house. After a few moments it came out, followed by a larger outline, and together they approached the gate.

"Man," said the harsh voice of Abu-al-Sikeen, when they had halted just inside the gate. "What do you want here?''

"I have offended the great sheik!" said Jami. "I didn't mean to—I swear I didn't mean to. But now the great sheik is offended with me, and I'm afraid, even though he promised to forgive me. Take me to him, Father of Knives. Take me to him. Justly, he took away from me one of the two things I most valued. Let him take the other thing, this woman I hold—it's all I have to give him—and turn his anger from me. Abu-al-Sikeen, help me to turn aside the anger of the great sheik!''

There was a long pause, and then a noise like that of a
man clearing his throat, and the taller outline spat into the
dust on the far side of the gate.

"It seems I was mistaken about you, filth!" he said.
"Wait here. I'll see if it would amuse the great sheik to see
you."

He turned and went across the courtyard into the house,
leaving the guard to stand and watch through the gate. Jami
squatted like a beggar on the ground and waited. After
several minutes, Abu-al-Sikeen returned and signaled that
the gate should be opened. Jami rose and came through,
carrying Light-of-Pearl, who was as quiet in his arms as if
she slept. Abu-al-Sikeen said nothing, but turned and led
the way, across the courtyard and into the house, and left to
the entrance of the room in which Jami had now faced
al-Birain twice before.

"Wait," Abu-al-Sikeen said, again.

He opened the door and stepped through, closing it behind him. After a moment, he came out again, held the door
open and jerked his head at Jami. Jami carried Light-of-
Pearl into the audience hall.

There was a strange, sweet spicy air to the atmosphere
within. Once more, al-Birain was surrounded only by a
dozen or so guards with their blue velvet scabbards. But on
the platform lay the Flower of Passion, still apparently
slumbering and wrapped as Jami had wrapped her in the red
bedspread taken from the temple of the Flowery Brethren.
At her head, in a space cleared of cushions, stood on three
tall legs a brazier, from which a blue haze arose to gather in
clouds under the high ceiling of the room and flavor the air
that Jami had smelled. Behind the brazier stood Mir Akbar,
and his eyes met Jami's briefly with a strange look that
seemed mingled of calculation and satisfaction.

Abu-al-Sikeen went before Jami to the edge of the platform, turned and jerked a thumb at Jami.

"This dog," he said, "begs you to smile on him once more, great Sheik."

Jami knelt, clumsily, holding Light-of-Pearl, who had now opened her eyes and was looking dully about the chamber as if searching for something.

"Great Sheik," said Jami. "I know you promised me forgiveness, as I asked, but I still tremble at the thought that I've offended you. I'm stupid, great Sheik—I didn't think; and the great sheik has justly punished me, after drinking coffee with me while his justice took one of the two creatures in this world I value; and giving me his oath of forgiveness only after that justice had been executed. I am afraid, great Sheik. I am afraid in spite of your promise."

He held out Light-of-Pearl at arm's length toward al-Birain.

"Take the other as well," he said. "Take her too and lift from me the burden of your displeasure."

On the platform, al-Birain smiled slowly.

"And what would I want with another slave?" he said. "Do you think something like that has any value in my eyes—do you think I could be brought to smile on you by anything that such as you could give?"

He stroked his beard for a second, watching Jami, and his eyes burned darkly. He looked over at Abu-al-Sikeen.

"She offends me," al-Birain said. "Take her and throw her to those on guard. Tell them she belongs to them, but I would not see her again in one piece."

Abu-al-Sikeen stepped forward as Jami rose to his feet and turned to face him.

"Now!" roared Jami.

He threw Light-of-Pearl from him toward the tall windows, black with the night beyond; and at the same time his foot lashed out, to double Abu-al-Sikeen upon the floor of the hall. Abu-al-Sikeen rolled over on his back, grimacing, and straightened himself with a jerk, his hand going in one of the slits in his robe as he still lay on the floor.

Jami took one step back and up onto the platform. With

one hand he snatched up the brazier by one of its tall tripod of legs, and slung the burning contents of it upon the fallen man. As he swung the top of the brazier forward, it collided with one of the lamps hanging overhead, tore it loose and smashed it, so that perfumed oil cascaded with the burning coals from the brazier upon the fallen man. Abu-al-Sikeen's robe blazed up like paper as the burning oil touched it and from the midst of the flame and smoke the Father of Knives howled like a dog, lurching to his feet and tearing the burning robe from his body. Beneath it, his chest was strapped with a cloth harness that held scabbards containing a multitude of knives, but this harness, too, had caught fire; and he tore it from him, throwing it aside.

Even as he did this, Jami turned and threw the emptied brazier at the nearest of the tall windows. It smashed through, disappearing into the dark beyond and scattering splinters of wood and glass; and, in that same moment, the first of the guards reached him, sword in hand. But Jami stepped aside from the sword swing of the first to reach him, caught the man's wrist, took his weapon and smashed the hilt into his face. The guard dropped, and Jami turned to face the next armed man, who was upon him.

"Jami!" shouted a voice—and Jami, engaged with the guards, hewing through them like a farmer through a field of ripe wheat, caught a momentary glimpse of Lukas, suddenly there in the now vacant window opening, standing spraddle-legged and reaching for Light-of-Pearl, who had run to the wall and, using a nearby pile of cushions, vaulted up to him even as Jami watched.

Lukas caught her, hauled her into place beside him, and put the rope he held into her hands. But then, instead of leaving, he himself drew his sword and leaped in and down, to the floor of the hall. A second later Pearl followed him, back into the room. Her arm reached out, seized something Jami could not see, and then whipped through the air. One of the swordsmen facing Jami dropped to the floor, choking, as a small but heavy brass bowl spun its edge sickeningly against his throat where his windpipe was.

"No!" howled Jami at both her and Lukas. "Leave me! Run!"

But neither made any move to run. Pearl continued to throw with murderous accuracy any small object she could lay her hands on; and Jami was fleetingly aware of Lukas, having fought his way to the room's entrance, swinging down the thick wooden bar that stood pivoted upright beside it, barring it shut against anyone trying to get in. Then Jami's whole attention was taken by the remaining guards, as they closed around him with bright swords reaching for his body.

It came on him then, the strange difference he had experienced only twice before in his life, but had heard about as soon as he had been old enough to understand the talk of the men around the fireside of his home. All at once things were narrowed-down, clear and simple. The blades aimed at him were there but he felt no more for them than if they had been painted sticks. His inner eye was filled by the image of Butterfly as she had been, alive; and a deep, heavy sorrow seemed to tear him apart within. He moved among his enemies; and they fell like stalks of grass, though it seemed his sword hardly touched them.

Suddenly there was space about him. Five men lay still on the floor of the room, but the rest of the guards were back against the walls, staring at him with pale faces and open mouths.

"Kill him!" thundered al-Birain.

But the men pressing against the walls only twitched, and did not move forward. Lukas, his own sword naked in his hand, still stood by the barred door. Only one figure moved—a towering, naked, red-seared figure with the ashy remnants of eyebrows and hair. Scooping a sword from beside one of the fallen bodies, it threw itself at Jami.

Jami blocked the downsweep of the sword held by Abu-al-

Sikeen with the blade of his own weapon and felt it break. The other's blade broke at the same time; and, throwing it aside, the hook-nosed desert warrior sobbed once, and threw his arms around Jami's body, locking hand to wrist. He tightened the cords of his arms and shoulders, gathering the pressure of his two fists against the incurve of Jami's backbone.

The image of Butterfly moved again before the eye of Jami's mind, working amongst her flowers in the courtyard. In turn he locked his own hands together behind the naked, scorched back of Abu-al-Sikeen and set his chin in the hollow of the other's shoulder. He put aside all awareness of his body but the power flowing up from his legs, across his back, into his shoulders and down his arms.

He increased his grip.

He felt the strength in the arms of Abu-al-Sikeen threatening to snap his spine, and thought of Butterfly once more. His own arms tightened. He felt the other man's backbone yield and break. Abu-al-Sikeen dropped to the ground like a man deprived suddenly of his legs.

Their eyes met.

"Kill me, man," husked Abu-al-Sikeen. "Don't leave me like this."

But the thought of Butterfly was still in Jami's mind, and he turned away to al-Birain. The sheik was standing on the platform, facing him, and holding now, with both hands, the heavy, bright length of the Grandfather of Swords. "I will kill you myself," said al-Birain.

"And what of your sons' souls you swore on?" said Jami.

Al-Birain snarled at him.

"You've attacked me in my house," he said. "The oath is broken by you. Since my forgiveness I've given you no reason for that."

"No," panted Jami, feeling a terrible rage growing from the heavy sorrow within him. "Your oath was good only from the moment the Veil was also in your hands. You were careful not to ask me to deliver it up to you until you knew your men had had time to do what you'd sent them to do. But the Flower of Passion and the Veil that wakens her were both in your possession, just now, when you would, far from protecting one of mine, have thrown her to your guards to use and do away with. The souls of your sons are cast aside, old man!''

For a moment al-Birain stared at him. Then he leaped from the platform, swinging the massive split-bladed sword in a whistling cut at Jami.

Jami had no time to find another sword. He stooped under the cut and jerked free the small black knife from his boot, bringing it up and out as he took one step forward, and the short, broad blade rang and ground against the large one next to the sword hilt, sending up a shower of sparks, but blocking the second blow.

He and al-Birain stood face to face and eye to eye. A flick of the wrist would free Jami's short blade for use, but there was no way the sheik could draw back his own massive weapon for use that easily. The difference and the exhilaration, all the concentration of battle, had taken over Jami completely, now, and he no longer saw the rest of the room or any of those in it. Even Pearl and Lukas did not exist for him at that moment and in a second more his knife would have been slid over the guard of the large sword and upwards between the ribs of al-Birain into the sheik's heart.

"Now," said Jami, between his teeth, "I'm going to kill you."

"*Seumas! Chan eil—*"

Only the words in his childhood language could have reached and checked him in that moment. But reach him they did. The voice had been the voice of Mir Akbar and he was suddenly aware of the Persian magician standing beside his hand that held the knife. Consciousness of the rest of the room flooded back into him; he looked around. Everyone was motionless. It was as if time had stopped. He stared back at Mir Akbar.

"Why are you so surprised?" said the magician, still in Gaelic. "You should know that there are spells that give the gift of tongues, and no one here but you will understand me when I speak in this one. You must not kill him."

"He is forsworn," said Jami, thickly, unthinkingly answering in Gaelic himself. "He shall die!"

"You would kill him not because he is forsworn," said Mir Akbar, "not even because of what he sent his men out to do to Butterfly before his oath had been paid for. You want to kill him only for the sake of a woman more than two years dead, whom no amount of killing will bring back to life."

"Yes," said Jami, still thickly. He stared into al-Birain's eyes and saw to his dull astonishment that, although the other was as motionless as everyone else except the magician and himself, the sheik seemed to be hearing what was said in this strange language he could not understand. "Yes, he should die for that, as she died—"

"And your friend Lukas? And the other girl, here, Light-of-Pearl? Should they die, and Butterfly stay slaughtered—all so you can feed your hunger for revenge?"

Jami looked numbly onto the floor of the room and saw both Lukas and Pearl, still on their feet and unharmed. But there were rings of swordsmen close around both of them. Mir Akbar was right. If Jami killed al-Birain, he himself would die—as he had been prepared to die when he walked into this room carrying Pearl. But these two he loved would die now with him, once the tribesmen saw their sheik slain. Whatever else happened, none of the three would leave the room alive.

"What else . . . ?" he said. But he said it almost more to himself than to Mir Akbar.

"I can give you back Butterfly, if you spare the sheik," said Mir Akbar in rapid Gaelic. "I can make sure you all

three live. There are matters at work here you don't understand. Only you, besides myself, could go into the *khaniqah*
and successfully bring out the Flower—this much I learned
from my calculations on the letters of your name. But only
the sheik could give you reason to go. He must live, though
he'll never become Sharif of Mecca. As for the Flower, she
was created for a higher purpose than to further the designs
of a Flowery Brotherhood or a desert sheik. She is a tool to
bridge the gap between this world and others like it—for
that purpose was she designed and made. But I can receive
her only as a free gift. You must give her to me."

"A gift from me?" Jami stared. "And how can you give
me back Butterfly? No one can raise the dead."

"Trust me!" said Mir Akbar. He switched suddenly from
Gaelic back into Arabic. "May all my knowledge wither
and my strength be lost if I can't give you what I promise.
But I tell you there's more at stake here than you could
understand, even if I told you everything. Let al-Birain live
and his oath must hold. He struck at you in a moment of
madness, but now he is no longer mad. For the sake of his
sons, neither he nor they will dare harm you. Take the
Flower of Passion, instead, to punish him; and give her to
me to pay for the return of Butterfly."

Al-Birain's eyes glittered from Jami to Mir Akbar.

"All this time!" he said to the sorcerer. "You!"

"I could neither go nor send anyone into the *khaniqah* of
the Brethren," retorted Mir Akbar. "The Flower's destiny
is for greater things than to be the toy of a desert king. Take
the Flower and go, Jami. For the sake of his honor, he
won't let any of his men stop any of you if you forgive him
his breaking of his oath just now."

"I'll forgive him when the damage he did is mended and
I see Butterfly alive again."

"I'll go with you then, and you needn't give the Flower
up to me until you have your Butterfly back," said the
sorcerer.

Jami looked at the barred door and saw Lukas still guarding it. He looked over toward the broken window and saw Light-of-Pearl standing under it. Her eyes were fixed on Mir Akbar in an expression of incredible hope.

Jami took a deep breath. Without putting the knife away, he looked at Pearl.

"Come," he said to her.

She walked through the naked swords surrounding her, and at a single sharp word from al-Birain, none of them were raised to stop her. Her eyes were clear and her face alive again. When she reached him, she put her arms around his neck and kissed him.

"Go with Lukas," he said to her, putting her on her feet. She went to the door. Jami came back and picked up the wrapped and slumbering Flower, still warily holding his knife. But al-Birain made no move to stop him and he turned toward the door, carrying the Flower.

As he passed Abu-al-Sikeen, however, a dry whisper stopped him.

"Man," whispered Abu-al-Sikeen, from the floor, "Don't leave me so. Have pity. Kill me!"

Jami looked at Mir Akbar, beside him.

"Can you cure him, too?"

"Mend his burns and his back where you broke it, so that he can walk again?" Mir Akbar looked casually down at the desert warrior. "That takes only simple art."

"Then that's another part of the price you pay for the Flower," Jami said. He looked down at Abu-al-Sikeen. "And the price you pay for having legs once more is that on your own soul you never raise a hand to any belonging to me, again."

"I will not. May God reward you," said Abu-al-Sikeen. "But one day I'll kill you for shaming my chieftain."

"If you can," said Jami, and went on past him with Mir Akbar, joining Lukas at the door and opening it to pass out of the room and the house.

"Go with them," ordered the voice of al-Birain behind them, sounding strange and old. "No one's to interfere."

One of the guards ran hastily from behind them, passed them up and went ahead crying out al-Birain's command.

They came back to Jami's house, walking with the donkey cart that carried the Flower of Passion in her red bedcover, and the gray cloth of the Veil. When they got to the front gate, a few windows were still alight on the second floor, marking where lamps lit earlier were still burning; but the street was empty of neighbors, except for Ibrahim the blacksmith, who turned out to have been standing guard there against thieves who might have already heard no one was at home.

Jami thanked the thick-set man; and the blacksmith went off to his own bed. They opened the gate and entered, Jami once more carrying the Flower, for safekeeping.

They were at the foot of the stairs leading to the front door when Jami noticed that Mir Akbar was not close beside them. He halted with the Flower still in his arms and turned about.

"Magician?" he said. "Where are you?"

"Here." The voice of Mir Akbar came back from the obscurity near the dark back wall of the garden. "Damn this darkness! Come help me, Light-of-Pearl. Where were those rosebushes I looked at yesterday? Which was your friend's favorite?"

There was the sound of snapping fingers and a pale blue witch-light appeared, burning from the fingertips of Mir Akbar's upraised right hand. He was revealed, standing in the midst of the flowerbed.

Revealed by the blue glow, Light-of-Pearl's eyes grew hard and she did not move.

"Go help him, Pearl," said Jami, "whatever it is."

Slowly, she went to the magician and led him to the bush of yellow roses Butterfly had loved.

"Here they are. But unless you've got a good reason—oh!"

She broke off on an odd note. Jami and Lukas followed her over to see what was going on and found her staring at a huge and perfect rose on a bare stem. Mir Akbar was holding up his witch-light at arm's length to examine the blossom.

"What Butterfly could have done with that!" murmured Light-of-Pearl. Her eyes filled with tears. "And she never even saw it!"

"Ah, the very one," muttered Mir Akbar, finishing his examination. "A bloom of extraordinary sweetness. Yes, that's right." Before any of the others could stop him, he had whisked out a small knife and cut through the stem.

Light-of-Pearl cried out, but Mir Akbar, carrying the cut flower, was already past them, standing at the foot of the stairs in the light from the windows.

"Stand back!" he warned them.

They stopped, only a few steps from him.

He lifted his hand that had sprouted the witch-light. But now the light was gone and his fingers made a circle in the air as he held his downturned hand at arm's length over the upright flower in his other hand. From his fingertips, a fine mist seemed to descend, sparkling like silver dust in the faint lamplight spilling into the courtyard. The mist came down, enclosed and hid the rose.

For a moment it sparkled there, then winked out of existence. Where the rose had been stood Butterfly.

" 'Fly!" Jami took one long step forward; but before his foot touched earth, Light-of-Pearl had already streaked to her. Butterfly's small face blinked dazedly up at Jami out of Light-of-Pearl's embrace.

"How did we get here?" she said. "Why is it night? Why are you hugging me so hard, Pearl?"

Mir Akbar laughed on a high, singing note. He turned and seized the Flower of Passion in Jami's arms.

"Just a minute," said Jami, holding to the sleeping form,

before the sorcerer could make off with it, "let's have an explanation first. Where's Butterfly been? What happened?"

"Let go!" snapped Mir Akbar. But Jami held on. "All right, then! Before I let Abu-al-Sikeen and his men inside, I made a simulacrum of Butterfly from the blossom I'd cut the day before—as the Flower of Passion had been made, though it was nowhere near the work of magic art that the Flower is. But this one didn't need to be. Then, I hid Butterfly herself as a rose among the other roses. You've got her back—now let me have my payment and go!"

Jami released the Flower.

"All right," he said. "But I'll be remembering it was you let the desert men in!"

"Think, Jami the Infidel," said Mir Akbar, looking at him. "How long would your gate have stopped them, that time? It was your own madness against al-Birain that started all this. Would you rather have gone through it without me? Without me you were doomed to destroy yourself and your friends in an effort to destroy him, like some frail craft dashing itself to death upon sea-bound rocks. Think what might have happened, not only to Butterfly, but to Light-of-Pearl, to Lukas, even to your friend the jeweler—as well as yourself, if I'd not been here!"

He spun on one heel as if to leave. But instead of stopping when he had turned about, he continued to spin, faster and faster until he was a blur in the darkness. Then, suddenly, he, the Flower of Passion, and the Veil were gone together.

Jami turned to the others. Butterfly and Light-of-Pearl, their arms around each other, were already disappearing through the front door of the living quarters at the top of the stairs. Wordlessly, Jami and Lukas followed them.

"We won't sail tonight, that's clear enough," said Lukas as they reached the foot of the stairs. "What do you say to my leaving you all to yourselves tonight? Then Shirin and I will stop by tomorrow, after the heat of the midday. We can celebrate together and then proceed to the boat.''

Jami nodded. They stepped up into the lamp-lit front room together.

"Yes, that sounds fine," Jami said; and walked aimlessly across the room, amidst the destroyed shards that were scattered about.

"I'll return tomorrow, then," said Lukas. But he paused, not leaving, but peering across the room into Jami's face.

"Why so sour?" he said. "You could frown the moon out of the sky, right now."

Jami grunted.

"It gnaws on me that I let Mir Akbar use me that way."

"Use you, brother?" said Lukas. "He only rode the tempest. And, speaking of tempests, do you hear the wind?"

"No," said Jami. "I haven't been list—"

He broke off. For now that he stopped to hear, there was no sound in the eaves of the house. The wind was gone.

"Once more it's passed," said Lukas. "Perhaps we should thank God for the wisdom to value what we have, and for not charging us over again the cost of our learning its true worth. For otherwise, I tell you, Jami, such learning might cost us dear, a second time. Look at what could so easily have been!"

He nodded to the platform at the back of the room. Jami, glancing over, saw the place where he had last thought he had seen Butterfly, lying dead. But now there was nothing there on the floor except a wilting rose and a long stem—but that stem and the rose itself had been savagely slashed and scattered by many knives.

ON MESSENGER
MOUNTAIN

I

IT WAS RAW, RED WAR FOR ALL OF THEM, FROM THE MOMENT the two ships intercepted each other, one degree off the plane of the ecliptic and three diameters out from the second planet of the star that was down on the charts as K94. K94 was a GO type star; and the yelping battle alarm of the trouble horn tumbled sixteen men to their stations. This was at thirteen hours, twenty-one minutes, four seconds of the ship's day.

Square in the scope of the laser screen, before the Survey Team Leader aboard the *Harrier*, appeared the gray, light-edged silhouette of a ship unknown to the ship's library. And the automatic reflexes of the computer aboard, that takes no account of men not yet into their vacuum suits, took over. The *Harrier* disappeared into no-time.

She came out again at less than a quarter-mile's distance from the stranger ship and released a five-pound weight at a velocity of five miles a second relative to the velocity of the alien ship. Then she had gone back into no-time again—but not before the alien, with computer-driven reflexes of its own, had rolled like the elongated cylinder it resembled, and laid out a soft green-colored beam of radiation which opened up the *Harrier* forward like a hot knife through butter left long on the table. Then it too was gone into no-time. The time aboard the *Harrier* was thirteen hours, twenty-two minutes and eighteen seconds; and on both ships there were dead.

"There are good people in the human race," Cal Hartlett had written only two months before, to his uncle on Earth, *"who feel that it is not right to attack other intelligent beings without warning—to drop five-pound weights at destructive relative velocities on a strange ship simply because you find it at large in space and do not know the race that built it.*

"What these gentle souls forget is that when two strangers encounter in space, nothing at all is known—and everything must be. The fates of both races may hinge on which one is first to kill the other and study the unknown carcass. Once contact is made, there is no backing out and no time for consideration. For we are not out here by chance, neither are they, and we do not meet by accident."

Cal Hartlett was Leader of the Mapping Section aboard the *Harrier*, and one of those who lived through that first brush with the enemy. He wrote what he wrote as clearly as if he had been Survey Leader and in command of the ship. At any moment up until the final second when it was too late, Joe Aspinwall, the Survey Leader, could have taken the *Harrier* into no-time and saved them. He did not; as no commander of a Survey Ship ever has. In theory, they could have escaped.

In practice, they had no choice.

When the *Harrier* ducked back into no-time, aboard her they could hear the slamming of emergency bulkheads. The mapping room, the fore weight-discharge room and the sleeping quarters all crashed shut as the atmosphere of the ship whiffed out into space through the wound the enemy's beam had made. The men beyond the bulkheads and in the damaged sections would have needed to be in their vacuum suits to survive. There had not been time for that, so those men were dead.

The *Harrier* winked back into normal space.

Her computer had brought her out on the far side of the second planet, which they had not yet surveyed. It was larger than Earth, with somewhat less gravity but a deeper atmospheric envelope. The laser screen picked up the enemy reappearing almost where she had disappeared, near the edge of that atmosphere.

The *Harrier* winked back all but alongside the other and laid a second five-pound weight through the center of the cylindrical vessel. The other ship staggered, disappeared into no-time and appeared again far below, some five miles above planetary surface in what seemed a desperation attempt to gain breathing time. The *Harrier* winked after her—and came out within five hundred yards, square in the path of the green beam which it seemed was waiting for her. It opened up the drive and control rooms aft like a red-hot poker lays open a cardboard box.

A few miles below, the surface stretched up the peaks of titanic mountains from horizon to horizon.

"Ram!" yelled the voice of Survey Leader Aspinwall, in warning over the intercom.

The *Harrier* flung itself at the enemy. It hit like an elevator falling ten stories to a concrete basement. The cylindrical ship broke in half in midair and bodies erupted from it. Then its broken halves and the ruined *Harrier* were falling separately to the surface below and there was no more time for anyone to look. The clock stood at thirteen hours, twenty-three minutes and four seconds.

The power—except from emergency storage units—was all but gone. As Joe punched for a landing the ship fell angling past the side of a mountain that was a monster among giants, and jarred to a stop. Joe keyed the intercom of the control board before him.

"Report," he said.

*   *   *

In the Mapping Section Cal Hartlett waited for other voices to speak before him. None came. He thumbed his audio.

"The whole front part of the ship's dogged shut, Joe," he said. "No use waiting for anyone up there. So—this is Number Six reporting. I'm all right."

"Number Seven," said another voice over the intercom. "Maury. O.K."

"Number Eight. Sam. O.K."

"Number Nine. John. O.K. . . . ."

Reports went on. Numbers Six through Thirteen reported themselves as not even shaken up. From the rest there was no answer.

In the main Control Section, Joe Aspinwall stared bleakly at his dead control board. Half of his team was dead.

The time was thirteen hours, thirty minutes, no seconds.

He shoved that thought from his mind and concentrated on the positive rather than the negative elements of the situation they were in. Cal Hartlett, he thought, was one. Since he could only have eight survivors of his Team, he felt a deep gratitude that Cal should be one of them. He would need Cal in the days to come. And the other survivors of the Team would need him, badly.

Whether they thought so at this moment or not.

"All right," said Joe, when the voices had ended. "We'll meet outside the main airlock, outside the ship. There's no power left to unseal those emergency bulkheads. Cal, Doug, Jeff—you'll probably have to cut your way out through the ship's side. Everybody into respirators and warmsuits. According to pre-survey"—he glanced at the instruments before him—"there's oxygen enough in the local atmosphere for the respirators to extract, so you won't need emergency bottles. But we're at twenty-seven thousand three hundred above local sea-level. So it'll probably be cold—even if the atmosphere's not as thin here as it would be at this altitude on Earth." He paused. "Everybody got that? Report!"

They reported. Joe unharnessed himself and got up from his seat. Turning around, he faced Maury Taller.

Maury, rising and turning from his own communications board on the other side of the Section, saw that the Survey Leader's lean face was set in iron lines of shock and sorrow under his red hair. They were the two oldest members of the Team, whose average age had been in the mid-twenties. They looked at each other without words as they went down the narrow tunnel to the main airlock and, after putting on respirators and warmsuits, out into the alien daylight outside.

The eight of them gathered together outside the arrow-head shape of their *Harrier*, ripped open fore and aft and as still now as any other murdered thing.

Above them was a high, blue-black sky and the peaks of mountains larger than any Earth had ever known. A wind blew about them as they stood on the side of one of the mountains, on a half-mile-wide shelf of tilted rock. It narrowed backward and upward like a dry streambed up the side of the mountain in one direction. In the other it broke off abruptly fifty yards away, in a cliff-edge that hung over eye-shuddering depths of a clefted valley, down in which they could just glimpse a touch of something like jungle greenness.

Beyond that narrow clefted depth lifted the great mountains, like carvings of alien devils too huge to be completely seen from one point alone. Several thousand feet above them on their mountain, the white spill of a glacier flung down a slope that was too steep for ice to have clung to in the heavier gravity of Earth. Above the glacier, which was shaped like a hook, red-gray peaks of the mountain rose like short towers stabbing the blue-dark sky. And from these, even as far down as the men were, they could hear the distant trumpeting and screaming of winds whistling in the peaks.

They took it all in in a glance. And that was all they had time to do. Because in the same moment that their eyes took in their surroundings, something no bigger than a man but tiger-striped and moving with a speed that was more than human, came around the near end of the dead *Harrier*, and went through the eight men like a predator through a huddle of goats.

Maury Taller and even Cal, who towered half a head over the rest of the men, all were brushed aside like cardboard cut-outs of human figures. Sam Cloate, Cal's assistant in the Mapping Section, was ripped open by one sweep of a clawed limb as it charged past, and the creature tore out the throat of Mike DeWall with a sideways slash of its jaws. Then it was on Joe Aspinwall.

The Survey Team Leader went down under it. Reflex got metal cuffs on the gloves of his warmsuit up and crossed in front of his throat, his forearms and elbows guarding his belly, before he felt the ferocious weight grinding him into the rock and twisting about on top of him. A snarling, worrying noise sounded in his ears. He felt teeth shear through the upper part of his thigh and grate on bone.

There was an explosion. He caught just a glimpse of Cal towering oddly above him, a signal pistol fuming in one big hand.

Then the worrying weight pitched itself full upon him and lay still. And unconsciousness claimed him.

II

WHEN JOE CAME TO, HIS RESPIRATOR MASK WAS NO longer on his face. He was looking out, through the slight waviness of a magnetic bubble field, at ten mounds of small rocks and gravel in a row about twenty feet from the ship. Nine crosses and one six-pointed star. The Star of David would be for Mike DeWall. Joe looked up and saw the unmasked face of Maury Taller looming over him, with the dark outside skin of the ship beyond him.

"How're you feeling, Joe?" Maury asked.

"All right," he answered. Suddenly he lifted his head in fright. "My leg—I can't feel my leg!" Then he saw the silver anesthetic band that was clamped about his right leg, high on the thigh. He sank back with a sigh.

Maury said, "You'll be all right, Joe."

The words seemed to trip a trigger in his mind. Suddenly the implications of his damaged leg burst on him. He was the Leader!

"Help me!" he gritted, trying to sit up.

"You ought to lie still."

"Help me up, I said!" The leg was a dead weight. Maury's hands took hold and helped raise his body. He got the leg swung off the edge of the surface on which he had

103

been lying, and got into sitting position. He looked around him.

The magnetic bubble had been set up to make a small, air-filled addition of breathable ship's atmosphere around the airlock entrance of the *Harrier*. It enclosed about as much space as a good-sized living room. Its floor was the mountain hillside's rock and gravel. A mattress from one of the ship's bunks had been set up on equipment boxes to make him a bed. At the other end of the bubble-enclosed space something as big as a man was lying zippered up in a gray cargo freeze-sack.

"What's that?" Joe demanded. "Where's everybody?"

"They're checking equipment in the damaged sections," answered Maury. "We shot you full of medical juices. You've been out about twenty hours. That's about three-quarters of a local day-and-night cycle here." He grabbed the wounded man's shoulders suddenly with both hands. "Hold it! What're you trying to do?"

"Have a look in that freeze-sack there," grunted the Team Leader between his teeth. "Let go of me, Maury. I'm still in charge here!"

"Sit still," said Maury. "I'll bring it to you."

He went over to the bag, and taking hold of one of the carrying handles he dragged it back. It came easily in the lesser gravity, only a little more than eight-tenths of Earth's. He hauled the thing to the bed and unzipped it.

Joe stared. What was inside was not what he had been expecting.

"Cute, isn't it?" said Maury.

They looked down at the hard-frozen gray body of a biped, with the back of its skull shattered and burnt by the flare of a signal pistol. It lay on its back. The legs were somewhat short for the body and thick, as the arms were thick. But elbow and knee joints were where they should be, and the hands had four stubby gray fingers, each with an opposed thumb. Like the limbs, the body was thick—almost waistless. There were deep creases, as if tucks had been taken in the skin, around the body under the armpits, around the waist and around the legs and arms.

The head, though, was the startling feature. It was heavy and round as a ball, sunk into thick folds of neck and all but featureless. Two long slits ran down each side into the neck and shoulder area. The slits were tight closed. Like the rest of the body, the head had no hair. The eyes were little pockmarks, like raisins sunk into a doughball, and there were no visible brow ridges. The nose was a snout-end set almost flush with the facial surface. The mouth was lipless, a line of skin folded together, through which now glinted barely a glimpse of close-set, large, tridentated teeth.

"What's this?" said Joe. "Where's the thing that attacked us?"

"This is it," said Maury. "One of the aliens from the other ship."

Joe stared at him. In the brighter, harsher light from the star K94 overhead, he noticed for the first time a sprinkling of gray hairs in the black shock above Maury's spade-shaped face. Maury was no older than Joe himself.

"What're you talking about?" said Joe. "I saw that thing that attacked me. And this isn't it!"

"Look," said Maury and turned to the foot of the bed. From one of the equipment boxes he brought up eight by ten inch density photographs. "Here," he said, handing them to the Survey Team Leader. "The first one is set for bone density."

Joe took them. It showed the skeleton of the being at his feet . . . and it bore only a relative kinship to the shape of the being itself.

Under the flesh and skin that seemed so abnormally thick, the skull was high-forebrained and well developed. Heavy brown ridges showed over deep wells for the eyes. The jaw and teeth were the prognathous equipment of a carnivorous animal.

But that was only the beginning of the oddities. Bony ridges of gill structures were buried under a long fold on either side of the head, neck and shoulders. The rib cage was enormous and the pelvis tiny, buried under eight or nine inches of the gray flesh. The limbs were literally double-jointed. There was a fantastic double structure of ball and socket that seemed wholly unnecessary. Maury saw the Survey Leader staring at one hip joint and leaned over to tap it with the blunt nail of his forefinger.

"Swivel and lock," said Maury. "If the joint's pulled out, it can turn in any direction. Then, if the muscles surrounding it contract, the two ball joints interlace those bony spurs there and lock together so that they operate as a single joint in the direction chosen. That hip joint can act like the hip joint on the hind leg of a quadruped, or the leg of a biped. It can even adapt for jumping and running with maximum efficiency. —Look at the toes and the fingers."

Joe looked. Hidden under flesh, the bones of feet and hands were not stubby and short, but long and powerful. And at the end of finger and toe bones were the curved, conical claws they had seen rip open Sam Cloate with one passing blow.

"Look at these other pictures now," said Maury, taking the first one off the stack Joe held. "These have been set for densities of muscle—that's this one here—and fat. Here. And this one is set for soft internal organs—here." He was down to the last. "And this one was set for the density of the skin. Look at that. See how thick it is, and how great folds of it are literally tucked away underneath in those creases.

"Now," said Maury, "look at this closeup of a muscle. See how it resembles an interlocking arrangement of innumerable tiny muscles? Those small muscles can literally shift to adapt to different skeletal positions. They can take away beef from one area and add it to an adjoining area.

Each little muscle actually holds on to its neighbors, and they have little sphincter-sealed tube-systems to hook on to whatever blood-conduit is close. By increased hookup they can increase the blood supply to any particular muscle that's being overworked. There's parallel nerve connections."

Maury stopped and looked at the other man.

"You see?" said Maury. "This alien can literally be four or five different kinds of animal. Even a fish! And no telling how many varieties of each kind. We wondered a little at first why he wasn't wearing any kind of clothing, but we didn't wonder after we got these pictures. Why would he need clothing when he can adapt to any situation—Joe!" said Maury. "You see it, don't you? You see the natural advantage these things have over us all?"

Joe shook his head.

"There's no body hair," he said. "The creature that jumped me was striped like a tiger."

"Pigmentation. In response to emotion, maybe," said Maury. "For camouflage—or for terrifying the victims."

Joe sat staring at the pictures in his hand.

"All right," he said after a bit. "Then tell me how he happened to get here three or four minutes after we fell down here ourselves? And where did he come from? We rammed that other ship a good five miles up."

"There's only one way, the rest of us figured it out," said Maury. "He was one of the ones who were spilled out when we hit them. He must have grabbed our hull and ridden us down."

"That's impossible!"

"Not if he could flatten himself out and develop suckers like a starfish," said Maury. "The skin picture shows he could."

"All right," said Joe. "Then why did he try a suicidal trick like that attack—him alone against the eight of us?"

"Maybe it wasn't so suicidal," said Maury. "Maybe he didn't see Cal's pistol and thought he could take the unarmed eight of us." Maury hesitated. "Maybe he could, too. Or maybe he was just doing his duty—to do as much damage to us as he could before we got him. There's no cover around here that'd have given him a chance to escape from us. He knew that we'd see him the first time he moved."

Joe nodded, looking down at the form in the freeze-sack. For the aliens of the other ship there would be one similarity with the humans—a duty either to get home themselves with the news of contact, at all costs; or failing that, to see their enemy did not get home.

For a moment he found himself thinking of the frozen body before him almost as if it had been human. From what strange home world might this individual now be missed forever? And what thoughts had taken place in that round, gray-skinned skull as it had fallen surfaceward clinging to the ship of its enemies, seeing the certainty of its own death approaching as surely as the rocky mountainside?

"Do we have record films of the battle?" Joe asked.

"I'll get them." Maury went off.

He brought the films. Joe, feeling the weakness of his condition stealing up on him, pushed it aside and set to examining the pictorial record of the battle. Seen in the film viewer, the battle had a remote quality. The alien ship was smaller than Joe had thought, half the size of the *Harrier*. The two dropped weights had made large holes in its midships. It was not surprising that it had broken apart when rammed.

One of the halves of the broken ship had gone up and melted in a sudden flare of green light like their weapons beam, as if some internal explosion had taken place. The other half had fallen parallel to the *Harrier* and almost as slowly—as if the fragment, like the dying *Harrier*, had had yet some powers of flight—and had been lost to sight at last on the opposite side of this mountain, still falling.

Four gray bodies had spilled from the alien ship as it broke apart. Three, at least, had fallen some five miles to their deaths. The record camera had followed their dwindling bodies. And Maury was right; these had been changing even as they fell, flattening and spreading out as if in an instinctive effort to slow their fall. But, slowed or not, a five-mile fall even in this lesser-than-Earth gravity was death.

Joe put the films aside and began to ask Maury questions.

The *Harrier*, Maury told him, would never lift again. Half her drive section was melted down to magnesium alloy slag. She lay here with food supplies adequate for the men who were left for four months. Water was no problem as long as everyone existed still within the ship's recycling system. Oxygen was available in the local atmosphere and respirators would extract it. Storage units gave them housekeeping power for ten years. There was no shortage of medical supplies, the tool shop could fashion ordinary implements, and there was a good stock of usual equipment.

But there was no way of getting off this mountain.

III

THE OTHERS HAD COME INTO THE BUBBLE WHILE MAURY had been speaking. They stood now around the bed. With the single exception of Cal, who showed nothing, they all had a new, taut, skinned-down look about their faces, like men who have been recently exhausted or driven beyond their abilities.

"Look around you," said Jeff Ramsey, taking over from Maury when Maury spoke of the mountain. "Without help we can't leave here."

"Tell him," said Doug Kellas. Like young Jeff, Doug had not shaved recently. But where Jeff's stubble of beard was blond, Doug's was brown-dark and now marked out the hollows under his youthful cheekbones. The two had been the youngest of the Team.

"Well, this is a hanging valley," said Jeff. Jeff was the surface man geologist and meteorologist of the Team. "At one time a glacier used to come down this valley we're lying in, and over that edge there. Then the valley subsided, or the mountain rose or the climate changed. All the slopes below that cliff edge—any way down from here—bring you finally to a sheer cliff."

"How could the land rise that much?" murmured Maury,

looking out and down at the green too far below to tell what it represented. Jeff shrugged.

"This is a bigger world than Earth—even if it's lighter," he said. "Possibly more liable to crustal distortion." He nodded at the peaks above them. "These are young mountains. Their height alone reflects the lesser gravity. That glacier up there couldn't have formed on that steep a slope on Earth."

"There's the Messenger," said Cal.

His deeper-toned voice brought them all around. He had been standing behind the rest, looking over their heads. He smiled a little dryly and sadly at the faint unanimous look of hostility on the faces of all but the Survey Leader's. He was unusual in the respect that he was so built as not to need their friendship. But he was a member of the Team as they were and he would have liked to have had that friendship—if it could have been had at any price short of changing his own naturally individualistic character.

"There's no hope of that," said Doug Kellas. "The Messenger was designed for launching from the ship in space. Even in spite of the lower gravity here, it'd never break loose of the planet."

The Messenger was an emergency device every ship carried. It was essentially a miniature ship in itself, with drive unit and controls for one shift through no-time and an attached propulsive unit to kick it well clear of any gravitic field that might inhibit the shift into no-time. It could be set with the location of a ship wishing to send a message back to Earth, and with the location of Earth at the moment of arrival—both figured in terms of angle and distance from the theoretical centerpoint of the galaxy, as determined by ship's observations. It would set off, translate itself through no-time in one jump back to a reception area just outside Earth's critical gravitic field, and there be picked up with the message it contained.

For the *Harrier* team, this message could tell of the aliens and call for rescue. All that was needed was the precise information concerning the *Harrier*'s location in relation to Galactic Centerpoint and Earth's location.

In the present instance, this was no problem. The ship's computer log developed the known position and movement of Earth with regard to Centerpoint, with every shift and movement of the ship. And the position of the second planet of star K94 was known to the chartmakers of Earth recorded by last observation aboard the *Harrier*.

Travel in no-time made no difficulty of distance. In no-time all points coincided, and the ship was theoretically touching them all. Distance was not important, but location was. And a precise location was impossible—the very time taken to calculate it would be enough to render it impossibly inaccurate. What ships traveling by no-time operated on were calculations approximately as correct as possible—*and leave a safety factor*, read the rulebook.

Calculate not to the destination, but to a point safely short enough of it, so that the predictable error will not bring the ship out in the center of some solid body. Calculate safely short of the distance remaining . . . and so on by smaller and smaller jumps to a safe conclusion.

But that was with men aboard. With a mechanical unit like the Messenger, a one-jump risk could be taken.

The *Harrier* had the figures to risk it—but a no-time drive could not operate within the critical area of a gravitic field like this planet's. And, as Jeff had said, the propulsive unit of the Messenger was not powerful enough to take off from this mountainside and fight its way to escape from the planet.

"That was one of the first things I figured," said Jeff, now. "We're more than four miles above this world's sea-level, but it isn't enough. There's too much atmosphere still above us."

"The Messenger's only two and a half feet long put

together," said Maury. "It only weighs fifteen pounds earthside. Can't we send it up on a balloon or something? Did you think of that?"

"Yes," said Jeff. "We can't calculate exactly the time it would take for a balloon to drift to a firing altitude, and we have to know the time to set the destination controls. We can't improvise any sort of a booster propulsion unit for fear of jarring or affecting the destination controls. The Messenger is meant to be handled carefully and used in just the way it's designed to be used, and that's all." He looked around at them. "Remember, the first rule of a Survey Ship is that it never lands anywhere but Earth."

"Still," said Cal, who had been calmly waiting while they talked this out, "we can make the Messenger work."

"How?" challenged Doug, turning on him. "Just how?"

Cal turned and pointed to the wind-piping battlemented peaks of the mountain looming far above.

"I did some calculating myself," he said. "If we climb up there and send the Messenger off from the top, it'll break free and go."

None of the rest of them said anything for a moment. They had all turned and were looking up the steep slope of the mountain, at the cliffs, the glacier where no glacier should be able to hang, and the peaks.

"Any of you had any mountain-climbing experience?" asked Joe.

"There was a rock-climbing club at the University I went to," said Cal. "They used to practice on the rock walls of the bluffs on the St. Croix River—that's about sixty miles west of Minneapolis and St. Paul. I went out with them a few times."

No one else said anything. Now they were looking at Cal.

"And," said Joe, "as our nearest thing to an expert, you think that"—he nodded to the mountain—"can be climbed carrying the Messenger along?"

Cal nodded.

"Yes," he said slowly. "I think it can. I'll carry the Messenger myself. We'll have to make ourselves some equipment in the tool shop, here at the ship. And I'll need help going up the mountain."

"How many?" said Joe.

"Three." Cal looked around at them as he called their names. "Maury, Jeff and Doug. All the able-bodied we've got."

Joe was growing paler with the effort of the conversation.

"What about John?" he asked, looking past Doug at John Martin, Number Nine of the Survey Team. John was a short, rugged man with wiry hair—but right now his face was almost as pale as Joe's, and his warmsuit bulged over the chest.

"John got slashed up when he tried to pull the alien off you," said Cal calmly. "Just before I shot. He got it clear across the pectoral muscles at the top of his chest. He's no use to me."

"I'm all right," whispered John. It hurt him even to breathe and he winced in spite of himself at the effort of talking.

"Not all right to climb a mountain," said Cal. "I'll take Maury, Jeff and Doug."

"All right. Get at it then." Joe made a little, awkward gesture with his hand, and Maury stooped to help pull the pillows from behind him and help him lie down. "All of you—get on with it."

"Come with me," said Cal. "I'll show you what we're going to have to build ourselves in the tool shop."

"I'll be right with you," said Maury. The others went off. Maury stood looking down at Joe. They had been friends and teammates for some years.

"Shoot," whispered Joe weakly, staring up at him. "Get it off your chest, whatever it is, Maury." The effort of the last few minutes was beginning to tell on Joe. It seemed to him the bed rocked with a seasick motion beneath him, and he longed for sleep.

"You want Cal to be in charge?" said Maury, staring down at him.

Joe lifted his head from the pillow. He blinked and made an effort and the bed stopped moving for a moment under him.

"You don't think Cal should be?" he said.

Maury simply looked down at him without words. When men work and sometimes die together as happens with tight units like a Survey Team, there is generally a closeness amongst them. This closeness, or the lack of it, is something that is not easily talked about by the men concerned.

"All right," Joe said. "Here's my reasons for putting him in charge of this. In the first place he's the only one who's done any climbing. Secondly, I think the job is one he deserves." Joe looked squarely back up at the man who was his best friend on the Team. "Maury, you and the rest don't understand Cal. I do. I know that country he was brought up in and I've had access to his personal record. You all blame him for something he can't help."

"He's never made any attempt to fit in with the Team—"

"He's not built to fit himself into things. Maury—" Joe struggled up on one elbow. "He's built to make things fit him. Listen, Maury—he's bright enough, isn't he?"

"I'll give him that," said Maury, grudgingly.

"All right," said Joe. "Now listen. I'm going to violate Department rules and tell you a little bit about what made him what he is. Did you know Cal never saw the inside of a formal school until he was sixteen—and then the school was a university? The uncle and aunt who brought him up in the old voyageur's-trail area of the Minnesota-Canadian border were just brilliant enough and nutty enough to get Cal certified for home education. The result was Cal grew up in the open woods, in a tight little community that was the whole world, as far as he was concerned. And that world was completely indestructible, reasonable and handleable by young Cal Hartlett.''

"But—"

"Let me talk, Maury. I'm going to this much trouble,'' said Joe, with effort, "to convince you of something important. Add that background to Cal's natural intellect and you get a very unusual man. Do you happen to be able to guess what Cal's individual sense of security rates out at on the psych profile?''

"I suppose it's high,'' said Maury.

"It isn't simply high—it just isn't,'' Joe said. "He's off the scale. When he showed up at the University of Minnesota at sixteen and whizzed his way through a special ordering of entrance exams, the psychology department there wanted to put him in a cage with the rest of the experimental animals. He couldn't see it. He refused politely, took his bachelor's degree and went into Survey Studies. And here he is.'' Joe paused. "That's why he's going to be in charge. These aliens we've bumped into could be the one thing the human race can't match. We've got to get word home. And to get word home, we've got to get someone with the Messenger to the top of that mountain.''

He stopped talking. Maury stood there.

"You understand me, Maury?'' said Joe. "I'm Survey Leader. It's my responsibility. And in my opinion if there's one man who can get the Messenger to the top of the mountain, it's Cal.''

The bed seemed to make a slow half-swing under him suddenly. He lost his balance. He toppled back off the support of his elbow, and the sky overhead beyond the bubble began to rotate slowly around him and things blurred.

Desperately he fought to hold on to consciousness. He had to convince Maury, he thought. If he could convince Maury, the others would fall in line. He knew what was wrong with them in their feelings toward Cal as a leader. It was the fact that the mountain was unclimbable. Anyone could see it was unclimbable. But Cal was going to climb it anyway, they all knew that, and in climbing it he would probably require the lives of the men who went with him.

They would not have minded that if he had been one of them. But he had always stood apart, and it was a cold way to give your life—for a man whom you had never understood, or been able to get close to.

"Maury," he choked. "Try to see it from Cal's—try to see it from his—"

The sky spun into a blur. The world blurred and tilted.

"Orders," Joe croaked at Maury. "Cal—command—"

"Yes," said Maury, pressing him back down on the bed as he tried blindly to sit up again. "All right. All right, Joe. Lie still. He'll have the command. He'll be in charge and we'll all follow him. I promise . . ."

IV

DURING THE NEXT TWO DAYS, THE SURVEY LEADER WAS only intermittently conscious. His fever ran to dangerous levels, and several times he trembled and jerked as if on the verge of going into convulsions. John Martin also, although he was conscious and able to move around and even do simple tasks, was pale, high-fevered and occasionally thick-tongued for no apparent reason. It seemed possible there was an infective agent in the claw and teeth wounds made by the alien, with which the ship's medicines were having trouble coping.

With the morning of the third day when the climbers were about to set out both men showed improvement.

The Survey Leader came suddenly back to clearheadedness as Cal and the three others were standing, all equipped in the bubble, ready to leave. They had been discussing last-minute warnings and advice with a pale but alert John Martin when Joe's voice entered the conversation.

"What?" it said. "Who's alive? What was that?"

They turned and saw him propped up on one elbow on his makeshift bed. They had left him on it since the sleeping quarters section of the ship had been completely destroyed, and the sections left unharmed were too full of equipment to make practical places for the care of a wounded man. Now they saw his eyes taking in their respirator masks, packs, hammers, the homemade pitons and hammers, and other equipment including rope, slung about them.

"What did one of you say?" Joe demanded again. "What was it?"

"Nothing, Joe," said John Martin, coming toward him. "Lie down."

Joe waved him away, frowning. "Something about one being still alive. One what?"

Cal looked down at him. Joe's face had grown lean and fallen in even in these few days but the eyes in the face were sensible.

"He should know," Cal said. His calm, hard, oddly carrying baritone quieted them all. "He's still Survey Leader." He looked around at the rest but no one challenged his decision. He turned and went into the corridor of the ship, down to the main control room, took several photo prints from a drawer and brought them back. When he got back out, he found Joe now propped up on pillows but waiting.

"Here," said Cal, handing Joe the photos. "We sent survey rockets with cameras over the ridge up there for a look at the other side of the mountain. That top picture shows you what they saw."

Joe looked down at the top picture that showed a stony mountainside steeper than the one the *Harrier* lay on. On this rocky slope was what looked like the jagged, broken-off end of a blackened oil drum—with something white spilled out on the rock by the open end of the drum.

"That's what's left of the alien ship," said Cal. "Look at the closeup on the next picture."

Joe discarded the top photo and looked at the one beneath. Enlarged in the second picture he saw that the white something was the body of an alien, lying sprawled out and stiff.

"He's dead, all right," said Cal. "He's been dead a day or two anyway. But take a good look at the whole scene and tell me how it strikes you."

Joe stared at the photo with concentration. For a long moment he said nothing. Then he shook his head, slowly.

"Something's phony," he said at last, huskily.

"I think so too," said Cal. He sat down on the makeshift bed beside Joe and his weight tilted the wounded man a little toward him. He pointed to the dead alien. "Look at him. He's got nothing in the way of a piece of equipment he was trying to put outside the ship before he died. And that mountainside's as bare as ours. There was no place for him to go outside the ship that made any sense as a destination if he was that close to dying. And if you're dying on a strange world, do you crawl *out* of the one familiar place that's there with you?"

"Not if you're human," said Doug Kellas behind Cal's shoulder. There was the faintly hostile note in Doug's voice still. "There could be a dozen different reasons we don't know anything about. Maybe it's taboo with them to die inside a spaceship. Maybe he was having hallucinations at the end, that home was just beyond the open end of the ship. Anything."

Cal did not bother to turn around.

"It's possible you're right, Doug," he said. "They're about our size physically and their ship was less than half the size of the *Harrier*. Counting this one in the picture and the three that fell with the one that we killed here accounts for five of them. But just suppose there were six. And the sixth one hauled the body of this one outside in case we came around for a look—just to give us a false sense of security thinking they were all gone."

Joe nodded slowly. He put the photos down on the bed and looked at Cal who stood up.

"You're carrying guns?" said Joe. "You're all armed in case?"

"We're starting out with sidearms," said Cal. "Down here the weight of them doesn't mean much. But up there . . ." He nodded to the top reaches of the mountain and did not finish. "But you and John better move inside the ship nights and keep your eyes open in the day."

"We will." Joe reached up a hand and Cal shook it. Joe shook hands with the other three who were going. They put their masks on.

"The rest of you ready?" asked Cal, who by this time was already across the bubble enclosure, ready to step out. His voice came hollowly through his mask. The others broke away from Joe and went toward Cal, who stepped through the bubble.

"Wait!" said Joe suddenly from the bed. They turned to him. He lay propped up, and his lips moved for a second as if he was hunting for words. "—Good luck!" he said at last.

"Thanks," said Cal for all of them. "To you and John, too. We'll all need it."

He raised a hand in farewell. They turned and went.

They went away from the ship, up the steep slope of the old glacier streambed that became more steep as they climbed. Cal was in the lead with Maury, then Jeff, then Doug bringing up the rear. The yellow bright rays of K94 struck back at them from the ice-scoured granite surface of the slope, gray with white veinings of quartz. The warmsuits were designed to cool as well as heat their wearers, but they had been designed for observer-wearers, not working wearers. At the bend-spots of arm and leg joints, the soft interior cloth of the warmsuits soon became damp with sweat as the four men toiled upward. And the cooling cycle inside the suits made these damp spots clammy-feeling when they touched the wearer. The respirator masks also became slippery with perspiration where the soft, elastic rims of their transparent faceplates pressed against brow and cheek and chin. And to the equipment-heavy men the *feel* of the angle of the steep rock slope seemed treacherously less than eyes trained to Earth gravity reported it. Like a subtly tilted floor in a fun house at an amusement park.

They climbed upward in silence as the star that was larger than the sun of Earth climbed in the sky at their backs. They moved almost mechanically, wrapped in their own thoughts. What the other three thought were personal, private thoughts having no bearing on the moment. But Cal in the lead, his strong-boned, rectangular face expressionless, was wrapped up in two calculations. Neither of these had anything to do with the angle of the slope or the distance to the top of the mountain.

He was calculating what strains the human material walking behind him would be able to take. He would need more than their grudging cooperation. And there was something else.

He was thinking about water.

Most of the load carried by each man was taken up with items constructed to be almost miraculously light and compact for the job they would do. One exception was the fifteen Earth pounds of components of the Messenger, which Cal himself carried in addition to his mountain-climbing equipment—the homemade crampons, pitons and ice axe-piton hammer—and his food and the sonic pistol at his belt. Three others were the two-gallon containers of water carried by each of the other three men. Compact rations of solid food they all carried, and in a pinch they could go hungry. But to get to the top of the mountain they would need water.

Above them were ice slopes, and the hook-shaped glacier that they had been able to see from the ship below.

That the ice could be melted to make drinking water was beyond question. Whether that water would be safe to drink was something else. There had been the case of another Survey ship on another world whose melted local ice water had turned out to contain as a deposited impurity a small windborn organism that came to life in the inner warmth of men's bodies and attacked the walls of their digestive tracts. To play safe here, the glacier ice would have to be distilled.

Again, one of the pieces of compact equipment Cal himself carried was a miniature still. But would he still have it by the time they reached the glacier? They were all ridiculously overloaded now.

Of that overload, only the Messenger itself and the climbing equipment, mask and warmsuit had to be held on to at all costs. The rest could and probably would go. They would probably have to take a chance on the melted glacier ice. If the chance went against them—how much water would be needed to go the rest of the way?

Two men at least would have to be supplied. Only two men helping each other could make it all the way to the top. A single climber would have no chance.

Cal calculated in his head and climbed. They all climbed.

From below, the descending valley streambed of the former glacier had looked like not too much of a climb. Now that they were on it, they were beginning to appreciate the tricks the eye could have played upon it by sloping distances in a lesser gravity, where everything was constructed to a titanic scale. They were like ants inching up the final stories of the Empire State Building.

Every hour they stopped and rested for ten minutes. And it was nearly seven hours later, with K94 just approaching its noon above them, that they came at last to the narrowed end of the ice-smoothed rock, and saw, only a few hundred yards ahead, the splintered and niched vertical rock wall they would have to climb to the foot of the hook-shaped glacier.

V

THEY STOPPED TO REST BEFORE TACKLING THE DISTANCE between them and the foot of the rock wall. They sat in a line on the bare rock, facing downslope, their packloads leaned back against the higher rock. Cal heard the sound of the others breathing heavily in their masks, and the voice of Maury came somewhat hollowly through the diaphragm of his mask.

"Lots of loose rock between us and that cliff," said the older man. "What do you suppose put it there?"

"It's talus," answered Jeff Ramsey's mask-hollowed voice from the far end of the line. "Weathering—heat differences, or maybe even ice from snowstorms during the winter season getting in cracks of that rock face, expanding, and cracking off the sedimentary rock it's constructed of. All that weathering's made the wall full of wide cracks and pockmarks, see?"

Cal glanced over his shoulder.

"Makes it easy to climb," he said. And heard the flat sound of his voice thrown back at him inside his mask. "Let's get going. Everybody up!"

They got creakily and protestingly to their feet. Turning, they fell into line and began to follow Cal into the rock debris, which thickened quickly until almost immediately they were walking upon loose rock flakes any size up to that of a garage door, that slipped or slid unexpectedly under their weight and the angle of this slope that would not have permitted such an accumulation under Earth's greater gravity.

"Watch it!" Cal threw back over his shoulder at the others. He had nearly gone down twice when loose rock under his weight threatened to start a miniature avalanche among the surrounding rock. He labored on up the talus slope, hearing the men behind swearing and sliding as they followed.

"Spread out!" he called back. "So you aren't one behind the other—and stay away from the bigger rocks."

These last were a temptation. Often as big as a small platform, they looked like rafts floating on top of the smaller shards of rock, the similarity heightened by the fact that the rock of the cliff-face was evidently planar in structure. Nearly all the rock fragments split off had flat faces. The larger rocks seemed to offer a temptingly clear surface on which to get away from the sliding depth of smaller pieces in which the boots of the men's warmsuits went mid-leg deep with each sliding step. But the big fragments, Cal had already discovered, were generally in precarious balance on the loose rock below them and the angled slope. The lightest step upon them was often enough to make them turn and slide.

He had hardly called the warning before there was a choked-off yell from behind him and the sound of more-than-ordinary roaring and sliding of rock.

He spun around. With the masked figures of Maury on his left and Doug on his right he went scrambling back toward Jeff Ramsey, who was lying on his back, half-buried in rock fragments and all but underneath a ten by six foot slab of rock that now projected reeflike from the smaller rock pieces around it.

*   *   *

Jeff did not stir as they came up to him, though he seemed conscious. Cal was first to reach him. He bent over the blond-topped young man and saw through the faceplate of the respiration mask how Jeff's lips were sucked in at the corners and the skin showed white in a circle around his tight mouth.

"My leg's caught." The words came tightly and hollowly through the diaphragm of Jeff's mask. "I think something's wrong with it."

Carefully, Cal and the others dug the smaller rock away. Jeff's right leg was pinned down under an edge of the big rock slab. By extracting the rock underneath it piece by piece, they got the leg loose. But it was bent in a way it should not have been.

"Can you move it?"

Jeff's face stiffened and beaded with sweat behind the mask faceplate.

"No."

"It's broken, all right," said Maury. "One down already," he added bitterly. He had already gone to work, making a splint from two tent poles out of Jeff's pack. He looked up at Cal as he worked, squatting beside Jeff. "What do we do now, Cal? We'll have to carry him back down?"

"No," said Cal. He rose to his feet. Shading his eyes against the sun overhead he looked down the hanging valley to the *Harrier*, tiny below them.

They had already used up nearly an hour floundering over the loose rock, where one step forward often literally had meant two steps sliding backward. His timetable, based on his water supplies, called for them to be at the foot of the ice slope leading to the hook glacier before camping for the night—and it was already noon of the long local day.

"Jeff," he said. "You're going to have to get back down to the *Harrier* by yourself." Maury started to protest, then shut up. Cal could see the other men looking at him.

Jeff nodded. "All right," he said. "I can make it. I can roll most of the way." He managed a grin.

"How's the leg feel?"

"Not bad, Cal." Jeff reached out a warmsuited hand and felt the leg gingerly. "More numb than anything right now."

"Take his load off," said Cal to Doug. "And give him your morphine pack as well as his own. We'll pad that leg and wrap it the best we can, Jeff, but it's going to be giving you a rough time before you get it back to the ship."

"I could go with him to the edge of the loose rock—" began Doug, harshly.

"No. I don't need you. Downhill's going to be easy," said Jeff.

"That's right," said Cal. "But even if he did need you, you couldn't go, Doug. *I* need you to get to the top of that mountain."

They finished wrapping and padding the broken leg with one of the pup tents and Jeff started off, half-sliding, half dragging himself downslope through the loose rock fragments.

They watched him for a second. Then, at Cal's order, they turned heavily back to covering the weary, strugglesome distance that still separated them from the foot of the rock face.

They reached it at last and passed into the shadow at its base. In the sunlight of the open slope the warmsuits had struggled to cool them. In the shadow, abruptly, the process went the other way. The cliff of the rock face was about two hundred feet in height, leading up to that same ridge over which the weather balloon had been sent to take pictures of the fragment of alien ship on the other side of the mountain. Between the steep rock walls at the end of the glacial valley, the rock face was perhaps fifty yards wide. It was torn and pocked and furrowed vertically by the splitting off of rock from it. It looked like a great chunk of plank standing on end, weathered along the lines of its vertical grain into a decayed roughness of surface.

The rock face actually leaned back a little from the vertical, but, looking up at it from its foot, it seemed not only to go straight up, but—if you looked long enough—to overhang, as if it might come down on the heads of the three men. In the shadowed depths of vertical cracks and holes, dark ice clung.

Cal turned to look back the way they had come. Angling down away behind them, the hanging valley looked like a giant's ski-jump. A small, wounded creature that was the shape of Jeff was dragging itself down the slope, and a child's toy, the shape of the *Harrier*, lay forgotten at the jump's foot.

Cal turned back to the cliff and said to the others, "Rope up."

He had already shown them how this was to be done, and they had practiced it back at the *Harrier*. They tied themselves together with the length of sounding line, the thinness of which Cal had previously padded and thickened so that a man could wrap it around himself to belay another climber without being cut in half. There was no worry about the strength of the sounding line.

"All right," said Cal, when they were tied together—himself in the lead, Maury next, Doug at the end. "Watch where I put my hands and feet as I climb. Put yours in exactly the same places."

"How'll I know when to move?" Doug asked hollowly through his mask.

"Maury'll wave you on, as I'll wave him on," said Cal. Already they were high enough up for the whistling winds up on the mountain peak to interfere with mask-impeded conversations conducted at a distance. "You'll find this cliff is easier than it looks. Remember what I told you about handling the rope. And don't look down."

"All right."

*   *   *

Cal had picked out a wide rock chimney rising twenty feet to a little ledge of rock. The inner wall of the chimney was studded with projections on which his hands and feet could find purchase. He began to climb.

When he reached the ledge he was pleasantly surprised to find that, in spite of his packload, the lesser gravity had allowed him to make the climb without becoming winded. Maury, he knew, would not be so fortunate. Doug, being the younger man and in better condition, should have less trouble, which was why he had put Doug at the end, so that they would have the weak man between them.

Now Cal stood up on the ledge, braced himself against the rock wall at his back and belayed the rope by passing it over his left shoulder, around his body and under his right arm.

He waved Maury to start climbing. The older man moved to the wall and began to pull himself up as Cal took in the slack of the rope between them.

Maury climbed slowly but well, testing each hand and foothold before he trusted his weight to it. In a little while he was beside Cal on the ledge, and the ascent of Doug began. Doug climbed more swiftly, also without incident. Shortly they were all on the ledge.

Cal had mapped out his climb on this rock face before they had left, studying the cliff with powerful glasses from the *Harrier* below. Accordingly, he now made a traverse, moving horizontally across the rock face to another of the deep, vertical clefts in the rock known as chimneys to climbers. Here he belayed the rope around a projection and, by gesture and shout, coached Maury along the route.

Maury, and then Doug, crossed without trouble.

Cal then led the way up the second chimney, wider than the first and deeper. This took them up another forty-odd feet to a ledge on which all three men could stand or sit together.

Cal was still not winded. But looking at the other two, he saw that Maury was damp-faced behind the faceplate of his mask. The older man's breath was whistling in the respirator. It was time, thought Cal, to lighten loads. He had never expected to get far with some of their equipment in any case, but he had wanted the psychological advantage of starting the others out with everything needful.

"Maury," he said, "I think we'll leave your sidearm here, and some of the other stuff you're carrying."

"I can carry it," said Maury. "I don't need special favors."

"No," said Cal. "You'll leave it. I'm the judge of what's ahead of us, and in my opinion the time to leave it is now." He helped Maury off with most of what he carried, with the exception of a pup tent, his climbing tools and the water container and field rations. Then as soon as Maury was rested, they tackled the first of the two really difficult stretches of the cliff.

This was a ten-foot traverse that any experienced climber would not have found worrisome. To amateurs like themselves it was spine-chilling.

The route to be taken was to the left and up to a large, flat piece of rock wedged in a wide crack running diagonally up the rock face almost to its top. There were plenty of available footrests and handholds along the way. What would bother them was the fact that the path they had to take was around a boss, or protuberance of rock. To get around the boss it was necessary to move out over the empty atmosphere of a clear drop to the talus slope below.

Cal went first.

He made his way slowly but carefully around the out-curve of the rock, driving in one of his homemade pitons and attaching an equally homemade snap-ring to it, at the outermost point in the traverse. Passing the line that connected him to Maury through this, he had a means of holding the other men to the cliff if their holds should slip and they have to depend on the rope on their way around. The snap-ring and piton were also a psychological assurance.

Arrived at the rock slab in the far crack, out of sight of the other two, Cal belayed the rope and gave two tugs. A second later a tug came back. Maury had started crossing the traverse.

He was slow, very slow, about it. After agonizing minutes Cal saw Maury's hand come around the edge of the boss. Slowly he passed the projecting rock to the rock slab. His face was pale and rigid when he got to where Cal stood. His breath came in short, quick pants.

Cal signaled on the rope again. In considerably less time than Maury had taken Doug came around the boss. There was a curious look on his face.

"What is it?" asked Cal.

Doug glanced back the way he had come. "Nothing, I guess," he said. "I just thought I saw something moving back there. Just before I went around the corner. Something I couldn't make out."

Cal stepped to the edge of the rock slab and looked as far back around the boss as he could. But the ledge they had come from was out of sight. He stepped back to the ledge.

"Well," he said to the others, "the next stretch is easier."

VI

IT WAS. THE CRACK UP WHICH THEY CLIMBED NOW SLANTED to the right at an almost comfortable angle.

They went up it using hands and feet like climbing a ladder. But if it was easy, it was also long, covering better than a hundred feet of vertical rock face. At the top, where the crack pinched out, there was the second tricky traverse across the rock face, of some eight feet. Then a short climb up a cleft and they stood together on top of the ridge.

Down below, they had been hidden by the mountain walls from the high winds above. Now for the first time, as they emerged onto the ridge they faced and felt them.

The warmsuits cut out the chill of the atmosphere whistling down on them from the mountain peak, but they could feel the pressure of it molding the suits to their bodies. They stood now once more in sunlight. Behind them they could see the hanging valley and the *Harrier*. Ahead was a cwm, a hollow in the steep mountainside that they would have to cross to get to a further ridge leading up to the mountain peak. Beyond and below the further ridge, they could see the far, sloping side of the mountain and, black against it, the tiny, oil-drum-end fragment of alien ship with a dot of white just outside it.

"We'll stay roped," said Cal. He pointed across the steep-sloping hollow they would need to cross to reach the further rocky ridge. The hollow seemed merely a tilted area with occasional large rock chunks perched on it at angles that to Earth eyes seemed to defy gravity. But there was a high shine where the sun's rays struck.

"Is that ice?" said Maury, shading his eyes.

"Patches of it. A thin coating over the rocks," said Cal. "It's time to put on the crampons."

They sat down and attached the metal frameworks to their boots that provided them with spiked footing. They drank sparingly of the water they carried and ate some of their rations. Cal glanced at the descending sun, and the blue-black sky above them. They would have several hours yet to cross the cwm, in daylight. He gave the order to go, and led off.

He moved carefully out across the hollow, cutting or kicking footholds in patches of ice he could not avoid. The slope was like a steep roof. As they approached the deeper center of the cwm, the wind from above seemed to be funneled at them so that it was like a hand threatening to push them into a fall.

Some of the rock chunks they passed were as large as small houses. It was possible to shelter from the wind in their lees. At the same time, they often hid the other two from Cal's sight, and this bothered him. He would have preferred to be able to watch them in their crossings of the ice patches, so that if one of them started to slide he would be prepared to belay the rope. As it was, in the constant moan and howl of the wind, his first warning would be the sudden strain on the rope itself. And if one of them fell and pulled the other off the mountainside, their double weight could drag Cal loose.

Not for the first time, Cal wished that the respirator masks they wore had been equipped with radio intercom.

But these were not and there had been no equipment aboard the *Harrier* to convert them.

They were a little more than halfway across when Cal felt a tugging on the line.

He looked back. Maury was waving him up into a shelter of one of the big rocks. He waved back and turned off from the direct path, crawling up into the ice-free overhang. Behind him, as he turned, he saw Maury coming toward him, and behind Maury, Doug.

"Doug wants to tell you something!" Maury shouted against the wind noise, putting his mask up close to Cal's.

"What is it?" Cal shouted.

"—Saw it again!" came Doug's answer.

"Something moving?" Doug nodded. "Behind us?" Doug's mask rose and fell again in agreement. "Was it one of the aliens?"

"I think so!" shouted Doug. "It could be some sort of animal. It was moving awfully fast—I just got a glimpse of it!"

"Was it"—Doug shoved his masked face closer, and Cal raised his voice—"was it wearing any kind of clothing that you could see?"

"No!" Doug's head shook back and forth.

"What kind of life could climb around up here without freezing to death—unless it had some protection?" shouted Maury to them both.

"We don't know!" Cal answered. "Let's not take chances. If it is an alien, he's got all the natural advantages. Don't take chances. You've got your gun, Doug. Shoot anything you see moving!"

Doug grinned and looked harshly at Cal from inside his mask.

"Don't worry about me!" he shouted back. "Maury's the one without a gun."

"We'll both keep an eye on Maury! Let's get going now.

There's only about another hour or so before the sun goes behind those other mountains—and we want to be in camp underneath the far ridge before dark!''

He led off again and the other two followed.

As they approached the far ridge, the wind seemed to lessen somewhat. This was what Cal had been hoping for— that the far ridge would give them some protection from the assault of the atmosphere they had been enduring in the open. The dark wall of the ridge, some twenty or thirty feet in sudden height at the edge of the cwm, was now only a hundred yards or so away. It was already in shadow from the descending sun, as were the downslope sides of the big rock chunks. Long shadows stretched toward a far precipice edge where the cwm ended, several thousand feet below. But the open icy spaces were now ruddy and brilliant with the late sunlight. Cal thought wearily of the pup tents and his sleeping bag.

Without warning a frantic tugging on the rope roused him. He jerked around, and saw Maury, less than fifteen feet behind him, gesturing back the way they had come. Behind Maury, the rope to Doug led out of sight around the base of one of the rock chunks.

Then suddenly Doug slid into view.

Automatically Cal's leg muscles spasmed tight, to take the sudden jerk of the rope when Doug's falling body should draw it taut. But the jerk never came.

Sliding, falling, gaining speed as he descended the rooftop-steep slope of the cwm, Doug's body no longer had the rope attached to it. The rope still lay limp on the ground behind Maury. And then Cal saw something he had not seen before. The dark shape of Doug was not falling like a man who finds himself sliding down two thousand feet to eternity. It was making no attempt to stop its slide at all. It fell limply, loosely, like a dead man—and indeed, just at that moment, it slid far upon a small, round boulder in its path which tossed it into the air like a stuffed dummy, arms and legs asprawl, and it came down indifferently upon the slope beyond and continued, gaining speed as it went.

Cal and Maury stood watching. There was nothing else they could do. They saw the dark shape speeding on and on, until finally it was lost for good among the darker shapes of the boulders farther on down the cwm. They were left without knowing whether it came eventually to rest against some rock, or continued on at last to fall from the distant edge of the precipice to the green, unknown depth that was far below them.

After a little while Maury stopped looking. He turned and climbed on until he had caught up with Cal. His eyes were accusing as he pulled in the loose rope to which Doug had been attached. They looked at it together.

The rope's end had been cut as cleanly as any knife could have cut it.

The sun was just touching the farther mountains. They turned without speaking and climbed on to the foot of the ridge wall.

Here the rocks were free of ice. They set up a single pup tent and crawled into it with their sleeping bags together, as the sun went down and darkness flooded their barren and howling perch on the mountainside.

VII

THEY TOOK TURNS SITTING UP IN THEIR SLEEPING BAGS, IN the darkness of their tiny tent, with Cal's gun ready in hand.

Lying there in the darkness, staring at the invisible tent roof nine inches above his nose, Cal recognized that in theory the aliens could simply be better than humans—and that was that. But, Cal, being the unique sort of man he was, found that he could not believe such theory.

And so, being the unique sort of man he was, he discarded it. He made a mental note to go on trying to puzzle out the alien's vulnerability tomorrow . . . and closing his eyes, fell into a light doze that was the best to be managed in the way of sleep.

When dawn began to lighten the walls of their tent they managed, with soup powder, a little of their precious water and a chemical thermal unit, to make some hot soup and get it into them. It was amazing what a difference this made, after the long, watchful and practically sleepless night. They put some of their concentrated dry rations into their stomachs on top of the soup and Cal unpacked and set up the small portable still.

He took the gun and his ice-hammer and crawled outside the tent. In the dawn light and the tearing wind he sought ice which they could melt and then distill to replenish their containers of drinking water. But the only ice to be seen within any reasonable distance of their tent was the thin ice-glaze—*verglas*, mountaineers back on Earth called it—over which they had struggled in crossing the cwm the day before. And Cal dared not take their only gun too far from Maury, in case the alien made a sudden attack on the tent.

There was more than comradeship involved. Alone, Cal knew, there would indeed be no hope of his getting the Messenger to the mountaintop. Not even the alien could do that job alone—and so the alien's strategy must be to frustrate the human party's attempt to send a message.

It could not be doubted that the alien realized what their reason was for trying to climb the mountain. A race whose spaceships made use of the principle of no-time in their drives, who was equipped for war, and who responded to attack with the similarities shown so far, would not have a hard time figuring out why the human party was carrying the equipment on Cal's pack up the side of a mountain.

More, the alien, had he had a companion, would probably have been trying to get message equipment of his own up into favorable dispatching position. Lacking a companion his plan must be to frustrate the human effort. That put the humans at an additional disadvantage. They were the defenders, and could only wait for the attacker to choose the time and place of his attempt against them.

And it would not have to be too successful an attempt, at that. It would not be necessary to kill either Cal or Maury, now that Doug was gone. To cripple one of them enough so that he could not climb and help his companion climb, would be enough. In fact, if one of them were crippled Cal doubted even that they could make it back to the *Harrier*. The alien then could pick them off at leisure.

*   *   *

Engrossed in his thoughts, half-deafened by the ceaseless wind, Cal woke suddenly to the vibration of something thundering down on him.

He jerked his head to stare upslope—and scrambled for his life. It was like a dream, with everything in slow motion—and one large chunk of rock with its small host of lesser rocks roaring down upon him.

Then—somehow—he was clear. The miniature avalanche went crashing by him, growing to a steady roar as it grew in size sweeping down alongside the ridge. Cal found himself at the tent, from which Maury was half-emerged, on hands and knees, staring down at the avalanche.

Cal swore at himself. It was something he had been told, and had forgotten. Such places as they had camped in last night were natural funnels for avalanches of loose rock. So, he remembered now, were wide cracks like the sloping one in the cliff face they had climbed up yesterday as, indeed, the cwm itself was on a large scale. And they had crossed the cwm in late afternoon, when the heat of the day would have been most likely to loosen the frost that held precariously balanced rocks in place.

Only fool luck had gotten them this far!

"Load up!" he shouted to Maury. "We've got to get out of here."

Maury had already seen that for himself. They left the pup tent standing. The tent in Cal's load would do. With that, the Messenger, their climbing equipment, their sleeping bags and their food and water, they began to climb the steeply sloping wall of the ridge below which they had camped. Before they were halfway up it, another large rock with its attendant avalanche of lesser rocks came by below them.

Whether the avalanches were alien-started, or the result of natural causes, made no difference now. They had learned their lesson the hard way. From now on, Cal vowed silently, they would stick to the bare and open ridges unless there was absolutely no alternative to entering avalanche territory. And only after every precaution.

In the beginning Cal had kept a fairly regular check on how Maury was doing behind him. But as the sun rose in the bluish-black of the high altitude sky overhead the weariness of his body seemed to creep into his mind and dull it. He still turned his head at regular intervals to see how Maury was doing. But sometimes he found himself sitting and staring at his companion without any real comprehension of why he should be watching over him.

The blazing furnace of K94 overhead, climbing toward its noontime zenith, contributed to this dullness of the mind. So did the ceaseless roaring of the wind which had long since deafened them beyond any attempt at speech. As the star overhead got higher in the sky this and the wind noise combined to produce something close to hallucinations . . . so that once he looked back and for a moment seemed to see the alien following them, not astraddle the ridge and hunching itself forward as they were, but walking along the knife-edge of rock like a monkey along a branch, foot over foot, and grasping the rock with toes like fingers, oblivious of the wind and the sun.

Cal blinked and the illusion—if that was what it was— was gone. But its image lingered in his brain with the glare of the sun and the roar of the wind.

His eyes had fallen into the habit of focusing on the rock only a dozen feet ahead of him. At last he lifted them and saw the ridge broaden, a black shadow lying sharply across it. They had come to the rock walls below the hanging glacier they had named the Hook.

They stopped to rest in the relative wind-break shelter of the first wall, then went on.

Considering the easiness of the climb they made remarkably slow progress. Cal slowly puzzled over this until, like the slow brightening of a candle, the idea grew in him to check the absolute altimeter at his belt.

They were now nearly seven thousand feet higher up than they had been at the wreck of the *Harrier*. The mask respirators had been set to extract oxygen for them from the local atmosphere in accordance with the *Harrier* altitude. Pausing on a ledge, Cal adjusted his mask controls.

For a minute there seemed to be no difference at all. And then he began to come awake. His head cleared. He became sharply conscious suddenly of where he stood—on a ledge of rock, surrounded by rock walls with, high overhead, the blue-black sky and brilliant sunlight on the higher walls. They were nearly at the foot of the third, and upper, battlement of the rock walls.

He looked over the edge at Maury, intending to signal the man to adjust his mask controls. Maury was not even looking up, a squat, lumpish figure in the warmsuit totally covered, with the black snout of the mask over his face. Cal tugged at the rope and the figure raised its face. Cal with his gloved hands made adjusting motions at the side of his mask. But the other's face below, hidden in the shadow of the faceplate, stared up without apparent comprehension. Cal started to yell down to him—here the wind noise was lessened to the point where a voice might have carried—and then thought better of it.

Instead he tugged on the rope in the signal they had repeated an endless number of times; and the figure below, foreshortened to smallness stood dully for a moment and then began to climb. His eyes sharpened by the fresh increase in the oxygen flow provided by his mask Cal watched that slow climb almost with amazement carefully taking in the rope and belaying it as the other approached.

There was a heaviness, an awkwardness, about the warmsuited limbs, as slowly—but strongly enough—they pulled the climber up toward Cal. There was something abnormal about their movement. As the other drew closer, Cal stared more and more closely until at last the gloves of the climber fastened over the edge of the ledge.

Cal bent to help him. But, head down not looking, the other hoisted himself up alongside Cal and a little turned away.

Then in that last instant the combined flood of instinct and a lifetime of knowledge cried certainty. And Cal knew.

The warmsuited figure beside him was Maury no longer.

VIII

REFLEXES HAVE BEEN THE SAVING OF MANY A MAN'S LIFE. In this case, Cal had been all set to turn and climb again, the moment Maury stood beside him on the edge. Now recognizing that somewhere among these rocks, in the past fumbling hours of oxygen starvation, Maury had ceased to live and his place had been taken by the pursuing alien, Cal's reflexes took over.

If the alien had attacked the moment he stood upright on the ledge, different reflexes would have locked Cal in physical combat with the enemy. When the alien did not attack, Cal turned instinctively to the second prepared response of his body and began automatically to climb to the next ledge.

There was no doubt that any other action by Cal, any hesitation, any curiosity about his companion would have forced the alien into an immediate attack. For then there would have been no reason not to attack. As he climbed, Cal felt his human brain beginning to work again after the hours of dullness. He had time to think.

His first thought was to cut the line that bound them together, leaving the alien below. But this would precipitate the attack Cal had already instinctively avoided. Any place Cal could climb at all, the alien could undoubtedly climb with ease. Cal's mind chose and discarded possibilities. Suddenly he remembered the gun that hung innocently at his hip.

With that recollection, the situation began to clear and settle in his mind. The gun evened things. The knowledge that it was the alien on the other end of the rope, along with the gun, more than evened things. Armed and prepared, he could afford to risk the present situation for a while. He could play a game of pretense as well as the alien could, he thought.

That amazing emotional center of gravity, Cal's personal sense of security and adequacy that had so startled the psychology department at the university was once more in command of the situation. Cal felt the impact of the question— why was the alien pretending to be Maury? Why had he adapted himself to man-shape, put on man's clothes and fastened himself to the other end of Cal's climbing rope?

Perhaps the alien desired to study the last human that opposed him before he tried to destroy it. Perhaps he had some hope of rescue by his own people, and wanted all the knowledge for them he could get. If so it was a wish that cut two ways. Cal would not be sorry of the chance to study a living alien in action.

And when the showdown came—there was the gun at Cal's belt to offset the alien's awesome physical natural advantage.

They continued to climb. Cal watched the other figure below him. What he saw was not reassuring.

With each wall climbed, the illusion of humanity grew stronger. The clumsiness Cal had noticed at first—the appearance of heaviness—began to disappear. It began to take on a smoothness and a strength that Maury had never shown in the climbing. It began, in fact, to look almost familiar. Now Cal could see manlike hunching and bulgings of the shoulder muscles under the warmsuit's shapelessness, as the alien climbed and a certain trick of throwing the head from right to left to keep a constant watch for a better route up the face of the rock wall.

It was what he did himself, Cal realized suddenly. The alien was watching Cal climb ahead of him and imitating even the smallest mannerisms of the human.

They were almost to the top of the battlements, climbing more and more in sunlight. K94 was already far down the slope of afternoon. Cal began to hear an increase in the wind noise as they drew close to the open area above. Up there was the tumbled rock-strewn ground of a terminal moraine and then the snow slope to the hook glacier.

Cal had planned to camp for the night above the moraine at the edge of the snow slope. Darkness was now only about an hour away and with darkness the showdown must come between himself and the alien. With the gun, Cal felt a fair amount of confidence. With the showdown, he would probably discover the reason for the alien's impersonation of Maury.

Now Cal pulled himself up the last few feet. At the top of the final wall of the battlements the windblast was strong. Cal found himself wondering if the alien recognized the gun as a killing tool. The alien which had attacked them outside the *Harrier* had owned neither weapons nor clothing. Neither had the ones filmed as they fell from the enemy ship, or the one lying dead outside the fragment of that ship on the other side of the mountain. It might be that they were so used to their natural strength and adaptability they did not understand the use of portable weapons. Cal let his hand actually brush against the butt of the sidearm as the alien climbed on to the top of the wall and stood erect, faceplate turned a little from Cal.

But the alien did not attack.

Cal stared at the other for a long second, before turning and starting to lead the way through the terminal moraine, the rope still binding them together. The alien moved a little behind him, but enough to his left so that he was within Cal's range of vision, and Cal was wholly within his. Threading his way among the rock rubble of the moraine, Cal cast a glance at the yellow orb of K94, now just hovering above the sharp peaks of neighboring mountains around them.

Night was close. The thought of spending the hours of darkness with the other roped to him cooled the back of Cal's neck. Was it darkness the alien was waiting for?

Above them, as they crossed the moraine the setting sun struck blazing brilliance from the glacier and the snow slope. In a few more minutes Cal would have to stop to set up the pup tent, if he hoped to have enough light to do so. For a moment the wild crazy hope of a notion crossed Cal's mind that the alien had belatedly chosen life over duty. That at this late hour, he had changed his mind and was trying to make friends.

Cold logic washed the fantasy from Cal's mind. This being trudging almost shoulder to shoulder with him was the same creature that had sent Doug's limp and helpless body skidding and falling down the long ice-slope to the edge of an abyss. This companion alongside was the creature that had stalked Maury somewhere among the rocks of the mountainside and disposed of him, and stripped his clothing off and taken his place.

Moreover, this other was of the same race and kind as the alien who had clung to the hull of the falling *Harrier* and, instead of trying to save himself and get away on landing, had made a suicidal attack on the eight human survivors. The last thing that alien had done, when there was nothing else to be done, was to try to take as many humans as possible into death with him.

This member of the same race walking side by side with Cal would certainly do no less.

But why was he waiting so long to do it? Cal frowned

hard inside his mask. That question had to be answered. Abruptly he stopped. They were through the big rubble of the moraine, onto a stretch of gravel and small rock. The sun was already partly out of sight behind the mountain peaks. Cal untied the rope and began to unload the pup tent.

Out of the corner of his eyes, he could see the alien imitating his actions. Together they got the tent set up and their sleeping bags inside. Cal crawled in the tiny tent and took off his boots. He felt the skin between his shoulder blades crawl as a second later the masked head of his companion poked itself through the tent opening and the other crept on hands and knees to the other sleeping bag. In the dimness of the tent with the last rays of K94 showing thinly through its walls, the shadow on the far tent wall was a monstrous parody of a man taking off his boots.

The sunlight failed and darkness filled the tent. The wind moaned loudly outside. Cal lay tense, his left hand gripping the gun he had withdrawn from its holster. But there was no movement.

The other had gotten into Maury's sleeping bag and lay with his back to Cal. Facing that back, Cal slowly brought the gun to bear. The only safe thing to do was to shoot the alien now, before sleep put Cal completely at the other's mercy.

Then the muzzle of the gun in Cal's hand sank until it pointed to the fabric of the tent floor. To shoot was the only safe thing—and it was also the only impossible thing.

Ahead of them was the snow-field and the glacier, with its undoubted crevasses and traps hidden under untrustworthy caps of snow. Ahead of them was the final rock climb to the summit. From the beginning, Cal had known no one man could make this final stretch alone. Only two climbers roped together could hope to make it safely to the top.

Sudden understanding burst on Cal's mind. He quietly reholstered the gun. Then, muttering to himself, he sat up suddenly without any attempt to hide the action, drew a storage cell lamp from his pack and lit it. In the sudden illumination that burst on the tent he found his boots and stowed them up alongside his bag.

He shut the light off and lay down again, feeling cool and clear-headed. He had had only a glimpse in turning, but the glimpse was enough. The alien had shoved Maury's pack up into a far corner of the tent as far away from Cal as possible. But the main pockets of that pack now bulked and swelled as they had not since Cal had made Maury lighten his load on the first rock climb.

Cal lay still in the darkness with a grim feeling of humor inside him. Silently, in his own mind he took his hat off to his enemy. From the beginning he had assumed that the only possible aim one of the other race could have would be to frustrate the human attempt to get word back to the human base—so that neither race would know of the two ships' encounter.

Cal had underestimated the other. And he should not have, for technologically they were so similar and equal. The aliens had used a no-time drive. Clearly, they had also had a no-time rescue signaling device like the Messenger, which needed to be operated from the mountaintop.

The alien had planned from the beginning to join the human effort to get up into Messenger-firing position, so as to get his own device up there.

He, too, had realized—in spite of his awesome natural advantage over the humans—that no single individual could make the last stage of the climb alone. Two, roped together, would have a chance. He needed Cal as much as Cal needed him.

In the darkness, Cal almost laughed out loud with the irony of it. He need not be afraid of sleeping. The showdown would come only at the top of the mountain.

Cal patted the butt of the gun at his side and smiling, he fell asleep.

But he did not smile, the next morning when, on waking, he found the holster empty.

IX

WHEN HE AWOKE TO SUNLIGHT THROUGH THE TENT walls the form beside him seemed not to have stirred, but the gun was gone.

As they broke camp, Cal looked carefully for it. But there was no sign of it either in the tent, or in the immediate vicinity of the camp. He ate some of the concentrated rations he carried and drank some of the water he still carried. He made a point not to look to see if the alien was imitating him. There was a chance, he thought, that the alien was still not sure whether Cal had discovered the replacement.

Cal wondered coldly where on the naked mountainside Maury's body might lie—and whether the other man had recognized the attacker who had killed him, or whether death had taken him unawares.

Almost at once they were on the glacier proper. The glare of ice was nearly blinding. Cal stopped and uncoiled the rope from around him. He tied himself on, and the alien in Maury's warmsuit, without waiting for a signal, tied himself on also.

Cal went first across the ice surface, thrusting downward with the forearm-length handle of his homemade ice axe.

When the handle penetrated only the few inches of top snow and jarred against solidity, he chipped footholds like a series of steps up the steep pitch of the slope. Slowly they worked their way forward.

Beyond the main length of the hook rose a sort of tower of rock that was the main peak. The tower appeared to have a cup-shaped area or depression in its center—an ideal launching spot for the Messenger, Cal had decided, looking at it through a powerful telescopic viewer from the wreck of the *Harrier*. A rare launching spot in this landscape of steeply tilted surfaces.

Without warning a shadow fell across Cal's vision. He started and turned to see the alien towering over him. But, before he could move, the other had begun chipping at the ice higher up. He cut a step and moved up ahead of Cal. He went on, breaking trail, cutting steps for Cal to follow.

A perverse anger began to grow in Cal. He was aware of the superior strength of the other, but there was something contemptuous about the alien's refusal to stop and offer Cal his turn. Cal moved up close behind the other and abruptly began chipping steps in a slightly different direction. As he chipped, he moved up them, and gradually the two of them climbed apart.

When the rope went taut between them they both paused and turned in each other's direction—and without warning the world fell out from underneath Cal.

He felt himself plunging. The cruel and sudden jerk of the rope around his body brought him up short and he dangled, swaying between ice-blue walls.

He craned his head backward and looked up. Fifteen feet above him were two lips of snow, and behind these the blue-black sky. He looked down and saw the narrowing rift below him plunge down into darkness beyond vision.

For a moment his breath caught in his chest.

Then there was a jerk on the rope around him, and he saw

the wall he was facing, a drop of perhaps eighteen inches. He had been lifted. The jerk came again, and again. Steadily it progressed. A strength greater than that of any human was drawing him up.

Slowly, jerk by jerk, Cal mounted to the edge of the crevasse—to the point where he could reach up and get his gloved hands on the lip of ice and snow, to the point where he could get his forearms out on the slope and help lift his weight from the crevasse.

With the aid of the rope he crawled out at last on the downslope side of the crevasse. Just below him, he saw the alien in Maury's clothing, buried almost to his knees in loose snow, half kneeling, half-crouching on the slope with the rope in his grasp. The alien did not straighten up at once. It was as if even his great strength had been taxed to the utmost.

Cal, trembling, stared at the other's crouched immobility. It made sense. No physical creature was possessed of inexhaustible energy—and the alien had also been climbing a mountain. But, the thought came to chill Cal's sudden hope, if the alien had been weakened, Cal had been weakened also. They stood in the same relationship to each other physically that they had to begin with.

After a couple of minutes, Cal straightened up. The alien straightened up also, and began to move. He stepped out and took the lead off to his left, circling around the crevasse revealed by Cal's fall. He circled wide, testing the surface before him.

They were nearing the bend of the hook—the point at which they could leave the glacier for the short slope of bare rock leading up to the tower of the main peak and the cup-shaped spot from which Cal had planned to send off the Messenger. The hook curved to their left. Its outer bulge reached to the edge of a ridge on their right running up to the main peak, so that there was no avoiding a crossing of this final curve of the glacier. They had been moving closer to the ice-edge of the right-hand ridge, and now they were close enough to see how it dropped sheer, a frightening distance to rocky slopes far below.

The alien, leading the way, had found and circled a number of suspicious spots in the glacier ice. He was now a slack thirty feet of line in front of Cal, and some fifty feet from the ice-edge of the rim.

Suddenly, with almost no noise—as if it had been a sort of monster conjuring feat—the whole edge of the ice disappeared.

The alien and Cal both froze in position.

Cal, ice axe automatically dug in to anchor the other, was still on what seemed to be solid ice-covered rock. But the alien was revealed to be on an ice-bridge, all that was left of what must have been a shelf of glacier overhanging the edge of the rocky ridge. The rock was visible now—inside the alien's position. The ice-bridge stretched across a circular gap in the edge of the glacier, to ice-covered rock at the edge of the gap ahead and behind. It was only a few feet thick and the sun glinted on it.

Slowly, carefully, the masked and hidden face of the alien turned to look back at Cal, and the darkness behind his face-plate looked square into Cal's eyes.

For the first time there was direct communication between them. The situation was their translator and there was no doubt between them about the meanings of their conversation. The alien's ice-bridge might give way at any second. The jerk of the alien's fall on the rope would be more than the insecure anchor of Cal's ice-hammer could resist. If the alien fell while Cal was still roped to him, they would both go.

On the other hand, Cal could cut himself loose. Then, if the ice-bridge gave way, Cal would have lost any real chance of making the peak. But he would still be alive.

The alien made no gesture asking for help. He merely looked.

Well, which is it to be? the darkness behind his faceplate asked. If Cal should cut loose, there was only one thing for the alien to do, and that was to try to crawl on across the ice-bridge on his own—an attempt almost certain to be disastrous.

Cal felt a cramping in his jaw muscles. Only then did he realize he was smiling—a tight-lipped, sardonic smile. Careful not to tauten the rope between them, he turned and picked up the ice axe, then drove it into the ice beyond and to his left. Working step by step, from anchor point to anchor point, he made his way carefully around the gap, swinging well inside it, to a point above the upper end of the ice-bridge. Here he hammered and cut deeply into the ice until he stood braced in a two-foot hole with his feet flat against a vertical wall, lying directly back against the pull of the rope leading to the alien.

The alien had followed Cal's movements with his gaze. Now, as he saw Cal bracing himself, the alien moved forward and Cal took up the slack in the rope between them. Slowly, carefully, on hands and knees like a cat stalking in slow motion a resting butterfly, the alien began to move forward across the ice-bridge.

One foot—two feet—and the alien froze suddenly as a section of the bridge broke out behind him.

Now there was no way to go but forward. Squinting over the lower edge of his faceplate and sweating in his warmsuit, Cal saw the other move forward again. There were less than ten feet to go to solid surface. Slowly, the alien crept forward. He had only five feet to go, only four, only three—

The ice-bridge went out from under him.

X

THE SHOCK THREATENED TO WRENCH CAL'S ARMS FROM their shoulder-sockets—but skittering, clawing forward like a cat in high gear, the alien was snatching at the edge of the solid ice. Cal suddenly gathered in the little slack in the line and threw his weight into the effort of drawing the alien forward.

Suddenly the other was safe, on solid surface. Quickly, without waiting, Cal began to climb.

He did not dare glance down to see what the alien was doing; but from occasional tautenings of the rope around his shoulders and chest, he knew that the other was still tied to him. This was important, for it meant that the moment of their showdown was not yet. Cal was gambling that the other, perhaps secure in the knowledge of his strength and his ability to adapt, had not studied the face of this tower as Cal had studied it through the telescopic viewer from the *Harrier*.

From that study, Cal had realized that it was a face that he himself might be able to climb unaided. And that meant a face that the alien certainly could climb unaided. If the alien should realize this, a simple jerk on the rope that was tied around Cal would settle the problem of the alien as far as human competition went. Cal would be plucked from his meager hand and footholds like a kitten from the back of a chair, and the slope below would dispose of him. He sweated now, climbing, trying to remember the path up the towerside as he had planned it out, from handhold to handhold, gazing through the long-distance viewer.

He drew closer to the top. For some seconds and minutes now, the rope below him had been completely slack. He dared not look down to see what that might mean. Then finally he saw the edge of the cup-shaped depression above him, bulging out a little from the wall.

A second more and his fingers closed on it. Now at last he had a firm handhold. Quickly he pulled himself up and over the edge. For a second perspiration blurred his vision. Then he saw the little, saucer-sloping amphitheater not more than eighteen feet wide, and the further walls of the tower enclosing it on three sides.

Into the little depression the light of K94 blazed from the nearly black sky. Unsteadily Cal got to his feet and turned around. He looked down the wall he had just climbed.

The alien still stood at the foot of the wall. He had braced himself there, evidently to belay Cal against a fall that would send him skidding down the rock slope below. Though what use to belay a dead man, Cal could not understand, since the more than thirty feet of fall would undoubtedly have killed him. Now, seeing Cal upright and in solid position, the alien put his hands out toward the tower wall as if he would start to climb.

Cal immediately hauled taut on the line, drew a knife from his belt and, reaching as far down as possible, cut the line.

The rope end fell in coils at the alien's feet. The alien was still staring upward as Cal turned and went as quickly as he could to the center of the cup-shaped depression.

The wind had all but died. In the semi-enclosed rock depression the reflected radiation of the star overhead made it hot. Cal unsnapped his pack and let it drop. He stripped off the gloves of his warmsuit and, kneeling, began to open up the pack. His ears were alert. He heard nothing from outside the tower, but he knew that he had minutes at most.

He laid out the three sections of the silver-plated Messenger, and began to screw them together. The metal was warm to his touch after being in the sun-warmed backpack, and his fingers, stiff and cramped from gripping at handholds, fumbled. He forced himself to move slowly, methodically, to concentrate on the work at hand and forget the alien now climbing the tower wall with a swiftness no human could have matched.

Cal screwed the computer-message-beacon section of the nose tight to the drive section of the middle. He reached for the propulsive unit that was the third section. It rolled out of his hand. He grabbed it up and began screwing it on to the two connected sections.

The three support legs were still in the pack. He got the first one out and screwed it on. The next stuck for a moment, but he got it connected. His ear seemed to catch a scratching noise from the outside of the tower where the alien would be climbing. He dug in the bag, came out with the third leg and screwed it in. Sweat ran into his eyes inside the mask faceplate, and he blinked to clear his vision.

He set the Messenger upright on its three legs. He bent over on his knees, facemask almost scraping the ground, to check the level indicator.

Now he was sure he heard a sound outside on the wall of the tower. The leftmost leg was too long. He shortened it. Now the middle leg was off. He lengthened that. He shortened the leftmost leg again . . . slowly . . . there, the Messenger was leveled.

He glanced at the chronometer on his wrist. He had set it with the ship's chronometer before leaving. Sixty-six ship's hours thirteen minutes, and . . . the sweep second hand was moving. He fumbled with two fingers in the breast pocket of his warmsuit, felt the small booklet he had made up before leaving and pulled it out. He flipped through the pages of settings, a row of them for each second of time. Here they were . . . sixty-three hours, thirteen minutes—

A gust of wind flipped the tiny booklet from his stiffened fingers. It fluttered across the floor of the cup and into a crack in the rock wall to his right. On hands and knees he scrambled after it, coming up against the rock wall with a bang.

The crack reached all the way through the further wall, narrowing until it was barely wide enough for daylight to enter—or a booklet to exit. The booklet was caught cross-ways against the unevenness of the rock sides. He reached in at arm's length. His fingers touched it. They shoved it a fraction of an inch further away. Sweat rolled down his face.

He ground the thickness of his upper arm against the aperture of the crack. Gently, gently, he maneuvered two fingers into position over the near edge of the booklet. The fingers closed. He felt it. He pulled back gently. The booklet came.

He pulled it out.

He was back at the Messenger in a moment, finding his place in the pages again. Sixteen hours—fourteen minutes—the computer would take four minutes to warm and fire the propulsive unit.

A loud scratching noise just below the lip of the depression distracted him for a second.

He checked his chronometer. Sixty-three hours, sixteen minutes plus . . . moving on toward thirty seconds. Make it sixty-three hours sixteen minutes even. Setting for sixty-three hours, sixteen minutes plus four minutes—sixty-three hours, twenty minutes.

His fingers made the settings on the computer section as

the second hand of his chronometer crawled toward the even minute . . .

There.

His finger activated the computer. The Messenger began to hum faintly, with a soft internal vibration.

The sound of scraping against rock was right at the lip of the depression, but out of sight.

He stood up. Four minutes the Messenger must remain undisturbed. Rapidly, but forcing himself to calmness, he unwound the rest of the rope from about him and unclipped it. He was facing the lip of the depression over which the alien would come, but as yet there was no sign. Cal could not risk the time to step to the depression's edge and make sure.

The alien would not be like a human being, to be dislodged by a push as he crawled over the edge of the lip. He would come adapted and prepared. As quickly as he could without fumbling, Cal fashioned a slipknot in one end of the rope that hung from his waist.

A gray, wide, flat parody of a hand slapped itself over the lip of rock and began to change form even as Cal looked. Cal made a running loop in his rope and looked upward. There was a projection of rock in the ascending walls on the far side of the depression that would do. He tossed his loop up fifteen feet toward the projection. It slipped off—as another hand joined the first on the lip of rock. The knuckles were becoming pale under the pressure of the alien's great weight.

Cal tossed the loop again. It caught. He drew it taut.

He backed off across the depression, out of line with the Messenger, and climbed a few feet up the opposite wall. He pulled the rope taut and clung to it with desperate determination.

And a snarling tiger's mask heaved itself into sight over the edge of rock, a tiger body following. Cal gathered his legs under him and pushed off. He swung out and downward, flashing toward the emerging alien, and they slammed together, body against fantastic body.

For a fraction of a second they hung together, toppling over space while the alien's lower extremities snatched and clung to the edge of rock.

Then the alien's hold loosened. And wrapped together, still struggling, they fell out and down toward the rock below accompanied by a cascade of rocks.

XI

"W"AKING IN A HOSPITAL," CAL SAID LATER, "WHEN you don't expect to wake at all, has certain humbling effects."

It was quite an admission for someone like himself, who had by his very nature omitted much speculation on either humbleness or arrogance before. He went deeper into the subject with Joe Aspinwall when the Survey Team Leader visited him in that same hospital back on Earth. Joe by this time, with a cane, was quite ambulatory.

"You see," Cal said, as Joe sat by the hospital bed in which Cal lay, with the friendly and familiar sun of Earth making the white room light about them, "I got to the point of admiring that alien—almost of liking him. After all, he saved my life, and I saved his. That made us close, in a way. Somehow, now that I've been opened up to include creatures like him, I seem to feel closer to the rest of my own human race. You understand me?"

"I don't think so," said Joe.

"I mean, I needed that alien. The fact brings me to think that I may need the rest of you, after all. I never really believed I did before. It made things lonely."

"I can understand that part of it," said Joe.

"That's why," said Cal, thoughtfully, "I hated to kill

160

him, even if I thought I was killing myself at the same time.''

"Who? The alien?'' said Joe. "Didn't they tell you? You didn't kill him.''

Cal turned his head and stared at his visitor.

"No, you didn't kill him!'' said Joe. "When the rescue ship came they found you on top of him and both of you halfway down that rock slope. Evidently landing on top of him saved you. Just his own natural toughness saved him— that and being able to spread himself out like a rug and slow his fall. He got half a dozen broken bones—but he's alive right now.''

Cal smiled. "I'll have to go say hello to him when I get out of here.''

"I don't think they'll let you do that,'' said Joe. "They've got him guarded ten deep someplace. Remember, his people still represent a danger to the human race greater than anything we've ever run into.''

"Danger?'' said Cal. "They're no danger to us.''

It was Joe who stared at this. "They've got a definite weakness,'' said Cal. "I figured they must have. They seemed too good to be true from the start. It was only in trying to beat him out to the top of the mountain and get the Messenger off that I figured out what it had to be, though.''

"What weakness? People'll want to hear about this!'' said Joe.

"Why, just what you might expect,'' said Cal. "You don't get something without giving something away. What his race had gotten was the power to adapt to any situation. Their weakness is that same power to adapt.''

"What're you talking about?''

"I'm talking about my alien friend on the mountain,'' said Cal, a little sadly. "How do you suppose I got the Messenger off? He and I both knew we were headed for a showdown when we reached the top of the mountain. And he had the natural advantage of being able to adapt. I was no match for him physically. I had to find some advantage to outweigh that advantage of his. I found an instinctive one.''

"Instinctive . . ." said Joe, looking at the big, bandaged man under the covers and wondering whether he ought not to ring for the nurse.

"Of course, instinctive," said Cal thoughtfully, staring at the bed sheet. "His instincts and mine were diametrically opposed. He adapted to fit the situation. I belonged to a people who adapted situations to fit *them*. I couldn't fight a tiger with my bare hands, but I could fight something half-tiger, half something else."

"I think I'll just ring for the nurse," said Joe, leaning forward to the button on the bedside table.

"Leave that alone," said Cal calmly. "It's simple enough. What I had to do was force him into a situation where he would be between adaptations. Remember, he was as exhausted as I was, in his own way; and not prepared to quickly understand the unexpected."

"What unexpected?" Joe gaped at him. "You talk as if you thought you were in control of the situation all the way."

"Most of the way," said Cal. "I knew we were due to have a showdown. I was afraid we'd have it at the foot of the tower—but he was waiting until we were solidly at the top. So I made sure to get up to that flat spot in the tower first, and cut the rope. He had to come up the tower by himself."

"Which he was very able to do."

"Certainly—in one form. He was in one form coming up," said Cal. "He changed to his fighting form as he came over the edge—and those changes took energy. Physical and nervous, if not emotional energy, when he was pretty exhausted already. Then I swung at him like Tarzan as he was balanced, coming over the edge of the depression in the rock.''

"And had the luck to knock him off," said Joe. "Don't tell me with someone as powerful as that it was anything but luck. I was there when Mike and Sam got killed at the *Harrier*, remember.''

"Not luck at all," said Cal, quietly. "A foregone conclusion. As I say, I'd figured out the balance sheet for the power of adaptation. It had to be instinctive. That meant that if he was threatened, his adaptation to meet the threat would take place whether consciously he wanted it to or not. He was barely into tiger-shape, barely over the edge of the cliff, when I hit him and threatened to knock him off into thin air. He couldn't help himself. He adapted.''

"Adapted!" said Joe, staring.

"Tried to adapt—to a form that would enable him to cling to his perch. That took the strength out of his tiger-fighting form, and I was able to get us both off the cliff together instead of being torn apart the minute I hit him. The minute we started to fall, he instinctively spread out and stopped fighting me altogether.''

Joe sat back in his chair. After a moment, he swore.

"And you're just now telling me this?" he said.

Cal smiled a little wryly.

"I'm surprised you're surprised," he said. "I'd thought people back here would have figured all this out by now. This character and his people can't ever pose any real threat to us. For all their strength and slipperiness, their reaction to life is passive. They adapt to it. Ours is active—we adapt it to us. On the instinctive level, we can always choose the battlefield and the weapons, and win every time in a contest.''

He stopped speaking and gazed at Joe, who shook his head slowly.

"Cal," said Joe at last, "you don't think like the rest of us."

Cal frowned. A cloud passing beyond the window dimmed the light that had shone upon him.

"I'm afraid you're right," he said quietly. "For just a while, I had hopes it wasn't so."

THINGS WHICH ARE CAESAR'S

"I know you," Jamethon said. *The dark skin of his face was like taut silk.* *"You are one of the Deniers of God."*

"An incorrect name for us," answered Padma. *"All men deny and believe at the same time—and each builds to his own heaven."*

Soldier, Ask Not (Childe Cycle: revised)

MEN AND WOMEN BORN OF CITIES FIND IT HARD TO REAL-
ize how utter a dark can come, outdoors, when the
last of the sunset goes and the moon is not yet up.
For a long hour of gradually fading twilight, the meadow
between the road and the lower woods had been almost as
visible as in full daylight. Now, suddenly, it was all dark as
an unlit cave. The few people already camped in the meadow
moved closer to their fires or lit lanterns inside their tents.

A few were caught away from the camping spaces they
had rented, visiting either at the store trucks selling food
and supplies alongside the road, or at one of the temporary
chemical toilets set up on the road's far side, where the
ground lifted in a wooded slope to the near horizon of the
hilltop. These stumbled and felt their way back to where
they thought they should be, not helped much by the limited
beams of flashlights, even if they were lucky enough to be
carrying such.

The only one who did not fumble his way was Ranald.
With neither sunset nor flashlight to help him, he kept
moving at a normal pace over the now invisible ground. In
the first breathing of the night wind his full, sandy beard
blew back around his neck under his chin. He did not

stumble over anyone, even those couples lying together in darkness. To his ears, each person there was a beacon of noise in the obscurity. Even those who were not talking, breathed, gurgled or rustled loudly enough to keep someone like himself from walking into them; and, even if they had not been so loud, he could smell each of them and their belongings from ten or fifteen feet away. Possessions or people, they all smelled, one way or another. Even those who thought of themselves as extremely clean stank of soap and dry-cleaning fluids and city smokes.

Ranald passed them by now; and he passed by their fires. Almost to a man or woman, these early-comers to the campground were loaded with outdoor gear of some sort or another. Most had brought food of their own, as well—the store trucks had barely begun to do the business their owners expected to do tomorrow or the next day. Ranald himself carried no camping equipment. But under each arm he had a chunk of log from a dry sugar maple. Behind him, now, he could hear some follower, someone heavy-footed and unsure, using him as a guide through the dark. Ranald grinned a little sadly in his beard and breathed deeply of the night breeze. Among and beyond the smells of the campers, he scented pine and spruce trees from downslope, swamp soil, and running river.

His searching gaze settled at last on one small fire and his nose found the reek of it right. Turning to it, he detoured around four city-dressed adults who were lying, talking in the total dark like children backyard camping for the first time. He came up to the small fire. It was a narrow blaze, fed by the ends of five pieces of oak limb, pointing to the burning area like wagon spokes to a hub. Just beyond the flames was a lean man, himself the color of peeled, old oak, dressed in Levi's and a red-and-white-checked wool shirt. He sat on an unrolled sleeping bag with a poncho staked at a rain slope above it.

He and Ranald looked at each other like strange dogs across the plains.

"Hard maple," said Ranald, dropping his two pieces of wood beside the fire. "Burns slow."

The other man stared for a moment at the chunks of wood, then reached off into the darkness behind him with his right hand and came back holding an aluminum coffeepot with its base blackened from the fire. "Tea?" he asked.

"I thank you," said Ranald. He sat down cross-legged himself; and he and the man behind the fire regarded each other in its light. The man who owned the fire was easily a foot taller than Ranald and looked competent. But Ranald, under his thin, worn leather jacket, was oddly wide across the shoulders and heavy-headed under a mass of sand-colored hair and beard, so that in a strange way he looked even more competent than the man with the fire.

"Dave Wilober's my name," said the man with the fire.

"Ranald," said Ranald.

The distance separating them across the flickering red flames was too far to reach across easily for the shaking of hands. Neither man tried.

"Pleased to meet you," said Dave Wilober. His accent was Southern and twangy. Ranald spoke almost like a Mid-westerner, except for a slight rhythm to his phrasing—not the singsong of someone with a Scandinavian inheritance of speech, but a patterning of words and emphasis that was almost Irish. The two looked at each other examiningly.

"And you," said Ranald.

The coffeepot on the white-glowing wood coals in the fire's center was beginning to sing already. Dave reached out and turned the pot to expose the curve of its other side to the greatest heat.

"I was thinking I'd probably sit by myself here," he said, half to Ranald, half to the fire. "Didn't guess anyone neighborly might come by."

"There'll be others," Ranald said. He frowned at the

fire, with his beard blowing about his face in the night breeze. In the unrelieved darkness behind him, he heard an uncertain shuffling of heavy hiking boots, and there was the sound of embarrassed breathing.

"Others?" Dave frowned a little. "Don't know about that. I'm not great for company."

"There'll be others," Ranald repeated. "There were the first time."

"The first time?" Dave raised an eyebrow and lifted the coffeepot off the coals. Inside it now, they could both hear the boiling water hammering at the metal sides. "There been a Sign in the Heavens before this? When?"

"Far back," said Ranald. He was tempted to say more, but the years had made him taciturn. "Long since."

Dave watched him for a moment. Ranald only gazed back.

"Any case," said Dave, taking the top off the hot pot with a quick, clever snatch of his fingers, and dropping it inside-up on the ground beside him. He poured some tea leaves from a bag into the pot. "Likely most anybody coming to something like this'd be churchy. I'm not."

He paused to glance at Ranald again.

"You neither?" he asked.

"That's right," said Ranald, softly. "There's nothing for me in god-houses."

Dave nodded.

"Not natural," he said, "going into a box—for something like that."

He half rose, to turn and produce a couple of plastic cups before sitting down again. As he did so, a small chinking noise came from him—so slight a noise that only ears like Ranald's could have caught it. Ranald cocked his head on one side like an interested bird, staring at the lower half of Dave's body, then raised his gaze to find Dave's eyes steady and unmoving upon him.

"Brother," said Ranald, peacefully, "you go your way, I go mine. Isn't that so?"

Dave's gaze fell away, back to the fire.

"Fair enough—" he began and broke off, turning his head to the right to look off into darkness. From the direction in which he stared came plainly now the noise of two pairs of feet, two breathing bodies, heavily approaching. After a moment a pair of people loomed into the illumination of the fire and halted, staring down at the seated men.

They were male and female both young. The man was only slightly taller than Ranald, and slighter of build. Like Ranald, he was bearded; but the dark-brown hair on his face was sparse and fine, so that with the wind blowing it this way and that it seemed as if he were only bearded in patches. Above the beard and narrow cheekbones his brown eyes had the dark openness of a suffering, newborn animal. Below the beard, his narrow body was thickened by layers of clothing. He walked unsurely. Beside him, the girl also was swollen with clothes. She was smaller than he, with long, straight-hanging blond hair, and a mere nub of a nose in a plate-round face that would not have looked old on a girl of twelve. But her arm was tightly around his waist. It was she who was holding him up—and she was the one who spoke.

"We've got to get warm," she said; and her tone of voice left no choice in the matter. "We've got to sit down by your fire."

Ranald glanced across at Dave. In the flickering firelight Dave's features were like a face carved in bas-relief on some ancient panel of dark wood. He hesitated, but only for a moment.

"Sit," he said. He reached behind himself once more and came back this time with two more plastic cups and an unopened can of vegetable beef soup.

The girl and the young man dropped clumsily down before the fire. Seated now, and clearly shown in the red light, the man was shivering. The girl kneeled beside him in her baggy, several layers of slacks; and placed the palm of her small, plump hand flat on his forehead. Her nails were top-edged in black; and to Ranald's nose she, like the young man, reeked of old dirt and sweat.

"He's got a fever," she said.

They were both wearing packs of a sort, his hardly more than a knapsack, hers sagging, heavy and large, with a blanket roll below the sack. She helped him off with his, then shrugged out of the straps that bound her, and opened up the blanket roll. A moment later she had him wrapped with a number of thin, dark-blue blankets, most of them ragged along their edges, as if something had chewed them.

Dave had opened the can of soup and emptied it into a pan on the fire. He rinsed out the can with water from a white plastic jug, then filled the can and the three cups with tea from the coffeepot. He handed the cups to Ranald and the other two, keeping the can for himself.

The girl's eyes had gone to Ranald as the cups were passed out. She had put her own cup down; and it was cooling beside her as she continued to urge tea into the young man. Ranald gazed back at her without particular expression, all the time Dave had been in constant activity.

"He's sick," the girl said to Ranald.

Ranald only continued to watch her, without moving.

Behind him, there was a sudden rush. The hiking boots that had followed him here, and which had been fidgeting in the background since, came forward with a rush, carrying a man in his mid-to-late thirties into the firelight. The light of the flames played on the boots, which were new-looking, with speed lacings, fastened tight to the tops of the thick corduroy pants above them with leather straps around the pant cuffs. He was zipped up in a plaid jacket, with a large backpack of yellow plastic strapped to an aluminum pack frame that glinted brilliantly in the firelight.

He smiled eagerly at them, turning his head to include

everybody. His face was softened and his waist thick with perhaps thirty pounds of unnecessary fat. His hair was receding, but what was left was black and curly. Only his long sideburns were touched with gray. He ended his smile upon the girl and squatted down beside her, getting out of his pack.

"I've got some antibiotics here . . ." he chattered, digging into the pack. "I couldn't help hearing you say your friend was sick. Here . . . oh, yes . . ."

He brought his fist out with a tube of bicolored capsules, red and black in the firelight. The eyes of both the young man and the girl jumped for a moment at the sight of the capsule-shapes, then settled back to quiet watching again.

"What's that?" asked the girl sharply.

"Ampicillin." The man in boots tilted one of the capsules out of the tube into the palm of his left hand, offering it to the girl. "Very good . . ."

She took the capsule and pushed it between the lips of the young man.

"Take it with the tea," she told him. He swallowed.

"That's right. And keep him warm—" the man in boots started to hand the tube of capsules to the girl, whose back was turned. He hesitated, then put the tube back in his pack. "Every six hours. We'll give him one. . . ."

He looked across at Dave and ducked his gaze away as Dave looked back. He glanced at Ranald, and looked away from Ranald back to Dave, almost immediately.

"My name's Strauben," he said. "Walt Strauben."

"Dave Wilober," said Dave.

"Ranald," said Ranald from the other side of the fire. Walt Strauben turned his face to the young man and the girl, expectantly.

"Letty," said the girl, shortly. "He's Rob."

"Rob, Letty, Dave . . . Ranald. Myself . . ." said Walt, busily digging into his pack. He came up with a heavy black thermos bottle and held it up. "Anyone care for some coffee—"

"Thanks," said Dave. "We've got tea."

"Of course. That's right. Well, I'll have some myself." Walt unscrewed the cap of the thermos and poured the cap half full of cream-brown liquid, closed the bottle again and put it away in his pack. He dug into his pack and came out with a folded newspaper. "Did you see today's paper? They're camping out all over the world just like us, waiting. Listen—'*The promise of a Sign from some supernatural power on the day of the vernal equinox has already, today, sent literally millions of people out into the fields all over the world to await the evidence of faith that rumor has promised for tomorrow. Expectation of some sort of miracle to celebrate the Christian year 2000, or simply to reward those who've been steadfast in their beliefs in any faith, continued to mount through the morning. All over the globe ordinary business is effectively at a standstill. . . .*'"

"That's all right," said Dave.

Walt stopped reading, lowered the paper and stared at Dave. The paper trembled a little in his hand. His heavy lower lip trembled a little as well.

"No need to read," said Dave. "You're welcome—for now."

"Oh all right. I just thought . . ." Walt cleared his throat and refolded the newspaper. Its pages crackled in the stillness as he thrust it back into his pack.

"Thank you," he said, speaking more into the packsack than in any other direction. "I appreciate . . ."

The girl, Letty, had been staring at him. Now, nostrils spread, she turned sharply to Dave as if to say something. Dave's eyes met her, still and steady. She turned back to Rob without speaking.

"Is that soup ready yet?" asked Rob. He had a sharp, high-pitched voice, with a ring to it that sounded just on the edge of excitement or anger.

"Soon, baby," said Letty to him, in a different voice. "Soon."

Dave sat drinking his tea from the soup can. Walt worked with his pack, unfolding an air mattress, blowing it up and unrolling a sleeping bag upon it. After a little while Dave took the pot holding the soup off the coals. Letty passed over the cup from which Rob had been drinking tea and Dave emptied the last of the liquid in it on the fire. It hissed and disappeared. Dave filled the cup with soup and handed it back to Letty.

"Thanks," she said, briefly, and held the cup for Rob. He sucked at it, not shivering visibly anymore.

". . . All the same," said Walt, now lying on his sleeping bag and beginning to talk so quietly that his voice came at the rest of them unexpectedly, "it's an amazing thing, all the same. Even if no miracle happens, even if no Sign is shown, everybody coming out to watch for it, like this, all over the world, has to count for something more than just hysteria. . . ."

Neither Dave nor Letty nor Rob answered him. Ranald watched him unmovingly, listening; but Walt, as he talked, avoided Ranald's eyes.

". . . So many people of different religions and cultures, getting together like this everywhere, has to be a Sign in itself," said Walt. "Spiritual values are beside the point. Personal weakness hasn't anything to do with it. We've all been *called* here when you think about it, in a sense. . . ."

Ranald's head lifted and his head turned. He listened and sniffed at the darkness behind him. After a second he got up and moved off away from the firelight so quietly that not even Dave's head turned to see him go.

Once he was well away from the fire, the pastureland between the road and the woods took shadowy form in his eyes. The moon was barely up above the hill, now—a fairly respectable three-quarters moon, but blurred by a high, thin cloud layer. Through this layer it spread enough cold light to show the upright objects in the pastureland as silhouettes, but left the ground surface still deep in obscurity.

Over this obscurity Ranald followed his nose and ears to a scent of perfume like lilacs, and an almost voiceless sound of crying. He came at last to a shape huddled on the ground, away from any fire or tent. Nose and ears filled in what his eyes could not see in the little light there was. Seated alone was another young woman or girl, tall, wearing shoes with heels made for hard cement rather than soft earth, a dress thin and tight for indoors, instead of out, and a coat cut for fashion, not warmth. Besides these things, she had nothing with her—no pack, no blankets, no lantern or shelter materials.

She sat, simply hunched up on the open ground, arms around her legs, face in her knees, crying. The crying was a private, internal thing, like the weeping of a lost child who has given up hope any adult will hear. No ears but Ranald's could have found her from more than six feet away; no other nose could have located her, huddled there in the darkness of the ground.

Ranald did not touch her. He sank down silently into a cross-legged sitting position, facing and watching her. After a while, the girl stopped crying and lifted her head, staring blindly in his direction.

"Who's there?" Her whisper was shaky.

"Ranald," said Ranald, softly.

"Ranald who?" she asked.

He did not answer. She sat staring toward him without seeing him in the darkness, as seconds slipped away. Gradually the tension of fear leaked away and she slumped back into the position in which he had found her.

"It doesn't matter," she said, to the darkness and to him.

"It always matters," said Ranald; but not as if he were answering her. He spoke out loud but absently, to himself, as if her words had pressed a button in him. "Every spring it matters fresh. Every fall it begins to matter all over again. Otherwise, I'd have given up a long time ago. But each time, every time, it starts all over again; and I start with it. Now and now.''

''Who *are* you?'' she asked, peering through the darkness without success.

''Ranald,'' he said.

He got softly to his feet, turned, and started back toward Dave Wilober's fire. Behind him, after a few steps, he heard her rise and follow the moon-limned silhouette of his body. He went with deliberate slowness back to Dave's fire, and all the way he heard her following. But after he had sat down he heard her come only to the edge of the thick shadow his own body cast from the fire flares. Having come that far she sat down, also, still slumped but no longer weeping.

''. . . What does someone like you know about it?'' Rob was saying sharply to Walt. ''What do you understand?'' Rob had straightened up and even thrown off most of his blankets. His face was damp and pink now above the beard, and the beard itself clung damply to his upper cheeks under the brown, yellow-lit eyes.

''Very little, very little. That's true. . . .'' Walt shook his head.

''You talk about how fine it is, everyone getting together out here, and every place. But what do you really know about it? What makes you think you know anything about why people are here? You don't know why Letty and I are here!''

''No, that's true. I don't deny it,'' said Walt. ''Who can know? No one knows—''

''Not 'no one'! You!'' said Rob. ''*You* don't know. You and the rest of the dudes. You don't know anything and you're scared to find out; so you go around making it big about nobody at all knowing. But that's a lie. I know. And Letty knows. Tell him, Letty.''

''I know,'' said Letty to Walt.

''I believe you. I really believe you,'' said Walt. ''But

don't you see, even if you think you're positive about something, you've got a duty to question yourself, anyway. You have to consider the chance you're wrong. Just to make sure—isn't that so?''

"Hell it is!" said Rob. "It's just a lot of junk you pile up to hide the fact you haven't got guts enough to face life the way it really is. Not other people. *You—*"

He broke off. Another pair of booted feet that Ranald had already heard coming toward the fire from the nearest fire downslope stepped into the firelight, and the flames showed them.

"No. That's a mistake, of course," Walt was saying in a voice that shook a little but was calm. He folded his hands together and closed his teeth gently on the middle knuckle of the first finger. "You don't—"

He caught sight of the boots and broke off in turn, raising his gaze to the man who had just joined them.

"All right, all of you. Let's see your permits."

As the firelight painted him standing there against the black frame of the darkness, the lawman now looming over them was shiny with leather. He was agleam with white motorcycle helmet, brown boots, and black jacket, unzipped in front to show the straps of a Sam Browne belt supporting a holstered revolver, glittering handcuffs and the dark, bloodsucker shape of a black leather sap. He had a heavy-boned, middle-twenties face with a short-bristled, full moustache, so light-colored of hair it was almost invisible in spite of its thickness.

"I said, permits," he repeated. His voice was a flat tenor.

Without saying anything, Dave reached behind himself once more and brought out a piece of printed blue paper. The man took it, looked at it, and handed it back. He took a similar paper from Walt Strauben, read it, and gave it back. His eyes slid along to Ranald, who had not moved, neither to produce a paper nor anything else. Eyes still locked with

Ranald, the lawman reached down to take the piece of paper upheld by Letty. With a sudden effort, then, he broke his gaze from Ranald's and looked down at Letty's permit.

He handed it back to Letty and looked at Rob.

"All right," he said to Rob. "Where's yours?"

"We're together," said Rob. His voice had thinned from the note it had held talking to Walt. The yellow glint was out of his brown eyes, leaving them dark and flat.

"He's my guest," snapped Letty. "The permit's good for a space ten feet by ten feet. That's all we take up, together."

"One person only to every ten-by-ten plot." The lawman turned back to her. "This isn't one of your garbage-heap camping grounds. The place is clean—it's going to keep clean. If your friend wants to stay, he'll have to get another permit."

"Who're you?" said Rob. His face seemed narrower now. It was pale and damp with sweat; and his voice was still thin. "This is private property."

"Pig," said Letty, strongly. She got to her feet. Standing, she looked no more than half the size of the lawman. "It's nothing to do with you. We'll talk it over with the owner."

"Now if you want trouble," said the lawman, answering her without lifting his voice, "you just keep on. There's deputies enough of us here on special duty from the county sheriff's office to keep things orderly. I'm not going to waste time arguing. You can buy another camping permit for twenty-five dollars; or one of you is going to have to clear out."

He stood, still holding the paper Letty had given him.

"Make your mind up," he said.

"He's sick, you bastard!" snarled Letty. "Sick, don't you understand? He can't clear out."

"All right," said the deputy, in the same tones. "Then we'll give him a ride into the hospital in Medora. If he's sick, they'll take care of him there. But nobody camps here without buying a permit."

"Do you buy and sell people the chance to know God exists?" asked Walt. But his voice trembled a little and was so low-pitched that what he said went ignored by both Letty and the deputy.

"What about *him?*" Rob said suddenly, nodding in the direction of Ranald. "Why just us? You aren't giving him a hard time for his permit!"

Ranald did not move. The deputy's eyes flicked a little in his direction, but not far enough for their gazes to lock together again.

"Never mind anyone else here," he said to Rob. "I'm talking to you. Get a permit to stay, or get on your feet and get moving."

He stepped forward and reached down as if to pull Rob to his feet out of the cone of blankets that swathed him.

"Wait! No, wait . . ." The words came tumbling out of Walt. "Here, officer. I'll take care of the permits. Just a minute now . . . wait. . . ."

He was digging into a side pocket of his corduroy pants. He came up with a wallet and thumbed out bills, which he handed up to the deputy.

"I'll take two of them," Walt said. "Fifty dollars—that's right?"

"Two." The deputy, still holding the bills, took out a pad of blue papers and a pen, scribbled a date and initials on two of the papers and tore them from the pack. He handed both to Walt, who passed one over to Letty and held out the other to Ranald.

"All right," said the deputy, putting money and pad of permits away. "Remember to keep the grounds clean. Pick up your own trash. And the comfort stations are across the road. Use them. That permit doesn't entitle you to make a nuisance of yourself. Any trouble by anyone and you'll still go out."

He stepped back into darkness and everyone there heard his boots going away.

Ranald reached out to take the permit Walt was still holding. He examined it for a moment and then turned to hand it to the girl he had found crying, and who all this while had hidden, crouched behind him.

"Who's that?" demanded Walt, twisting to stare at her.

"I'm . . . Maybeth Zolovsky," the girl said. Her voice was thin, as Rob's had been.

Walt opened his mouth and saw Ranald mildly watching him. Walt's eyes shifted; he closed his mouth and turned back to find himself facing the round, childish, hard features of Letty.

"The world's as much ours as anyone else's," she said. "He's got no inherent right to keep us off any part of it, when we aren't doing any harm, any more than we've got a right to keep him off."

Rob said something inarticulate, endorsing. Walt shook his head and looked away from them down into the flames of the fire.

"*You* thank him, if you want," said Rob, turning to Ranald. He added, "But I guess you don't need to. You weren't going to get asked for a permit anyway, were you? How come? Why didn't he ask you?"

Ranald looked back at him silently, the night breeze blowing in his beard.

"Don't want to tell us?" said Rob. "All right. But I'd like to know. What makes you a special case? —You don't want to tell me, is that it?"

Dave snorted a little, filling his soup-can cup again from the teapot. Rob looked back across the fire at him.

"Now you're laughing," Rob said. "How about letting the rest of us in on the joke?"

Dave lifted his soup can, drank some hot tea, and looked across the rim of the container at the younger man.

"You want to know why that deputy didn't ask a man

like him for a permit?'' Dave said. ''Whyn't you find out for yourself? He gave the permit away to the young lady there. Whyn't you just go try to take it back from her?''

Rob stared at Dave.

''What?'' he said, after a moment.

''I said,'' Dave went on, ''you want to know why the deputy done what he done, you go do something like it. Go take the permit back from''—he hesitated, looking at the dark-haired girl—''Maybeth?''

She nodded back at him, only half-sheltered now behind Ranald.

''Take it away—'' Rob's voice cracked. ''What do you think I am? Why'd I want to do something like that?''

''To learn,'' said Dave.

''Learn? You mean learn how to be like that?''

''No.'' Dave looked directly at him. ''Learn why you'd never try to do it, even if you wanted to—no more than that deputy'd try it. Look at him—'' Dave's voice went a little harsh. ''I say, look at *him!*''

Rob turned and stared again at Ranald. Ranald gazed back, sitting quietly bathed by the moving firelight. In its red and yellow light he was a short man in a thin leather jacket; but he was strangely wide across the shoulders and heavy-headed under his mass of sand-colored hair and beard. His blue eyes watched Rob without blinking.

For several seconds Rob looked at him in silence. Then he gave something like a start and a shudder combined, and jerked his gaze back to the fire. He sat hunched toward the flames and muttered something under his breath.

Letty lifted one of the dropped blankets to wrap about him, again, meanwhile throwing a brief, fierce glance first at Ranald and the dark-haired girl, then at Dave. She tucked the blanket about Rob's huddled shape.

''Baby . . . ?'' she murmured, feeling his forehead once more. Rob pulled his head back from her touch.

''Never mind!'' he said. ''I tell you, never mind!''

"You see?" said Dave, from across the fire. "It'd have been more trouble to a man, than it was worth—for that deputy to mess with Ranald—or for you to."

"Or for you," muttered Rob to the flames.

Dave looked down at his tin-can cup for a second without speaking.

"Could be," he said, quietly.

A silence came down on them all, which lasted several minutes. Then Walt Strauben stirred. He turned to his pack and dug out a blue-and-white blanket three times the thickness of any of the dark blankets wrapping Rob. He held the blanket out to Maybeth Zolovsky.

"Come in next to the fire?" he said.

Maybeth hesitated, glancing at Ranald. But he looked back at her with no particular expression. She got up and came forward to sit down beside Walt, wrapping the blanket around her, hugging it to her.

"Thanks," she whispered.

From across the fire, Letty gave her a grim glance.

"Coffee?" Walt said, pouring from his thermos.

"Thank you," she said. She turned to Dave. "Thank you."

"Welcome," said Dave.

"You must have made up your mind to come out here on the spur of the moment . . ." Walt said to her.

They fell into low-voiced conversation. Dave let them talk, only feeding the fire from time to time. Ranald sat back in silence, listening to other sounds of the evening. After a while, Letty began to rearrange the blankets enclosing Rob, until she and he were wrapped up together in a sort of cloth cocoon that was bed and tent in one for them both. A little after that, Walt produced another blue-and-white blanket and made up a bed of sorts for himself, turning his own sleeping bag over to Maybeth. The three-quarters moon traveled upward, burning its way slowly through the low-lying cloud layer and climbing at last into a star-clear sky, so that the pastureland with its people and tents and pin-points of fire or lantern light showed up like the negative of a photograph taken by daylight.

When the moon was almost straight overhead, Dave stirred from where he had sat feeding the fire all this time, reached back behind him to come up with some middle-sized, dark object, and rose to his feet. He went off toward the woods at the lower end of the pasture.

Ranald silently got up and followed the taller man.

The moon was bright enough now so that Dave walked almost as surely as Ranald had walked earlier in full dark-ness. Dave threaded his way between the fires, and to anyone's hearing but Ranald's, his going was utterly silent. But to Ranald's ears, each stride of the taller man produced the same faint chinking noise Ranald had heard earlier by the fire.

Dave went downslope across the pastureland to its lower edge and moved in among the trees. He went some little distance, until the ground under its layer of dead grass and leaves began to feel soft—if not yet damp. The sound of the running river was close, now. In a little open space, in the moonlight, Dave sat down on a dead and fallen tree trunk. For a second or two he simply sat; not exactly slumped, but with his back gently curved like the back of a man who has been carrying a heavy pack through a long day. Then he stirred, lifted the shape he had carried away from the camp-ground, and unscrewed the top of it.

The moonlight showed the shape of a large bottle in black silhouette against the stars as he drank. He lowered the bottle, sat again for a moment, then recapped it and put it aside. Leaning forward, he began to rake together some of the ground trash and fallen twigs before him. Once or twice Ranald heard the small snap of a dead branch, breaking.

In a pool of moon-shadow cast by a twisted oak-trunk, Ranald sank into a squatting position on his heels. The darkness around him hid him utterly as he watched Dave's hands, like independent small creatures squirrel-busy at some instinctive task, glean the makings of a fire from ground that hardly appeared to bear anything worth burning. Once, Dave stopped to drink again from his bottle, but otherwise the craft of his hands seemed a reflexive, automatic thing—as if wherever he went, there had to be fire.

After a little, he finished. A match scratched and spurted yellow light in the darkness. The flame caught among the twigs and other stuff of the little conical pile of twigs before the log on which he sat. The flame spread and rose. In its new light, Dave got up briefly to go a few steps aside for larger pieces of dead branch, which he returned and fed into the fire, end-on, as he had done with the fire above in the pasture.

This was a smaller fire, however, than that earlier one. A private fire. Still, its light pushed back the shadows; and, as Dave lifted the bottle to drink a third time, the flickering of the flame illuminated Ranald, squatting at the base of the oak.

Dave drank and lowered the bottle.

"You?" he said. "I came here to get away from the crowd."

Ranald said nothing.

"True," said Dave, "you're not like the rest. Come to the fire."

Ranald rose, approached the other side of the flames and squatted again. There was a naturalness and ease about the way he sat on his heels, as if he could remain that way for hours with as much comfort as another man in an armchair.

"Drink?" said Dave. He held out the bottle.

"I thank you," said Ranald. He lifted the bottle and swallowed. Its content was store-sold bourbon. Not the best, perhaps, but store-sold and distillery-made, a half-gallon bottle heavy against the firelight.

He handed the bottle back to Dave, who drank again.

"It's happened before," Dave said, setting the open bottle down to one side of the fire, but equidistant between them. "You said that. You told me there'd been a Sign in the Heavens before. Long ago. How long? Fifty years?"

"Longer," said Ranald.

"A hundred? Five hundred? A thousand—"

"About that," said Ranald.

"But you remember it?" Dave gestured to the bottle. "Help yourself."

Ranald reached for the bottle, drank and replaced it exactly where it had sat a moment before.

"You remember?" repeated Dave.

"I remember," Ranald answered.

"Could be," said Dave, looking at him across the fire. "Could be—anything. But here you are with the rest of us; and you said there was nothing for you in god-houses."

"I've found nothing there. That's true," answered Ranald. "But there's no telling. Maybe I'll go to a god-house in the end, to die."

"Maybe they'll bury me out of a church someday, too," said Dave, thoughtfully. "Maybe . . . And here we are, all of us sitting out here, waiting for a great Sign of Faith. God, his own self, is going to come down and walk among us in glory, amen. Tonight, maybe, or tomorrow. All over the world at once, there's going to be proof it's been true, all this time and—then what?"

"I don't know," said Ranald.

"But you've seen it once before, you said." Dave made a motion toward the bottle. "Drink. Drink when you feel like it. I can't go drinking myself, with you waiting for an invite each time."

Ranald reached out and drank.

"All these people," said Dave, drinking after him. "That Letty and Rob. That Walt Strauben. That deputy even, and that Maybeth girl you pulled out of a hip pocket—that deputy sure didn't want to make trouble with you, now, did he? Mighty queer how a man can get to be the way you are, and another man just know it without being told. No one ever monkeys with you, do they?"

"Odin," said Ranald, "had one eye."

"Odin?"

"Another god," said Ranald. "He gave his eye for wisdom, they said. But any man who wants to give the price for anything, can buy, like that. Having bought, it shows on him. And so it goes. Each buys his own want and pays the price. That part never changes."

"What changes, then?" asked Dave. His tongue stumbled a little on the *ch* sound.

Ranald shook his head.

"I don't know," he said. "Every season, every year, the thought of living comes fresh and new to me. Fresh and new—and I go on again. But nothing changes. Over a thousand years, now." He looked across the fire to Dave. "Why do I keep on starting and starting again, if there's no change? If you can, tell me; and I can rest."

"Nothing I can tell you. Take a drink," said Dave. "It'll help you think."

Ranald drank.

"Thanks," he said, "I give you thanks." His tongue had not thickened as had Dave's; but there was a different note, of something like an echo chamber's echo of melancholy in his voice.

"Welcome, brother," said Dave, lifting the bottle himself. "Welcome and rest yourself. Tomorrow the Sign comes, the papers say—and the world changes. We'll all change—"

He put down the bottle and began to sing, a little hoarsely but in key with a light baritone voice.

> *"There was a rich man and he lived in Jerusalem.*
> *Glory, Hallelujah, hi-ro-de-rum!*
> *He wore a top hat and his clothes were very*
> *spruce-ium.*
> *Glory, Hallelujah, hi-ro-de-rum!*

Hi-ro-de-rum, hi-ro-de-rum!
Skinna-ma-rinky doodle-doo, skinna-ma-rinky
     doodle-doo,
Glory, Hallelujah, hi-ro-de-rum!

Now, outside his gate there sat a human wreckium.
  Glory, Hallelujah, hi-ro-de-rum!
He wore a bowler hat in a ring around his neckium.
  Glory, Hallelujah . . ."

"Sing!" Dave interrupted himself to say to Ranald. Ranald cocked his head on one side, listening, as Dave started a new verse.

   ". . . Now the poor man he asked for a piece of
       bread and cheesium—"

"*Glory, Hallelujah, hi-ro-de-rum!*" sang Ranald along with him. Dave nodded. "*. . . The rich man said, I'll call for the police-ium,*" Dave went on. "*Glory, Hallelujah, hi-ro-de-rum!*" They sang together:

   "*Hi-ro-de-rum, hi-ro-de-rum!*
   Skinna-ma-rinky-doodle-doo, skinna-ma-rinky-
       doodle-doo!
   Glory, Hallelujah, hi-ro-de-rum! . . ."

The singing, the firelight, the bottle passing back and forth, made something like a private room for them in the midst of the darkness. They went on through other verses of the same song and other songs after that, while the fire burned down toward the coals and they came back to talking again. Or rather, Dave came back to talking.

"*. . .* that Walt," he was saying, no longer stumble-tongued, but with a deliberate slowness of pronunciation. "I smell preacher on him. Maybe not now he's a preacher, but he's been one. So, that's why he'd be here. He'd come to see a Sign because he needed one to preach. But that Letty and Rob—what do they want with a proof of God?''

"To know, perhaps," said Ranald.

"To know?"

"To find out what actually is. —For themselves, as men and women always do each generation, over and over again."

"And Maybeth? What do you say for that Maybeth girl?"

"Lost," said Ranald, "with nowhere else to go. Maybe she came here, hoping."

"Hoping?" Dave said. "Come here praying, you mean. Praying for a miracle, to set everything right for her without her having even to lift a finger for herself."

"A broken finger," Ranald looked across the dying flames at him, talking in a voice that showed no trace of effect from the liquor, "lifts hard. Broken legs don't run easy nor broken wings fly, brother."

"Can't fly or run, you can walk. Can't walk, can crawl. I been there. I know."

"You know," said Ranald, softly. "But do you know all there is to know?"

"Enough," said Dave. "Been there, I say. Could have given up anytime. Never did. You know why? Even with everything else gone, broke or rotted—there was still air, dirt, and water. Air to breathe, dirt to grow in, water to wash life down into the dirt. Running water. Rain. Black dirt. Green stuff. Trees."

"Yes," said Ranald, his eyes going past the fire and Dave for a moment. "New and new—each fresh season. I know that part, too."

"And I damn near lost it all," said Dave. "Things nearly turned me away from that part of it." He lifted the bottle to his lips, but it was empty. He stared at it for a moment, then set it down carefully. "Three sisters of mine, four brothers, all died before they were old enough to go to school. My daddy died. I got born last, after he was put in the ground.''

''A sickness?'' Ranald said.

''Yes. No. Killed.'' Dave stared hard across the fire coals at Ranald. ''Worked too hard, they said. Mine—coal mine and then field-work. No. People killed him. Other people killed him, taking him away from dirt and water, and air. . . .

> *''—Down in the mountain, in a fall of the coal,*
> *Buried in the mountain is O'Shaunessy's soul . . .*

''—they buried my daddy aboveground, but his soul was buried down in the mine like O'Shaunessy's, just the same. All the people of the world, with their mines, their coal, their things—they put my dad down in a mine to kill and bury him; and when I asked why, they sent me to church for answer. Church!''

The breath of his last word fanned the red coals of the fire momentarily white.

''Looky here,'' said Dave. He bent forward and rolled up his right pants-leg, uncovering what looked like a bulky white bandage covering his leg from the ankle to low on the calf. ''I was the last alive of the children. Ma near on frantic to keep me from the chance of dying too and making it all for nothing—babies and husband, all in the grave. Now, she was one believed what people told her. She asked around and they said, 'Take the boy to church. Take him to the preacher. Ask help of the Lord.' So she took me.''

Dave started to reach for the now-empty bottle, checked his hand halfway there and let it drop back on his knee.

''She took me to a preacher and he prayed over me,'' Dave went on. ''Middle of the week too. Just into May; apple blossoms, peach blossoms on the trees, and all. No one in the church, but we three went and knelt there before the altar with the windows open and the bird noise sounding all around outside. 'Guard this boy, Lord. The last of the flock. . . .' And then we all waited for an answer on our knees, with the preacher's eyes closed, Ma's eyes closed— mine supposed to be, too, but I got tired holding them shut. . . .''

Dave's voice ran down. Ranald sat perfectly still, watching him and listening—not just like someone who is merely attentive, but like someone waiting, and who has been waiting a long time for an answer.

"Preacher opened his eyes, at last," Dave went on, suddenly. "I got mine closed again just in time. 'God has answered,' he told Ma and me. 'There's a way to make this boy of yours safe, but only one way. Straight and narrow is the road to the gate. Straight the road he must walk. You got to give him to the Lord; and he must know the Lord is with him, the hand of the Lord is on him, guiding him, night and day. . . .' And Ma believed him; and —looky here."

Dave reached down and began to unwind the cloth around his leg and ankle. It fell away, so that Ranald saw a section of limb just above the ankle that looked blackened and crusted—as it might have been by dirt, but was not. The darkness and the ribbed skin were the markings of callouses and old scars, very nearly solid callous and scar tissue for six inches from the ankle upward. And what had caused this still circled the ankle—a loose loop of tractor chain with two-inch links, shiny with age and rubbing against itself and the leg it encircled.

Dave turned his ankle to the firelight and the chain slipped, chinking as Ranald had heard it chink earlier.

"It would come off," said Ranald, looking at the chain. "A hacksaw, a file—even a good knife. It wouldn't be hard to take off."

Dave laughed. It was only the second time he had laughed in Ranald's hearing.

"Oh, I had it off," Dave said. "Ma died when I was sixteen; and I took out for other places. First night away from home, I had it off me. Crowbar and hatchet. Stuck a crowbar end through a link, chopped the link open with a hatchet, then buried the chain in some woods. Five years I walked around with no weight on my ankle.''

"Then what?''

"No 'then what,' '' answered Dave. ''Bit by bit it come back on me. I moved around; but everywhere I went—city, town, farm or backwoods—there wasn't no notch, no wrinkle, no fold, no place for me to back myself into like everybody else was backed into and settled. Bit by bit, then, I come to understand. That chain hadn't been just something I could chop off and throw away. It was part of a deal my ma had made for me with someone that wasn't there, far as I was concerned. But the fact that someone wasn't there for me, though, didn't make no difference. Takes two to make a bargain; and there had been a bargain made. Only I hadn't kept my end.''

"Odin gave his eye,'' said Ranald.

"Like that. I'd taken, but I hadn't given. My not believing didn't matter, long as I wore the chain; because the chain stood for what I hadn't got to give—that believing I couldn't do, no matter how much my ma wanted me to. But when I took the chain off . . .''

Dave sighed.

"So,'' he said, ''I put it back on, without nobody telling me to. Just like you see now. And then things began to straighten out for me. I found my way back to my own country; and I found out how it was I had to live. Alone with the fields, the barns, and all; and got along with neighbors all right, long as we didn't visit together too much. But I had my honest dirt, water, and plain air—and peace out of it all.''

He stopped talking. For nearly a minute the silence filled the moment between the little cracklings of the dying fire.

"Now, it was *my* mother,'' murmured Ranald, looking at the red and white wood coals, ''said I would never find my way home again, if I went. But our ships sailed out that spring; and I was twelve. I went with them; in time, to many places. But, when years later I sailed north again, I could not find where I'd been born. It had been a small place always; and maybe some other ships had put in to raid and burn there, killing or making slaves of all—and afterwards it went back to forest. Or maybe it was only that all the old people I'd known there were dead; and I did not recognize the place when I saw it again, remembering it only the way a boy remembers things, bigger than they are. But my mother was right. I'd gone, and after that I could never find home again.''

He hesitated, gazing at what was left of the fire.

"That's when I first thought I would die, because there was no reason for me to live longer,'' he said, softly. "But I found I could not bring myself to it; and since, I go on and on.''

He raised his head from its tilt toward the cooling embers and looked across at Dave. Sometime since, Dave had slid from his seat on the log to a seat on the ground, with his back against the thick round of the log from the dead and fallen tree. Now his hands were limp, palms-upward on his thighs. His chin was down on his chest and his eyes were closed.

Ranald lifted his head and sniffed the night air. The moon was low on the far horizon, and the breeze blew from a different direction, bringing a chill with it. Ranald made no attempt to build up the fire, but lay down on his side and drew his arms and legs in toward his body, curling up animal-fashion. Like Dave, he slept.

Dawn woke them both. They rose without conversation, left the dead, small fire, and went back to the campground. There, Dave silently revived the earlier fire he had left unattended and cooked them both a breakfast of bacon and pancakes. As they were finishing this, the others—Maybeth, Letty, and Rob—began to wake and stir in their various bed-shelters. These looked with attention at the remains of breakfast; but Dave made no move to invite them to eat. It was Walt, struggling out of his blankets with a stubble of a twenty-four-hour beard gray on his face and under-chin, who finally produced a small Coleman stove, cookware, and breakfast materials for himself and the other three.

As the morning warmed, the pastureland rapidly began to fill. There was a steadily growing feeling-in-common above the tents and shelter-halves and groundsheets that blossomed all about. A feeling like excitement, but not like a holiday sort of excitement. A tense thread of apprehension laced like a red vein through the body of eager expectancy that enclosed them all, there between the comfort stations and the woods stretching below down to swamp and river. It was a cloudless day, promising to become hot.

As it warmed and grew close to noon, the pressure of the tensions in the people increased; as if they were all under water that was becoming steadily deeper. By eleven o'clock it was hard to believe that any space in the pasture remained unsold; and there were a number of deputies of the local county sheriff to be seen, sweating under their equipment and uniforms. The particular deputy who had checked those around Dave's fire for permits the night before now passed by frequently, as if their space were within an area he had to patrol. In the daylight he looked much younger than he had the night before; and it was possible to see that he wore not only a star-shaped gold badge, but a nameplate below it with white block letters spelling out TOM RATHKENNY on a blue background.

In the daylight, some of the certainty he had shown during the dark hours earlier was missing. He no longer stood out among the crowd of people who had bought space in the pastureland, but seemed more to fit in among them—a little shorter and less heavily-boned, a little more of flesh and less of leather. Sweat gleamed on his chin in the sunlight and his glance shifted more frequently from person to person as he walked past.

Just past eleven thirty, the pressure broke. The universal ocean-wash of voices was interrupted by a moving wave of silence that traveled across the pasture and, on the heels of that moving silence, a man walked among them.

". . . him"—the word erupted everywhere in the crowd as the man passed—". . . him . . . him . . . him . . ."

He went by not fifteen feet from Dave's fire, walking swiftly and apparently alone; a thin, brown-faced man, beardless, with shaven head and eyes spaced widely above sharp cheekbones. He was barefoot and wearing what seemed to be only a loose gown of coarse and heavy brown cloth, the skirt of which rippled with the length of his strides. Beneath the hem of that skirt, his feet were mottled with dirt.

". . . *him,*" echoed Walt as the voices took up after the man had passed. "The prophet. The one who promised the world a Sign. But what brings him here, out of everywhere else on the Earth? Why to this one little place? Him . . ."

"Him . . . him . . ." said Letty and Rob and Maybeth, and all the other people crowding in the wake of the one who had passed. "Here . . . here of all places. *Him . . .*"

Dave had gotten to his feet with the rest. Now he sat down again to face Ranald, who had not risen.

"Why's he here?" Dave asked. "Is there something special here?" He looked steadily at Ranald. "It's not because of you?"

Ranald shook his head.

"Was he really here?" said Ranald. "Perhaps they're seeing him everyplace where people have gotten together to wait for the Sign."

"What're you talking about?" Walt turned suddenly to stand above Ranald. "He was here. I saw him. We all saw him. Didn't you?"

Ranald shook his head again.

"I saw, but that was all. I heard no one passing. I smelled no one," he said.

"Heard?" echoed Rob. "Smelled? In this crowd? Who could hear or smell anyone in a crush like this?"

Ranald glanced at the younger man.

"In any case," Ranald said, "he would only be a messenger."

"You can't know that," Letty said. "He could be the Sign, himself. Maybe that's what he was."

Ranald looked at her, almost mildly.

"When Signs come," he said, "there's no question."

And there was none. Just at noon, just as Ranald remembered from the time before, there was a shock that went through everyone and everything. A shock like that of a great gong being struck in a place where no sound was permitted—so that the effect was not heard, but felt, in great shudders that passed through all living and nonliving things like light through clear water. And when the shock had passed, a knowledge of sorts came into them all, as if a part of their minds which had been asleep until this moment had now been awakened to report what it witnessed. Above them, the sun had ceased apparent movement. They felt the fact that it no longer moved. It stood still in a sky without clouds.

Earth, also, stood still under their feet. They could feel its new lack of motion, as well. The laws of the universe were no longer touching sun, or Earth, or people. Something like a hand was now holding them apart from such things.

In the pasture, the crowd too was stilled. No one moved or spoke. In the woods downslope no birds sang, no insects hummed. Even to the ears of Ranald, the river seemed to have ceased its murmur. Matters were as he remembered them happening that earlier time, before he had learned that he could never find his way home again—back when he had been already far from home. He sighed silently inside himself, now, lowering his head and closing his eyes; and, sharp as a burn, fresh-branded on his inner eyelids, was suddenly the image of that home as he remembered it in the moment just before he sailed. The shore, the ships, the log buildings in the green clearing by the sea came back to him across more than a thousand years, with such immediate pain that he could almost believe he might open his eyes to see it there after all, alive again instead of lost forever.

He got to his feet, still holding his eyes tightly closed to keep the picture to him. Moving by sense of hearing and smell alone, like a blind man with radar, he drifted through the silent, unstirring crowd toward the sanctuary of the woods. It was not until he had left the crowd behind him and felt the shade of the trees on his face and his exposed lower arms and hands that he paid any attention to the fact that once more boots had followed him, familiar boots.

This time, however, they caught up with him.

"Forgive me . . ." said the voice of Walt, trembling and a little breathless behind him. "But I have to talk to you. You *knew*, didn't you? You're a Messenger yourself, aren't you—or something more than mortal?"

Ranald stopped. The picture on the inner surface of his eyelids was already fading. His shoulders sagged. He opened his eyes.

"No," he said.

"Oh, but I know you are. —Aren't you?" Walt came walking around to face him. They stood, surrounded by thick oaks, dappled themselves with oak shade in the hot, still air. "I mean—if you are, I don't want to intrude. I don't want to pry. If you don't want to say anything about yourself, that's all right. But I have to talk to you about myself. I have to explain to . . . a part of God, anyway, to some man who's part of God Eternal."

Ranald shook his head again.

"I'm no god, nor god-man," he said.

"But I was," said Walt eagerly. "I was a God-man—or at least, a man of God. That's what makes talking to you now important. It's as if this has all happened just between God and me. Do you understand what I'm saying?''

Ranald sat down wearily cross-legged on the ground with his back against an oak trunk.

''Yes,'' he said.

''Then you can see what it means—'' Walt squatted also, facing Ranald, but found the position awkward and ended up sitting down clumsily with an unsuccessful effort to cross his legs as easily as Ranald had, ''—means to me. And if it means that much to me, what it must mean to the whole world. I don't flatter myself it was just for me, of course. But that's the essence of miracle, that it works for everyone as if it were just for him, alone. Isn't it?''

Ranald shook his head, without answering. Walt made a wide gesture at the sky and the unmoving noontide sky overhead.

''Now we've had the Sign,'' Walt went on. ''Now we'll never be the same again—each of us, as individuals, never the same again. Now all our doubts are answered, finally and completely. And now that my own doubts, my special doubts, have been answered, I can see how little, how shameful, how sinful they were. Do you know what my particular sin and crime was? Doubt itself. Not just plain doubt—simple doubt—but doubt for doubt's sake. Can you imagine that?''

Ranald nodded.

''Yes,'' said Walt, his face pink-brown in the pinto shade-and-sunlight. ''I played a game with the Creator. Even my choosing religion as a lifework was part of that game. I knelt and prayed *'I believe, Lord,'* but the words were a lie. What I meant was *'Prove to me that I should believe, Lord.'* ''

He paused, looking at Ranald; but Ranald only sat watching.

''You understand?'' said Walt. ''I had to be continually testing God. Not only God directly, but God as He was made manifest in the world—in other men and women, in the things man had built, in nature itself. *Render unto*—do you know the verse from Matthew, Chapter twenty-two, Verse twenty-one—"

"Yes," said Ranald. "I was a slave in a monastery for a while, and I served the tables while they ate and one read to the others."

"There were no slaves in monasteries," said Walt. "Matthew twenty-two, twenty-one has to do with the questioners that the Pharisees sent to test Jesus. What do you think their question was?"

"Whether it was lawful to give tribute to Caesar or not," said Ranald.

"They asked Him whether it was lawful to give tribute to Caesar or not," said Walt. "And you know what He answered? *'Why tempt me, ye hypocrites?'* He made them show Him the tribute money with the image of Caesar on it, and told them, *'Render unto Caesar the things which are Caesar's—'* "

"Render *therefore* unto Caesar—" murmured Ranald.

" *'—And unto God the things that are God's,'* " continued Walt. "Two thousand years ago He said those words; but all down those millenniums this has been our major confusion. We confuse our duties to Caesar with our duties to God. In essence, we tend to think of God as just another Caesar—to be paid tribute, if necessary, but also to be questioned. This has been my sin, in particular; a sin which men like you and Dave, gifted with a simple response to nature, have learned instinctively to avoid. Now, you two are naturally free in this respect, so free neither of you even suspected I had something like that in me. But that young man Rob did. You remember how he kept saying it was *my* particular fault, my own lack, that I saw in the world and other people. —You remember that, yesterday?"

"Yes."

"Well," said Walt, slapping the pants-cloth stretched

tightly over his bent right knee, "he was right! Absolutely right. That's been my missing part all along, a lack of simple faith. Faith like you have, and Dave Wilober has. But now I have it, like everybody else; and now that I *know* this, I can do something about it, I can learn—from people like you and Dave."

He leaned forward, eagerly, his heavy shirt creasing over his belly.

"Talk to me," he said. "Tell me how you see the world."

He stayed leaning forward, waiting. Ranald gazed at him for a long moment, then shook his head.

"No," he said, getting to his feet.

"Wait . . ." Walt began to scramble to his own feet. "What do you mean—'No'?"

"It's no use," said Ranald.

He turned and went off through the woods. Behind him, he heard Walt calling him by name and trying to follow, but the other man crashed noisily among the trees, tripping over roots and blundering into bushes; and Ranald soon left him behind.

Once he was free again, Ranald turned and went back to the pasture. On the way, he met others of the campers, wandering under the unmoving sun, as if the suspension of physical laws had suspended all responsibility as well; and there was no longer any requirement upon them but to follow the whim of each second, through a noonday pause that was unending.

The sound of a steady metal-on-metal hammering drew him back to the campfire he had shared with Dave and the others. Dave was seated on his bedroll, singing to himself, cutting with a chisel and hammer through a link of his ankle chain, laid upon a hatchet-blade for support. Maybeth was half seated, half kneeling beside him, watching. Across the now small fire, with flames nearly invisible in the bright sunlight, were three people close together. The deputy, Tom

Rathkenny, was huddled up on the ground with his head in
Letty's lap. She was stroking his short, pale-blond hair
soothingly; and the new-softened weapon of her gaze was
turned on him, rather than Rob, who was standing, looking
down at the two of them.

". . . The whole world's changed," Rob was saying to
Letty. She did not look up at him.

". . . *Now the poor man died,*" sang Dave in tune to the
clink of his hammer on the head of the chisel. . . .

> ". . . *and his soul went to Heavenium.*
> *Glory, Hallelujah, hi-ro-de-rum!*"

"Are you listening to me, Letty?" demanded Rob.

> ". . . *He danced with the angels till a quarter
> past elevenium . . .*"

"—I said, are you listening?"

But Letty did not answer him. Her head was bent forward, her hair falling over the head in her lap.

"Poor baby," she was murmuring. "All right, baby. All
right. I'm here . . ." She interrupted herself to speak briefly
to Rob. "Go to hell! Can't you see I'm busy?"

> "*Skinna-ma-rinky doodle doo! Skinna-ma-rinky doo-
> dle doo!*
> *Glory, Hallelujah, hi-ro-de-rum . . .*"

"All right," said Rob.

He straightened up. In the noonday heat, he had shed
more of his layers of clothing. The antibiotics seemed to
have conquered his illness and his fever. With his beard no
longer plastered to his face by the wind and his face no

longer damp with sweat he looked slim, but supple and strong, in both determination and body. He turned and walked over to stand above Maybeth, who looked away from Dave and up at him.

"Come on," said Rob to her.

She hesitated and looked back at Dave. But Dave was occupied only with his chiseling and his singing.

> "*. . . Now the rich man died and he didn't fare so wellium . . .*"

"I said, come on!" repeated Rob.

Maybeth looked at him again, and from him to Ranald. Ranald met and returned her gaze with the same open, uncommenting stare with which he had dealt with her from the beginning.

"It's happened, don't you understand?" said Rob to her. "It's the New Age. We've had the Sign and it'll never be the same again. Now, everyone *knows;* and the world's going to be completely different. Don't you understand? Some of us don't want to face that. Letty there, she doesn't— and look at that mess over there in her lap, scared out of his wits because what really *is* has caught up with him. It's too much for him and her—but not for people like you and me. For us it's the New Age of Actuality; it's the Garden of Eden really for the first time. Come on! What're you waiting for? You don't belong here with a couple of failures, and two old men."

Maybeth looked down at the ground before her. Slowly she got to her feet without looking again at Dave or Ranald. She went off with Rob and they disappeared among the moving figures of the crowd that was still in the pasture.

> "*. . . couldn't go to Heaven, so he had to go to Hellium.*
> *Glory, Hallelujah—*"

With a final *clink* the chisel cut through the link on which it had been biting; and Dave broke off his song. The chain parted and slithered snakelike from around Dave's scarred and calloused ankle to the hard, heel-beaten ground of the pasture. Dave picked up the links and laid them, with the hammer and chisel, carefully back into his pack behind his sleeping bag. He looked up at Ranald and laughed.

"Sing!" he said. "I got me religion at last. Don't need no chain anymore to stand for no faith I never had. All it took the Lord was a little old stopping of the sun at midday to set me free—from that, anyhow. Now I can give to folks without thinking I'm paying back for something."

"You always could," said Ranald. "And did." His mind was half lost in time.

Dave frowned for a second.

"What?"

" *'For owre ioye and owre hele. Iesu Cryst of hevene,'* " said Ranald, " *'In a pore mannes apparaille pursueth us evere . . .'* "

"What?" repeated Dave. "Say it again?"

"It's part of a poem," said Ranald, "that the priests used to use for a text in sermons. All week long, up and down hall, the priest was nothing to the gentles. But on Sunday all the good families around would come into chapel and the priest could say his sermon with a god's voice, paying them all back. And so he would tell them how Piers the plowman was closer to God than they. And those listening used to weep to hear it—people do not believe that now, but all were more open with weeping in those days. They wept, knights, ladies, all matter of warm-dressed folk. But later, after chapel, it made no difference you could see."

Dave fingered his chin, which was now lightly shadowed by twenty-four hours of beard.

"I've plowed," he said. "But I'm no 'pears-to-be-a-plowman.' I'm Dave Wilober."

"That, and more too," said Ranald. "But all of us are

something more, with the sun straight overhead the way it is now.''

Dave glanced briefly at the unmoving daystar above them.

"Could be. Could well be," he said. He laughed again. "Never mind, I'm free."

"Let's go get something to drink, come back and talk."

Tom Rathkenny lifted a crumpled face from Letty's knees.

"There's no alcoholic beverages out here," he said in a choked voice. "Every truck's been told . . ."

"Still, always something around," said Dave. He jerked his head at Ranald. "Come on, brother."

They went off to the line of trucks by the road; and, the third truck they came to was occupied by a drunken driver-owner who first tried to share his own half-empty bottle; then offered to give them an unopened one, but only if they would take it for nothing. Quietly telling the man that he took things for nothing only from neighbors or friends, Dave tucked bills unnoticed into the pocket of the driver's shirt and accepted the fresh bottle.

He and Ranald went back to their camping place. Letty and Tom Rathkenny were gone, now. Rob, Maybeth, and Walt had none of them returned. Ranald and Dave sat down on opposite sides of the fire with the bottle to one side of them, uncapped. But although Dave poured cups half full of the tepid, blended whiskey, neither of them drank. It was hot and the air was without movement. They forgot the liquor and became lost in talk; which went down mines, up mountains, and from the California shore to the Ob River half a world away. Their words swung them through all sorts of places and seasons; from winter through summer and fall and back to winter again. Meanwhile, the sun stayed in place above them and the hours without time went by.

". . . A knife like that with a deer-antler handle," Dave heard himself saying at one moment. "I had a knife like that, and lost it commercial fishing—handlining sharks at the mouth of the Tampico River down in Mexico."

"Sharkskin soon spoils any knife edge," said Ranald. "Sponge-dredging off the Libya coast . . ."

Unremarked, alone, Maybeth crept quietly back to join them, sitting down back a little from the fire and listening. She nodded after a while, lay down with her head just on a corner of the foot of Dave's sleeping bag, and fell asleep.

Later, yet, Rob came back by himself. He glanced at the sleeping Maybeth without smiling and then lay down on the pile of blankets he and Letty had occupied the night before. Shortly, he began a light, easy snoring.

It was some hours later that Letty returned with Tom Rathkenny. The former deputy now wore only shirt, motorcycle breeches, and boots, and the shirt was open at the neck. While the shadow of beard on Dave's lean face stood out darkly in the sunlight, Tom's blond features looked as clean-shaven as they had the night before. Letty took one of the thin blankets not pinned to the earth by the weight of Rob's sleeping body and, with Tom helping, set it up on two sticks as a sloping sunshade to keep the eternal noontide glare out of their eyes. In the shadow of this, they both also lay down and slept.

Similar things were happening all about the pasture. People were yielding everywhere to the weariness of the unchanging noon day. Like wilting flowers, they were returning back to the earth beneath them and falling into deep, unmoving slumber. The sound of the voices of those left awake slowed, diminished, and fell silent at last; and that same silence crept in the end even between Dave and Ranald.

"Me, too," said Dave, at last looking around at the pasture full of unconscious figures. "Whatever comes next, for now there's got to be some time to rest." He glanced back at Ranald. "How about you?"

"Soon," said Ranald.

Dave picked up his untouched cup and poured the liquor

in it back into the bottle without spilling a drop. Ranald picked up the cup from which he himself had not drunk and began to pour its contents back as well.

"You don't have to do that," said Dave. "Keep the bottle with you."

"Later," said Ranald. "Now's no drinking time."

"Maybe right," Dave answered. He turned, saw the head of Maybeth on the corner of his sleeping bag and carefully stretched himself out on it without disturbing the girl. He put his hand up to his face to shield his eyes from the sunlight. "Talk to you later, then."

"Yes," said Ranald.

Ranald closed his eyes. Smoke-thin across the inner lids, misty and unsubstantial, drifted the vision of home that had been so clear to him before. The heat of the sunlight beat on his closed eyes like the silent shout of a god demanding to be heard. He dozed.

—And woke, with animal instinct, a second before her hand touched him. Maybeth had crept close until she was seated just beside him and her fingers were inches from the fingers of his right hand. At the sight of him, awake, she drew back and looked down away from his pale-blue gaze.

"I'm sorry . . ." she whispered.

"There's no magic in me," said Ranald. "Touch me if you like, but nothing will change."

Her head bent lower on her neck until she looked only at the earth.

"Why won't you like me?" she said, barely above her earlier whisper.

"There's no magic in that, either," said Ranald. "In time, even love and hate wear out. Not all the way out . . . each new season a little comes back again. But near out. Your god has spoken above you. Turn to him for magic."

She lifted her face to him at that.

"But He's your God, too," she said. "Now that He's proved Himself. Isn't He?"

"No god have I," said Ranald.

"But He's stopped the sun at noon. He's stopped the Earth."

"Yes," said Ranald. "But I neither thank nor curse him for it. It's long since I hardly remember giving up praying at every sound of thunder, or touch of the dry, hot wind that threatens drought. Gods may stop Earths and suns, but none of them can give me back my home again, or make me what I was—and it's I, not he or any other, that keeps me going on, and on, from season to season, when I see no sense in it any longer. I do that to myself, against myself, and don't know why. But no god has any hand in it."

She sat, staring at him.

"You aren't afraid—" she began.

But at that moment Walt Strauben came back to them. He was flushed and panting, barefoot now and stripped to the waist, the hair on his head and the rolls of fat on his chest and belly grayed and darkened with what looked like dirt. Trickles of sweat had cut streaks of meandering cleanliness down his upper body. In his right hand he carried a cardboard sign nailed to the neck of a cross made of two pieces of lath; and on the sign in grocer's crayon was written "RENDER UNTO CAESAR . . ." In his left hand he carried a newspaper which he threw down between Ranald and Maybeth as he collapsed, panting, into a sitting position on the ground beside them.

"Look—" he gasped.

They looked. Two words filled the upper half of the front page of the paper—SUN EVERYWHERE. Below that headline, the page was black with type with no pictures showing.

"Everywhere!" said Walt. "The sun's at noon everywhere around the world. Every place there were people gathered together, they saw the Messenger, just the way we did here. The sun's stopped at noon all over the Earth."

"Everywhere?" asked Dave. He had woken up and now

lay propped on one elbow, watching them. "Don't make sense. Earth's round, isn't it? Has to be dark on one side."

"Can you ask a question like that after what you've seen happen here?" Walt turned on him. "If it's true here, why not everywhere? Why not anything? Why not?"

"Have to show me something more than a newspaper," said Dave. He shut his eyes and lay down again.

"There'll be some lacking enough faith—even now," said Walt, turning back to Ranald and Maybeth. "But read the paper. Read it. A few people stayed with their jobs to make sure it was printed; and because of that we know that God has indeed touched this Earth with a Sign of His power. Not just for our few numbers here in this meadow—but for everyone, everywhere."

He reached out clumsily to the edge of the dead fire and scraped up a handful of ashes, which he added to what was already thickening his disordered hair.

"Glory, glory!" A good share of the ashes he had scraped up had clung to the palm of his sweaty hand instead of falling on his head. He wiped the hand clumsily on the hard ground beside him. "I'm my God's man now, truly, at last!"

He met Ranald's eyes directly for the first time, with a glint of defiance.

"This was all it took, this news about the sun everywhere," he said, "it cleared up my last shred of doubt."

Ranald looked back at him without answering.

"But not people like Dave! Not you—" Walt's voice rose. "You don't believe in Him, do you? Even now, you don't believe He exists!"

"I believe," said Ranald.

"It's a lie! You—"

"It's not a lie," said Maybeth, out of nowhere. "Of course he believes. It's just that he doesn't have to be jolted, or shook up, or frightened, like we do. He just takes God for granted."

"Sin—sin! Blasphemy!" shouted Walt, pounding the butt end of his sign's post on the ground. "To take God for granted—"

"Walt," said Ranald.

Walt looked defiantly back at him; and this time Ranald caught and held the other man's eyes with his own.

"Walt," he said, "look around. All these people here are tired. So are you. You need sleep. Sleep now."

He held Walt's eyes unmovingly with his own.

"I . . ." Walt began, and broke off as his mouth, opened to speak, opened wider and wider into an enormous yawn. "I said . . . I . . ."

His eyelids fluttered and closed. He leaned sideways to the ground and half curled up there, hugging his sign to him. Within five breaths he was inhaling and exhaling deeply in slumber.

"We need sleep, too," said Ranald.

He lay down and closed his eyes once more against the sunlight. He heard Maybeth lie down near him; and a second later he felt the touch of her hand creeping into his.

"If you don't mind," he heard her murmur, "I'll hold on, anyway."

This time Ranald fell into full sleep.

He woke, briefly and instinctively, some time later. His body had felt a sudden cutting off of the sun's heat, and he opened his eyes to look up into a night sky full of stars. Once again, from the woods and the river he heard bird and water sounds, and the whisper of a breeze. He went back to sleep.

The next day found the people in the meadow more normal after their night's sleep, but still under the influence of the timeless noontide that had held them awake to the point of exhaustion. They were like people who had been stunned, and were now conscious again, but unsure of themselves, as if at any moment dizziness might make the ground rock beneath their feet. In the meadow, this unsureness showed itself in the reluctance of those there to leave their encampment and go back to whatever place it was from which they had come.

—And there were other aftereffects.

Walt was not the only one with something like ashes in his hair and a sign or cross or other symbol in hand. There were a number like him; and they were mostly busy speaking either to small groups in near-privacy, or from stumps or boxes to any who would listen. Many listened, others had withdrawn into meditation or trance, ignoring the noise around them. There were those who sang and prayed together; and those who sang and prayed alone. There were those in the store trucks parked along the roadway who had given away all their goods, and those like the driver-owner from whom Dave had bought drink the day before, who still sat numb with drink or drugs in their vehicles and indifferent to anyone who wanted to help himself to what was there.

Letty and Tom Rathkenny had gone off once more by themselves early. Walt, still holding his sign and smeared with the dirt of ashes, was wildly preaching to a group farther down the meadow. Rob, either high on something obtained from one of the trucks or self-hypnotized into a near-trance state, was engaged in a meditative process, seated cross-legged on the ground by himself, staring at the few grass blades upon the trodden earth between his knees.

"This is too much holy for me," said Dave finally, when a natural noon sun had passed its high point in the sky. He looked around the meadow and back at Ranald and Maybeth. "Far as I'm concerned, a hallelujah or two in the morning ought to take care of it, and then a man could get down to other things. I'm going to walk off a piece. How about you two?"

Ranald got to his feet and Maybeth followed. The three of them wove their way through the crowd downslope, into the trees and away through the trees, skirting the soggier spots until they came to a firm bank opening between trees on the clear-running water of the river. It was a middle-sized stream, perhaps two hundred feet across at this point, and shallow with midsummer dryness so that the pebble shoals could be seen under the clear water reaching out for some distance from the bank. They came to a halt there and stood watching the running water. Insects buzzed by their ears; and now and then a bird call sounded not far from them. It was cooler here, down by the river and under the thick-leaved branches.

"Never stops running, does it?" said Dave, after a while. "Somewhere, always, there's water running downhill to the sea."

"I think it may have stopped yesterday," said Ranald. "When everything else was stopped, too. I didn't hear it."

"Held up a bit was all, probably," said Dave. There was almost a loving note in his voice as he spoke about the moving river. He bent, picked up a pebble and threw it far out to midstream. The pebble made a single neat hole in the water, going in, and then there was no sign it had ever fallen. "Stopped for good is dead. Like with that shark-fishing, down in Mexico. *Finito,* and you're through for the day; *acabo,* and the sharks got you. This river just got finitoed along with everything else, for a little while. That was all."

"You're not afraid of things, either of you, are you?" said Maybeth, unexpectedly. "I've always been afraid. I tried to pretend I wasn't for sixteen years, and then, when I got away from home, I didn't have to pretend any more and I faced it."

"If you faced it, what's the difference?" said Dave. "I can get scared like anybody."

He looked over at Ranald. But Ranald shook his head.

"Not often for me, any more," he said. "I was telling her—things wear out. Love, hate . . . also fear."

"You don't understand, either of you," said Maybeth.

"I'm always afraid. Of everything. It's a terrible feeling. I keep hunting for something to stop it. I thought this would, but it didn't. Even stopping the sun didn't do it. I'm just as afraid as ever. What if there is a God? He doesn't really care about me."

"Nobody used to expect gods to care without reason," said Ranald. "It's only the last few hundred years—" He stopped speaking rather abruptly. Something or someone was crashing through the underbrush in their direction. Ranald stepped forward to the riverbank, bent down and picked up a handful of sandy soil. As he straightened up, Tom Rathkenny, carrying a revolver, burst through the leaves of the brush behind them to join them.

"What'd you do with her?" the young deputy sheriff shouted, pointing the revolver at them. "Where'd you—"

At this point, he saw the handful of sand, which Ranald had already flung, coming at him through the air like a swarm of midges. The flung soil fell well short, but Tom ducked instinctively and the revolver went off, pointing at the sky.

Before he could pull its muzzle and his gaze back to earth again, Ranald had reached him—running very quickly but effortlessly with what looked like abnormally long strides— and as Tom tried once more to aim the revolver, Ranald hit him. It was a blow with clenched fist, but as odd in its way as Ranald's method of running. The fist came up backhand from the region of Ranald's belt level in a sweep to the side of the other man's jaw. It snapped Tom's head around sideways; and he took a step backward, fell, and lay apparently unconscious. Dave, who had come up meanwhile, reached down and picked up the revolver.

"What got into him?" asked Dave. He squatted down comfortably on his heels beside Tom, holding the gun loosely on one knee with his right hand and waiting for Tom to come to.

"Letty," said Maybeth. "Maybe he thought she was with you instead of me."

Tom opened his eyes, blinked stupidly at them all, and tried to sit up, reaching for the revolver. Dave pushed him back to the ground.

"Can't go shooting around like that," Dave said. "Lay there for a minute and cool off. Then maybe you can tell us what got you worked up."

"She isn't here?" Tom said. "Letty isn't?"

"Last I saw of her she was with you," Dave said.

Tom let himself go limp. His head rolled back on his neck so that he stared bitterly at the sky. He lay for a moment.

"She went off," he said, then. "She expects me to read her mind. For God's sake, I don't know what she's thinking!"

Dave, Ranald, and Maybeth watched him.

"She got mad," Tom said to the sky. "She wants me to change; but she's got all these crazy ideas of what I am. And I'm not. How can I change from something I'm not? How can I tell what she's thinking when she doesn't tell me?"

He waited, as if for an answer. None of them offered any.

"Guess you can get up," said Dave, getting to his own feet. Tom scrambled upright. His eyes went to his gun, now tucked into the belt of Dave's Levi's.

"That's mine," he said hoarsely. "Give it back."

"Guess I will," said Dave, "when I figure you can be trusted with it again."

"That's stealing," said Tom. "I could arrest you for that."

"You still a sheriff's man?" Dave said. "You don't look it much, right now. Anyway, how do you know there's still a sheriff?"

He stood. Tom leaned forward a little as if he might try to

take the revolver back, but kept his arms down. He turned, suddenly, and plowed off into the brush.

"We'll just hold on to this for now," said Dave, patting the revolver butt fondly. "He'll be all right once he gets his head clear. How if we move on down the river?"

He turned and led the way along the bank, downstream. Ranald and Maybeth went with him.

"She's like you two," said Maybeth, a little bleakly as they went. "She's not afraid of anything. That's why it always happens to people like her."

But as they moved on beside the river, her mood improved. Some time later, the two men even heard her humming almost inaudibly to herself. They followed the curving stream until the bank began to rise and they found themselves at last on what was actually a small bluff, looking through a screen of birch and maple trees down a vertical drop of perhaps eighty feet to a small open area like a valley. There a road emerged on the right below the bluff to run straight ahead, until the trees of a wooded slope to its right seemed to move in and swallow it up in the distance; and the river emerged on the left to run right beside the road with only a small strip of bank between them.

"That'll be the farther part of the road from back where we're camped," Dave said. "This way must be the way to Medford. Let's go back. Thought I saw a pool up a ways with some fish in it."

They went back the way they had come for perhaps an eighth of a mile to the pool Dave had seen. He produced a fishing handline and hooks from a leather folder in his right hip pocket and discovered some earthworms under a log. He turned the line and worms over to Ranald and went to build one of his reflexive fires. By the time he had it going and burned down to a useful set of coals, Ranald had, in fact, caught four middling-sized brook trout.

"Let me do that," said Maybeth, when the fish were cleaned and spitted on twigs over the coals.

There was actually nothing more for her to do but watch the fish and turn them occasionally. But she sat keeping an intent watch on them and the two men heard her humming once more to herself.

When the fish were done, they ate the flaky, delicate flesh with their fingers, using some salt Dave produced in a fold of wax paper from the same leather folder that had contained, and now contained again, the fishline and hooks. The four trout made next to nothing of a lunch for three people, but by this time the day had heated up to noon temperature and none of them were very hungry. After eating, they put the fire to rest with river water and walked back upstream.

It was quite warm. Maybeth took off the sweater Walt had lent her and carried it. Dave took off his jacket, folded it, and tucked it under the belt of his Levi's, in back. Only Ranald stayed dressed as he was, indifferent to the temperature.

They passed the spot where they had first come upon the riverbank and Tom had burst out on them with his revolver. They went on up the river's edge, detouring only here and there when some small bay or close stand of brush barred the direct route. Returning from one of these small detours, they heard ahead, through a stand of young oak and elm trees, a sound of voices in relaxed and comfortable argument.

"That's Rob and her, now," said Maybeth.

They came up through the stand of young trees and looked out on a wide, shallow stretch of the river. Letty and Rob were there in the water, naked in the sunlight. Rob was seated on a fallen log that had its upper edge barely out of the river's surface; and Letty, standing behind him, was washing his hair. Up to her knees in water, she worked her fingers industriously and had succeeded in raising a good lather. The sun gleamed on her pale, compact back and firm buttocks; and wads of lather dripped from Rob's narrow and bent, but sinewy, shoulders to float off like foam flecks on the current downstream.

". . . that's your trouble," Rob was saying, "you always want to run things."

"Like hell I do," she answered.

"The hell you don't."

"The hell I do—sit still, you son of a bitch," said Letty. "Anyway, hold your head still."

"This log . . ." said Rob, shifting his weight uncomfortably.

Dave laughed softly.

"Just as well I kept that Tom's gun," he said, low-voiced. He turned away. They went off from there without any further words.

"I think I'll go back," said Maybeth unexpectedly, when they were once more out of sound of the voices from the two in the river. She was not humming now, and her face had gone back to its old expression. She turned, and stopped. "Which way is it?"

Ranald pointed through the woods.

"Just keep the sun at your back," said Dave. "If you don't hit the meadow, you'll run into the road. If it's the road, turn left and the meadow'll be down a ways, only."

She left.

"Well, now," said Dave, looking after her. "And I was just about figuring she'd come out of it."

"Nothing changes," said Ranald. "As I said."

Dave glanced at him.

"You really hold to that," Dave said.

"I'd like to believe it's not so," said Ranald. "But it's what I've learned. All that's left to know is why I go on, knowing it, getting a new start each time spring turns to summer, summer to fall—to winter—to spring again."

"Go on because you're wrong," said Dave. They were walking on together, once more, following the riverbank upstream. He pointed to the moving water. "See there?

Riverbed's changing all the time. No spring's like any other spring. No two trees alike. That tree there''—he pointed to a young birch—''there never was one like it before. After it's grown big and died and fallen, never be another like it. There never was another like it, from the beginning of the world until now. Same with people. Anyone, he dies, no one just like him's ever going to come again.''

''What profit in that?'' Ranald said, ''—if all he does is what men have always done—no more, no less. What gain is there in his special differences if he comes from nowhere just to walk the same treadmill in one spot before going back into nowhere again?''

''Why bother to argue it with me if you think that's so?'' said Dave. ''If you're so sure of it and we're just saying what's been argued all out, time and again, before?''

''Because I wish you were right and I was wrong. Still,'' said Ranald, ''that's the one thing I can't understand. Why I go on, why I still hope. —Also, you aren't like most men, brother.''

''That's a kind word,'' said Dave. ''Well, listen to my side of it, then. You're wrong thinking people never get nowhere. We've come a long ways. Apes once, wasn't we?''

''Or something like that. What of it?'' said Ranald. ''As apes we walked in the woods like this and the sun made us hot, like this. Where are you and I different, now? What difference Rob and Letty, naked in the river? They were naked there as apes, also.''

''Not washing hair.''

''Grooming each other. As apes and monkeys do, today.'' Dave laughed.

''Might be right about that,'' he said. ''But even if you're winning the argument, you're still not changing my mind. I still feel you're wrong—know you're wrong.''

''You have your god,'' said Ranald. ''That may be the difference.''

"Have Him?" Dave said. "I believe He's there, sure enough. I can't hardly say no to that after seeing the sun stopped over my head the way it was. But *have* God? No more than I ever had when He was just a chain around my ankle."

"He'll be a chain around your ankle again," said Ranald. "Nothing changes."

"What it is I believe in, that says you're wrong," said Dave, "that's not God or religion. That's what I got from what I've seen—everything I seen all my life long. I tell you a tree lives and dies and there never was nothing like it before, nor can't anything ever be like it again—nor it don't make sense things ever be the same after it's once lived and died. Trees, everything's that way. People can't be any different—and they're not. I know it by feel, inside me."

"I felt like that once—now only my foolish self goes on acting as if I did," said Ranald. " *'Render therefore unto Caesar the things which are Caesar's.'* That's the verse Walt's taken for his text. *'—and unto God the things that are God's.'* Meaning that when all the dues of the world are paid, faith remains. But what if one pays all dues and then finds no faith, nothing left over?"

They walked on a little way without talking, their feet finding level and uncluttered space without conscious thought on either man's part.

"You told me you went through this once before," said Dave. "The sun stopped—"

"No," said Ranald. "That time it was a matter of darkness at midday. A hand held the light of the sun away from the Earth."

"Eclipse, maybe?" suggested Dave.

Ranald shook his head.

"A hand," he said. "We were made to know it. The sun was there, unmoving as it was this time. We could see it. But a hand held its light from reaching us and the other things of Earth. And so matters stayed for some time, for about as long as it happened in the meadow to you and me and the rest. But afterward, there was no difference. Just as there was no difference a little later after the gentlefolk had wept at chapel at hearing that Piers Plowman was closer to God than they. Soon afterward, no man or woman stayed changed.''

"Everyone's been changed this time, far as I can see."

"At first. It seemed all those there were changed, too, that earlier time. But it was like in the chapel, for a small time only. Very soon after the hand was gone, any difference it had made was gone from those who had seen it.''

"Maybe," said Dave. "Got to see it myself to believe it. Got to see it *in* myself, to believe it.''

They went on a few more miles up the river, then turned and came back to the meadow in the midafternoon. Maybeth was not by the dead ashes of their campfire, nor Letty, Rob, or Tom. But Walt was there, no longer preaching, sitting on his sleeping bag, still dirty and shirtless with his sign face down on the ground by him. Newspapers were spread around him; and he pushed front pages from these into the hands of Dave and Ranald as they came up.

"Read!" he said. "The counterattack of those who hate God. The lies of the atheists.''

Headlines on the sheet in Ranald's hand took up nearly half the available white space there.

ACT OF GOD
OR
ACT OF NATURE?

The paper Dave had been given had smaller headlines.

MIRACLE MAY BE AN ILLUSION

"Not all," said Walt, "could testify to the truth. There had to be those few who had to try to tear it down." He waved his hand at the snowdrift of other newspapers scattered around him. "All these other papers are honest, reporting the new era as it is." His voice trembled a little. "But among the sheep there have to be a few goats—a few wolves, wolves would be a better name for them; and they're tearing at the truth, trying to tear it down. Pity them, as I do. Pity them!"

"Says here," said Dave, bending his head over the newssheet he held, "the whole thing could have been the result of massive auto-hypnosis. Guess not. I don't hypnotize well. Man tried it once on me some years back, then said I kept fighting him. I wasn't fighting; just sitting there waiting to see what it felt like. He said that was the same thing as fighting."

Ranald was reading below the headlines on the page in his hand. . . .

"We owe at least this much to nearly three millennia of scientific thought and work," Nobel Prize winner Nils Hjemstrand said today, *"not to throw out all possibility of a natural explanation for this apparent miracle before a thorough investigation is made by competent physicists, astronomers, and students of any other scientific disciplines which might have been involved in what seemed to happen. . . ."*

"Their investigation won't work," said Walt, looking up at Ranald's face. "They'll learn that."

Ranald handed the paper back down to him and looked over at Dave.

"Tomorrow you'll begin to see it for yourself," he said to Dave. "It'll begin."

"Fools," muttered Walt, staring down at the paper Ranald had just given back to him, "doubting fools, clinging to a superstition called science. . . ."

That night Maybeth rejoined them, and the praying and the singing of religious songs was louder in the meadow than it had ever been. But at dawn there were gaps among the line of store trucks parked along the road and the number of campers in the meadow was noticeably less. During the morning, Walt washed himself, put on a clean shirt, and gathered an audience around him. Standing on a wooden egg crate, he lectured his listeners earnestly on the chance, now, to form a new society, a new world. Maybeth stood in the audience with Walt's other listeners for perhaps an hour, then she left and came back to the campsite where Dave and Ranald, Rob and Letty were turning a loaf of bread and two cans of corned beef into lunch.

She sat down, but made no move to reach for the bread and meat. Her shoulders were curved and she stared down at the gray-black ashes where the fire of last night had glowed.

"Walt's right," she said, without looking at any one of them in particular. "It shouldn't be lost, what we all know happened here. The people who went through it ought to get together and change things."

"Not his way," said Rob. "People tried it his way for hundreds of years—and look what it led to. He just wants to set up more of the same. But that won't work—anymore."

Maybeth looked at him as if she would argue, then gazed back at the ashes without saying anything.

"You don't believe me?" Rob got to his feet. "I'll prove it to you—it's not going to work."

He went off toward the road and the store trucks. Letty started to rise and follow him, then sat back down again. She looked for a moment hard at Maybeth, but Maybeth was still staring at the fire's dead ashes.

It was over an hour before Rob returned; but when he came he brought with him almost as many newspapers as Walt had surrounded himself with the day before. They were a new day's editions, and he dumped them on the ground before the seated Maybeth.

"Read those," he said. "Half of them, anyway, have already switched over. Half of them don't believe anymore it was a miracle. They're full of articles by scientists saying how it could have happened without anything supernatural about it.''

"But there was!" Maybeth said. "Don't you remember? It wasn't just the sun stopping, it was what we all felt. Remember? We all *knew* it was God doing it, then.''

"What if we did? What if it was?" Rob said. "What matters isn't what happened, but what people are going to think happened, a year from now.''

"Oh, no!" said Maybeth.

"Oh, yes," he said. "You damn right, yes. That's how things happen. You just have to face it.''

She looked hopefully at Dave and Ranald. Dave, however, was occupied in using a wire pad to clean fire-black from the bottom of his soup pan, and did not even see the glance she gave him. Ranald met her eyes in open, unresponsive silence.

She looked down again at the headlines on the newspapers before her.

"I'm no good arguing," she said. "Walt'll answer you. Why don't you try to make him believe it's going like that?''

"That's what I'm sitting around here waiting for," said Rob, the yellow glints showing in his eyes. "Just that.''

It was early afternoon before Walt gave up his efforts long enough to come back to the place where the rest of them were, to make himself a sandwich and a cup of coffee. All the others, though they had strayed some little distance away from time to time since Rob and Maybeth had talked, came drifting back to their common campsite when Walt sat down with his coffee cup and a pressed-ham sandwich.

He ate and drank hungrily, saying nothing. Rob spoke to him.

"It's not working, is it?" Rob said.

Walt looked at him and bit into the sandwich without answering.

"It isn't, is it?" said Rob. "I mean, you talking to them.

It's not doing any good, not keeping them from changing their minds?''

Walt swallowed the last of his sandwich. His back was bent as Maybeth's shoulders had been bent, earlier.

"Forgive me," he said. "I'm all talked out for the moment."

"Are you? Are you?" Rob, who had been sitting down, got to his knees and walked several steps on his knees clumsily to bring himself right in front of Walt and only half a body's length away. "You sure it's not just you don't want to discuss it—I mean, really discuss it, not just stand up there and shout while people pretend to listen?''

"I think," said Walt, holding his voice very even, "some at least were listening."

"The ones who want to be brainwashed, you mean?" Rob said. "Look around, for Christ's sake. This place hasn't got half the people it had yesterday, or when it happened."

"Then you admit it happened," said Walt heavily.

"Happened? Happened? It happened, all right," said Rob, leaning forward. "But what's 'happened' mean? According to you it's supposed to mean something great, is that it? Well, it doesn't. *Nothing*—that's what it means!''

"You don't believe in God," said Walt. "That's what makes you talk this way."

"Believe? I don't not-believe and I don't believe. I don't give a damn one way or another. Because it doesn't *matter*— don't you understand? Haven't you seen these latest papers?''

"I looked," said Walt, not looking at them. "There's nothing new there. A few dissenters—"

"Not a few," said Rob. "A lot. Half of them, at least. And even the ones who're still shouting miracle are starting to tone down and go cautious on it—keeping an open mind, that's how they put it. But toning down, all the same!''

"I repeat," said Walt, slowly and deliberately, "you

don't believe in God. If you believed in Him, then what you saw here would have been a revelation for you, too.''

"Revelation!" Rob laughed. "Do you know what it was to me? You never saw anything like the sun stand still in the sky before. That was really something for you, wasn't it? And so you think it had to be really something for everybody else, too. Well,'' Rob leaned even closer, "I'm telling you now, it wasn't; no matter what people like you want to make out of it. I'll tell you what it was. An experience— that's all. A trip, man! And you never had one before, so you thought it was something to turn everybody in the world inside out.''

Walt shook his head and turned to face away from Rob. Rob scrambled around on his knees to keep them nose to nose.

"You think that's the first time I saw something like the sun standing still?'' Rob demanded. "I've seen lots of things—things you couldn't even dream up; and not just from being high, either. A trip, that's all it was; and there's all kinds of trips. I don't care where this one came from. It was a trip, that's all. Just that and nothing else.''

"The two things," said Walt, staring at him now, "don't compare in any way. What you're talking about is subjective. What we all saw here was objective.''

"All right, call it objective. You think that makes any difference? God exists and He made the sun stand still,'' said Rob. "You think that impresses me with Him? If He wanted to get to me, why didn't He feed a million people that are starving right now in the world? Now, that's something I've never seen done. Why didn't He clean all the smog out of the air everywhere and make it that there couldn't be any more? Why didn't He stop the wars and the killing and heal everybody in the hospitals and out of the hospitals who're sick or hurt?''

"These are our own sins," said Walt, heavily. "We have to cure them ourselves.''

"But we're already curing them, old man." Rob sat back on his heels. "We. Us. —Not you. We're already not making smog, or polluting, or killing people. It's people like you who keep on doing that, talking one thing and doing another. You and your *'Render unto Caesar—'* How'd you like your own quotations to turn around and bite you? What was it Jesus was supposed to say when they came to ask him that question about what was Caesar's and what was God's? '. . . *Why tempt ye me, ye hypocrites?'* Wasn't that it? Who do you suppose the hypocrites are now, with this miracle business—us? Or you people?"

Walt jerked the last coffee in his cup out onto the dead ashes, staining the gray dust black. He put the empty cup in his packsack and got to his feet.

"You're twisting things," he said, "and you know it. You're doing it quite deliberately. I think you know you're not being fair or honest."

He walked away. From the other side of the campfire ashes, Letty looked at Rob.

"You stink, every so often," she said. "You know that?"

Rob did not look back at her. He had picked up a small stick and was digging one sharp end of it furiously into the ground before him, watching the dirt break and move.

"Shut up," he said. "Will you just for once shut up?"

That night, though at least half of the original crowd had gone, the singing and praying in the meadow was as loud as it had been the night before. If anything, the prayers were more sonorous and the songs more shouted. There were also more intoxicants in evidence. Several times during the early evening, when all the campfires were alight, fights broke out and there were men and women to be seen staggering about, or lying sprawled and thickly breathing in unlikely or inconvenient places.

The late editions of the newspapers, when they reached the meadow, contained many stories that backed off even farther from putting the name of miracle to what had happened. Now, less than a third of the press took for granted that a Sign of some kind had been given to the people of the Earth. And there were news stories in opposition to the idea of miracle that used words like "gullible" and "frenzied" in their descriptions of those who might still be whole-heartedly believing.

Meanwhile, as the evening grew, Dave had been sitting by the evening fire, seeming to become bonier of jaw and more bleak of eye as the noise and activities in the meadow increased. Now, a few hours after full dark, he rose suddenly and disappeared into blackness in the direction of the woods lower down. This time Ranald did not go after him. Instead, he stayed by the fire with Maybeth, who was the only other person still there. When Dave left she moved closer to Ranald, who sat cross-legged now, in the midst of the meadowful of noisy people, with the light of the flames playing yellow variations on the rusty colors of his beard, like a magician surrounded by the demons and other dark figures of his conjurations.

"This is going to be the last night here, isn't it?" she asked him.

He did not answer.

"You know," she said, after a little while, "I think I really have been changed."

His face lifted then, and he turned his head to look at her. His gaze was completely unblinking and the firelight reflected from his eyes as if they had themselves caught fire. She had never faced such a brilliant and piercing look in her life; and after a second she looked away from him, down at the ground.

"Never mind," he said. "You meant well. But after these many years I've learned the ways people look when they lie."

"I—" She had intended to speak out loud, but her throat hurt so from tears she did not dare let loose, that her voice could only come out in a whisper. "—just wanted to give you something."

"I know," he said. "And you have, as much as anyone can. But no one person's changing can be an answer to my trouble. The answer I need has to be one that fits everybody. If I can know why I want to go on living, then I'll know why the whole race wants to keep on living when it rejects all gods and keeps trying the impossible as if it were possible."

"But maybe it *isn't* impossible," she said. "Maybe it's possible and you just can't see it."

"I?" he asked; and the single questioning syllable tore to dustrags the fine fabric of the argument she was forming in her mind. Without an argument and without hope, she went on talking, anyway.

"It could be because you're different," she said. "After all, you're immortal."

"No," he answered. "I've only lived a long—a very long time. And that's the problem of it. I'm mortal, all men and women are mortal, the human race is mortal. That's why it makes no sense. An immortal would want to keep the eternal life he had. But people are like climbers on a cliff too high even to imagine. Each knows he can struggle up only a little distance before he dies and drops off and another climber takes his place. —Still, when a god comes winging close like some great bird, ready to carry at least some of them toward the top, they reject him—turn their heads away and insist they're alone on the cliff."

"But, as you say," she said, "you've lived so long. Maybe it looks different to you from how it really is for the rest of us."

"No, it doesn't look different," he said, staring at the flames, "and I'm no different. I turn my back on gods, just like the rest. I want to climb, too."

"Instinct," she said.

He shook his head.

"Instinct's to find a safe notch in the cliff face and stay there. To climb goes against that."

"Maybe, then," she said, "that's what they mean by 'soul.' "

"A soul is a god-thing," he replied. "A soul would reach for the god who comes swooping by just like the instinct-part would try to find a safe spot and live there without pain and effort. But in spite of soul and instinct, the climbing goes on."

He rocked a little on his hips. It was the first physical sign of emotion she had ever seen in him.

"And still I keep going on," he said. "And on. And on."

Two dark figures broke from the clutter of the crowd in the darkness downslope and came running toward their fire, a larger shape chasing a smaller. As they broke into the firelight the pursuer grabbed for the smaller figure, which dodged with the easy smoothness of much faster reflexes and cut around the fire to stand behind Ranald and Maybeth. Panting on the other side of the fire, the pursuer showed himself to be Tom Rathkenny.

"Yellow—" he gasped. "Why don't you stand still? You, doing all that talking about not being afraid of anything—anybody."

"Who's—afraid?" said the voice of Rob, behind Ranald and Maybeth. "You just want me to give you all the advantages. If I weighed forty more pounds, I'd stand still. So, I don't. So, let's see you catch up with me."

"I'll kill you," panted Tom.

"Sure—you will." Rob was getting to be breathing almost normally. "That's all you can do. You can't win the argument, so you'll kill me. You can't catch me, so you'll kill me. Sure, pig, come kill me!"

"Yug—" It was a sound without words. Tom started straight ahead through the fire at the two seated people and direction of Rob's voice.

Ranald got to his feet without touching his hands to the ground, so suddenly that his appearance in Tom's path was almost like a stage trick.

Tom checked, the flames licking about his boot tops.

The heavy-boned young man swayed on his feet for a second like an animal caught in a trap. Then he turned and plunged off down the slope into the darkness and the crowd. From behind Ranald and Maybeth came a long, slightly shuddering outbreath.

"Woo," said Rob, gustily. He came around and dropped down at the fire in a sitting position facing them. Ranald reseated himself.

"I'm not afraid of him," said Rob, in a calm voice. "Not afraid of him at all. That's something somebody like him can't understand. I'm not afraid of"—he glanced at Ranald, then hesitated slightly and looked back at the fire— "hardly anything."

"You shouldn't drive him crazy like that, anyway," said Maybeth.

Rob looked at her.

"Well," he said. "The great silent one speaks."

"I'm just telling you," said Maybeth. "It's dangerous to get anybody—anybody, even—that mad at you. If people get mad enough they don't care what they do." He grinned and she turned to Ranald. "You tell him."

Ranald looked at her and at Rob, but said nothing.

"Please," she said. "Tell him. He'll believe you. —And shouldn't someone tell him?"

Ranald looked directly at Rob.

"He'll kill you," Ranald said.

"Kill me?" said Rob; but, eye to eye with Ranald, he did not grin. "Maybe he might even try it, at that. But he'd have to catch me first."

"I did not say what he might do," said Ranald. "I said what he will do."

Rob stared at him. Face to face across the fire, both short

and wiry, silky beard and high white forehead facing full beard and brown skin faintly wrinkled about the eyes, the flames made them look for a moment like older and younger brothers. Then Rob jerked his head aside and scrambled to his feet.

"No," he said, "you don't—"

He broke off. Letty was coming upslope into the firelight to join them. She stopped in front of Rob.

"I got him to promise to stay away from you," Letty said, flatly. "And you're going to stay right here the rest of the night. I promised him that."

"You, too?" said Rob. "Oh, Mama!"

He sat down again with a thump, as if all his muscles had given way at once. Letty knelt beside him and put an arm around his shoulders.

"You can't help being a bastard," she said tenderly. "I know you can't. But he's a straight. He doesn't understand; and he could hurt you."

"Mama, Mama," said Rob. "No—*Aunt* Letty." He looked across the fire. "Mama Maybeth. Daddy Ranald." ·

"Will you stop it?" said Letty. She put her other arm around him and tried to pull him over backwards. After a second he gave in and they both fell back on the ground intertwined. The firelight played on the soles of their boots, but the upper parts of their bodies were in shadow. Rob laughed and muttered unintelligibly.

"Who cares?" said Letty, indifferently.

Maybeth looked sideways at Ranald. But Ranald's gaze went through and beyond the two on the other side of the fire as indifferently as if they had been half-sketched figures in some old drawing that familiarity had made practically invisible.

His face had shown little but calmness in the time she had known him; and there were no explicit lines of emotion on it now. But a shadow of sadness seemed to have appeared like a visor over his eyes; and he stared off into the distance at nothing, or at least nothing she could see. Timidly she rested a hand on his arm; but he neither moved nor spoke to her. It was like touching a carving in wood.

The fire burned down to red coals and Dave did not return. But close to midnight, Walt came heavily back to join them and dropped into a sitting position on his sleeping bag. After a minute, he reached out for some of the thicker pieces of dead oak limbs Dave had collected in a neat pile nearby, and put them on the coals. Little flames licked up immediately, feeding on the loose bark but leaving the heavy center wood no more than darkened.

"How many did you convert tonight?" Rob asked, from across the fire.

Walt ignored him, staring at the pieces of oak branch with the little flames feeding with temporary ease on the rough bark.

"Didn't hear me?" said Rob, raising his voice. "I asked you "

"I heard you," said Walt. He sagged, a roll of belly bulging his shirt out above his belt as he sat on the sleeping bag. He still did not look up; and his voice was hollowed by weariness. In the new light of the little flames, his eyes showed bloodshot.

"But you didn't answer me."

"If you don't mind," Walt said with great effort, still not looking up, "I'm not in much shape to talk, right now."

"Hey, that's too bad," said Rob.

Walt sat silent and unmoving.

"I said," said Rob, "that's too bad." He raised his voice again. "Too bad—I said."

"Why don't you quit talking?" said Letty.

"Yes, that's a shame," said Rob. "Shows how little real faith there is in people. God says one thing and the newspapers say another; so naturally, they take the word of the newspapers. Here, instead of the converted growing in numbers, they've been staying just the same. —Or maybe they've even been falling off the bandwagon. Is that right?"

He paused; but Walt still did not respond.

"Come to think of it, it seemed to me there were fewer people standing around listening to you and the rest preach tonight, than there were earlier today. —To say nothing of last night. The congregations've been getting smaller and smaller all along, here. In fact, haven't the people been peeling off until there wasn't anyone left for you to talk to at all? —Walt?"

Walt stirred. He did not look up from the pieces of oak limbs which were now beginning to catch fire in the true sense and to grow rows of little flames flickering and running along their undersides. But he shifted his weight on the sleeping bag and the ground on which the bag was lying.

"God is not mocked," he said.

"No, of course not," said Rob.

Maybeth, still seated beside Ranald, tugged a little at his arm.

"Ranald . . ." she whispered.

Ranald's full attention came back slowly, as if from a thousand miles and a thousand years away. He looked at her, and around the fire at Walt, Rob, and Letty, and back to her again. Then he went away once more into distance and time.

Maybeth dropped her hand strengthlessly to her lap.

"God can't be mocked," Rob was saying, "because that wouldn't be right. Or do I mean 'righteous'? That's right, I mean righteous. It wouldn't be righteous for God to be mocked; the way He is here when people begin to decide they don't believe in Him even after His stunt with the sun—"

"They believed," said Walt in a near whisper, staring at the fire.

"Of course they believed," said Rob. "After all, it happened, didn't it? And they should have gone on believing. You ought to have made sure they go on believing. After all, that was your job, wasn't it?''

"Please," said Walt, staring at the fire. "If you don't mind . . ."

"But I mean that really hurts me, those people who listened to you acting like this," said Rob. "They should have gone off in every direction after hearing you, like a batch of disciples, to spread the faith. And here they do just the opposite. They back off from the faith themselves, dropping away one by one until you haven't got anyone there listening to you. How could that happen? How could you let it happen?"

Walt was no longer looking even at the fire. His head hung down now, so that he stared directly at the barren, heel-trampled earth between his thighs.

"Leave him alone," said Letty, getting to her feet. "Come on."

"No," said Rob, not looking around at her, watching and speaking only to Walt, "I can't let something like that happen without trying to understand it. Something that rotten can't happen without a reason, some big reason. I mean—something besides the newspapers must have been working on those people listening to you, to drive every one—every single one of them—away from you, like that."

Walt shuddered a little, but he still sat without answering, staring at the ground.

"Rob," said Letty.

"Be with you in a minute, Let," said Rob, not moving from the ground. "I just want to find out how anybody could have a hundred percent failure, like that. Even the law of averages ought to give one or two converts, shouldn't it? Here now, it's almost as if Walt had been preaching against their believing in the miracle, instead of for it. Hey, do you suppose a man actually could do something like that? I mean, subconsciously? Say one thing, but say it so the people listening realized he was really lying to them? Like, for example, he would be saying out loud to them, 'Abandon doubt, believe and enter the kingdom of heaven . . .' but at the same time the way he'd say it he'd actually be telling them that even if they thought they were positive about something, they had a duty to question themselves about it anyway. —As if he was telling them sort of behind his words that they really had to consider the chance they were wrong. As if they ought to try doubt on for size, just to make sure—"

Walt made a choking sound. Then another. It was suddenly clear that he was sobbing, crying where he sat, making no effort to move or wipe away the tears.

"After all," said Rob, raising his voice a little over the sounds Walt was making, "it's true enough. —I don't see how any thinking person can deny it. You've got a duty to keep an open mind, no matter how much faith you have. That's the only good way, the enlightened way—"

"LEAVE HIM ALONE!"

The fury of Letty's scream was incandescent. Like a sudden eruption of white light in darkness, it left them all momentarily numb and dazzled; and it silenced not only Rob, but everyone in the meadow for fifty yards in all directions. Having exploded, Letty said nothing more, but stood waiting until Rob, after a moment, scrambled to his feet. Then she turned and stalked away. He went after her.

Walt looked after them, then turned to Maybeth and Ranald with a face in which the lines seemed to have deepened like the eroded gullies in some dry desert riverbed.

"He's right," Walt said. "I preached doubt to them. I preached my own doubt, after all. From the second day— right after those newspapers began to doubt, I began to doubt again, too."

"You shouldn't care," said Maybeth. "You did it in spite of what you were thinking. That's harder than doing it with no doubts at all. Doing something in spite of yourself is the hardest thing there is."

He shook his head and went back to looking down at the earth. She looked bleakly at the ground, herself. It had been no use, like throwing a kiss to a starving man; but it was all she knew to say to him.

The noise dwindled in the meadow and at last, with the moon small and high overhead and the fires low, there was silence. It was then that Dave came back and found all of them asleep but Ranald, who was still sitting as he had been.

"Two bells, and all's well," said Dave, sitting down and tossing one of the oak limbs on the once more nearly dead fire. A scent of whiskey came across the fire with his words to Ranald. Just as in the woods, only a deliberateness about Dave's speech backed up the evidence reaching Ranald's nose.

"Party's over, I take it?" asked Dave.

Ranald stirred and came back, as he had briefly for Maybeth earlier, from the distance of his mind.

"Tomorrow everyone will go," Ranald said. His eyes went to the bottom pants leg covering that ankle of Dave's he had seen dark with scar and callouses.

"No," said Dave, following the direction of Ranald's gaze, "I didn't put it back on. Don't intend to, either; but I don't know as it makes any difference. Turned out the covenant between me and the Lord wasn't something you could put on and off like a chain, anyhow."

"So," said Ranald, almost to himself, "like the gentlefolk leaving chapel, like these around us here, there's to be no change for you either, brother?"

Dave frowned.

"Don't know," he said. "I won't know until I get the sight and stink of this place out of my eyes and nose." He reached into his pocket and pulled out the cut chain. It glittered like a living metal thing in his grasp. "The day comes I can throw this away, I'll know I found something here—found it for good."

He turned, unzipped his sleeping bag and opened it. He lay down in it, throwing the unzipped top flap loosely over him.

"Paying Caesar never really worried me none," he said, looking up at the night sky. "It was paying God. Actually, a man ought to be able to pay them both off—and be free. I'll see about that after I'm clear of this place. Well, party's over. Night."

"Farewell," said Ranald.

In a moment Dave was asleep and the meadow held only one waking mind under the moon and the stars.

Dawn rose on a meadow empty of more than nine tenths of the crowd that had filled it when it was most full. And these that were left now went about the business of leaving, themselves. Even before the sun was above the hill beyond the road where the trucks had lined up, most of the last few campers were gone or on their way; and, now that the meadow was clearing, it was possible to see the signs they had left behind them.

The crowd had been good about collecting their litter and trash in the beginning. But the last couple of days, all order had begun to disintegrate. Now that the surface of the meadow was no longer hidden by people, it showed all sorts of discarded material, as if the ground had sickened with a disease called humanity; and the illness showed now in a rash of useless items. Torn newspapers, unclean plastic and paper plates, empty cans, abandoned, punctured air mattresses in various gaudy colors, bits of tents and clothing, shoes and garbage, all blotched the gentle slope where sparse but tough green grass had covered loose, brown soil. Above, the morning sky was high and blue with clouds as fluffy and clean as if they had just been born out of the pure upper air. It was cool, with a fair, small wind blowing from the northwest, from the hill down toward the unseen river.

Around Dave's campfire, they were also getting ready to leave, packing up along with the two dozen or so other people remaining in the meadow. There were two of the sheriff's deputies in uniform going from group to group. One of these was Tom Rathkenny. He came up to the fire with a paper in his hand, as shiny in leather helmet, boots, and Sam Browne belt as he had been the first time they had seen him. Only the holster at his belt was empty, though the fact that the holster flap was closed and buttoned down helped to disguise its emptiness.

"I'll take my gun back," he said to Dave, holding out his free hand.

Dave, seated as he filled his pack, looked at the hand for a second, then reached into the pack, pulled out the revolver and handed it up. Tom unbuttoned his holster and put the weapon into it; but he did not button down the flap again. He held the paper up.

"This is a legal notice," he said. "Your license to camp here has expired and the county court orders you to vacate the premises, after cleaning up any litter you have left, repairing any damage you have done, and returning the area you have occupied to the condition it enjoyed before you occupied it."

"I never was much for being able to grow grass in one day," said Dave.

The younger man ignored him. Tom was looking at Rob only, and running the thumbnail of his right hand back and forth along the top curve of his unbuttoned holster flap. Rob, busy packing the tattered blankets he owned with Letty, ignored the attention he was getting. Ranald, the only one of them unmoving, still seated as if he had not even shifted once from his position the night before, watched both of the younger men.

"Yang and Yin," said Ranald to Tom, without warning, "love and hate. *'Abou Ben Adhem, may his tribe increase, awoke one night from a great dream of peace; and saw within the moonlight of his room—'* "

It was a moment before they all realized he was reciting

verse; and, when they did realize, they continued to listen—
for the moment all stopped from what they were doing—as
if caught by the magic of primitive people listening to an
incantation.

" 'Making it rich,' " Ranald went on, as if no one but Tom
were there.

> ". . . *and like a lily in bloom,*
>   *An angel writing in a book of gold.*
> *Exceeding peace had made Ben Adhem bold;*
>   *And to the presence in the room he said,*
> *'What writest thou?' The Vision raised his head;*
>   *And with a look made of all sweet accord,*
> *Answered, 'The names of those who love the Lord.'*
>   *'And is mine one?' asked Abou. 'Nay, not so,'*
> *Replied the Angel. Abou spake more low,*
>   *But cheerily still, and said, 'I pray thee, then,*
> *Write me as one that loves his fellow men.'*
>   *The Angel wrote and vanished. The next night,*
> *He came again with a great wakening light;*
>   *And showed the names whom love of God had bless'd;*
> *And lo! Ben Adhem's name led all the rest.*

". . . and there are others," Ranald said, without pause
or change in his voice. *'Le temps a laissé son manteau, De
vent, de froidure, et de pluie . . .'* Also, *'He prayeth well
who loveth well both man and bird and beast . . .'* But it
doesn't matter. I was too young the first time this happened.
Each one must build or break his own god. —And I, like
all . . ."

Then, as they still watched and waited, his attention went
away off from them again into time and space, as it had the
day before. They sat or stood, still without speaking—there
was something in the air, something fearful promised to
whoever might break the silence first.

"What was that about?" asked Dave.

He asked the question of Ranald, but Ranald did not answer and he looked around at the others.

"That . . . that last bit about praying was from Coleridge—'The Ancient Mariner,' " said Walt, unsurely, staring at Ranald. "The French bit was from the fourteenth-fifteenth century—a poem about how wonderful spring was, written by a man who'd been locked in prison for years, I think . . . Charles d'Orléans. That first verse is by some nineteenth-century poet." He looked at Maybeth and Letty and Rob in turn. "I can't remember who. Do you know?"

They stared at him, and shook their heads.

"All three things he quoted have something to do with loving—people or things . . ." Walt said. "I . . . don't understand."

Dave looked at Tom Rathkenny. Tom's features were pale and tight. It was impossible to tell whether his expression was one of fear, or rage, or only of simple embarrassment. He wore a statue's or an idol's face; and, as Dave's eyes hit him now, Tom turned and plunged away, off down the slope of the meadow toward another group of late departees.

Rob looked after him for a moment, then turned back to stuff the last blanket into the pack he, himself, would be carrying, and buckled it closed. Getting to his feet, he put the pack on. Letty already bore hers.

"Well," said Rob, half turned to go. He hesitated, looking at Maybeth and Walt. "We've got the promise of a ride in the last panel truck down there. The driver wants somebody along to help him change tires. He could take some more people besides us."

Walt got slowly to his feet, then shook his head.

"No," he said. "I've got to be alone—a while."

He snatched up his pack and went off away from the road, downslope, but not in the direction Tom had taken, until he disappeared into the woods between meadow and river. They watched him go; and neither Tom nor the other sheriff's deputy was watching as he went.

"Well," said Rob, after he had gone, "anyone who wants a ride better come along in a hurry. That trucker's ready to pull out."

He and Letty took their gear and went toward the road. Maybeth looked after them, hesitated, and looked back at Dave and Ranald.

Ranald's eyes, once more lost on the view of his inner vision, looked through and past her. Dave returned her look.

"Better go," Dave said.

"I can't stay with you," she said, "even a little longer?"

Dave shook his head slowly.

"Not me," he answered. "Someday, maybe, if it turns out this changed things, I may want a woman around steady, neighbors in to dinner, and all the rest of it. But that's someday."

He buckled tight the last buckle of his pack on its pack-frame and stood up, sliding his arms through the straps. Maybeth looked at Ranald.

"Good-bye, Ranald," she said.

He came a little way back from where he had gone, to speak to her.

"Go with a god," he said. "Your god, if may be. But any god will do."

She turned abruptly and almost ran after Rob and Letty, who were now standing talking to a short, brown-shirted man beside the left front door of a somewhat battered blue panel truck—the only vehicle left in the meadow except for two motorcycles of the sheriff's deputies. Dave looked after her for a moment as she joined them, and they all got into the truck. It pulled away, back down the route up which they had all come.

"The other way, for me," said Dave, "up that road

alongside the river we saw, into Medora or whatever they call it. A day or so's walking'll clear my head.''

He looked back at Ranald.

"So long, then," Dave said. "Maybe we'll run into each other again."

"I don't think so," said Ranald. His voice and eyes were a little strange because of his being only partway back. "I will turn away a little, then turn back and find you are dust. Unless . . ."

"Unless?" Dave stared at him curiously.

"Unless . . ." said Ranald, still from the in-between of two places, "you turn away, then turn back to find me dust. I was too young the first time I saw this."

"You figuring on dying?" said Dave, bluntly.

"No. Yes—eventually. Maybe, soon . . ." Ranald came almost all the way back and looked up at Dave with strangely clear eyes. "I do not know if I want to. I do not know if I should. I don't know if I will."

Dave stared at him.

"What makes you so sure anything'll happen?" he asked.

"Always," said Ranald. "People always do the same things. A curse makes a blow—makes—wounding—makes a killing."

Dave grunted slightly under his breath.

"Man ought to know what's he doing."

"I belong to no god," said Ranald. "And no more do I belong to any people, so that their ways are a law to me. I belong, though, to myself—to Ranald; and I do not know what Ranald is going to do. It's a little thing to die after three score years and ten. To die after much longer is a hard problem. How can I be sure this moment is so worthwhile? Will it be worth all those other times before when I refused death, fought it off and said—'Not yet'?"

Dave hesitated. Then he took a step closer and held out his hand.

"Luck," he said.

Ranald reached up and took hold; but with his hand grasping Dave's forearm above the wrist, so that Dave had no choice but to fold his own fingers around Ranald's forearm in return. They let go.

"If I'm to die soon," said Ranald, "I'd like to see you free first, Brother Piers." He added, almost muttering under his breath, " *'Cessez, cessez, gens d'armes et piétons—de piller et manger le bonhomme . . .'* "

"You're full up with poems, today," said Dave.

"It's Walt and his question about Caesar that opened my memory to them," said Ranald. "Walt was right. His question is the question, after all. . . ."

He stopped talking as if he had run down.

"As I say, luck, then," said Dave after a second. But this time Ranald did not answer. Dave shook his head, turned, and went off with a loose, swinging stride toward the far end of the meadow where the trees came together, hiding the road to Medora.

Near the middle of the road beside the openness of the meadow, the two deputies watched him go. Then they turned back. Ranald was the last left amidst the litter of the open space, sitting cross-legged and unmoving. One of the deputies started toward him; but the other, who walked like Tom Rathkenny, caught the first by the arm and turned him around. They went to their motorcycles, the other got on his and left in the opposite direction Dave had taken, back toward the city. Tom started his own bike after a minute and slowly followed. Ranald was alone in the meadow.

Now that there was no human activity around to retreat from, he came all the way back into the present, opening all his senses to the land around him and its inhabitants. Already half a mile distant, the other sheriff's deputy droned on his motorcycle back toward his headquarters. Tom Rathkenny, just out of sight beyond the meadow, had pulled his machine off the road behind a willow clump and stopped. He put the kickstand down carefully and got off.

A few hundred yards beyond and out of sight on the winding road from Tom, the panel truck had stopped with a flat tire, which Rob was just now replacing with a spare from inside the truck, while the driver stood by and watched.

In the opposite direction, already out of sight beyond the meadow, Dave swung along the people-empty route to Medora, the sound of his bootsoles in the loose gravel on the shoulder of the roadway noisy in the noon silence. Down beside the river, beyond the woods and not moving—possibly on his knees—Walt was praying out loud.

". . . I'm this way because this is the way You made me, Lord," he was praying. "No, I don't mean to put all the responsibility on You; but You ought to share in what I am. . . ."

All these things—the rushing of the river, the rustling of tree leaves, the drone of a nearby wasp—came clearly and unavoidably to Ranald's acute hearing. There was a flutter of wings, and a male Western song sparrow came to a perch on the end of a leaning tent-pole near Ranald, a tent-pole abandoned, but still stuck in the earth and semi-upright. The song sparrow threw back his head and sang, and Ranald understood. Like the intentions of humans, the messages of birds and animals had become clear to him through long time and familiarity. But he had never understood a bird as clearly as this one, at this moment.

"*I am me!*" cried the song sparrow. "*Me. Me! And this meadow is mine! Mine—and no other's! Mine—and no other's!*"

". . . Lord," Walt was praying to a God in whom he had no trust, no hope, "You should help me. . . ."

". . . All right," Rob was saying to the driver of the panel truck, "suppose you get something into your head. We came along to *help* with your flat tires; not do all the work while you stand around juicing! The next tire that goes flat, you're going to do as much fixing as we do!"

"That's what you get for trying to do favors," said the

driver, climbing back into the front seat of the truck. "To hell with you. Just to hell with you! You can walk into town!"

He closed the door of the truck, started the panel up and drove off.

"Wait—" Maybeth called after him.

"Let him go," said Rob. "They're all alike. I ought to've known."

Dave had begun to whistle as he strode along. Walt was still praying. Tom Rathkenny had left his motorcycle and was walking down the curve of the wooded road toward Rob and the others, although he could not yet be close enough for them to see him. The breeze blowing against the left side of Ranald's face ceased for a moment. Abruptly, he sprang upright; and headed down the road in the direction everyone but Dave and Walt had taken, breaking into a run.

He ran with the oddly long strides he had used down by the river when he had taken the gun from Tom. His running was effortlessly swift, so that he seemed to soar slightly with each step, the way a deer soars with each bound. He crossed the road and headed on a direct line through the trees, toward that spot beside the road where Rob and Letty were dividing up some of the load in their packs, so that Maybeth could help them carry it on foot back into town.

Ranald ran. Up ahead of him, out of sight beyond the trees, Tom Rathkenny came around a curve and walked up to the three as they were redistributing the load they had to pack.

"So, you're still here," said Tom.

Rob's answer was lost to Ranald. He was in full stride, now. He coursed the woods like a wild animal, hurdling fallen logs and small bushes in his path as if some instinct deep within him told him when to go over, and when around. The slope of the hillside and its sun-dappled tree trunks swam around him; and the late morning breeze was cold on face and neck where he had begun to sweat. Ahead, talk between Tom and the others had become some kind of an argument between Tom and Rob; and as Ranald rocketed down the wooded slope, close to the others now, Rob's voice reached clearly through the leaves and pine needles.

"You and Letty?" Rob was saying. "Oh, sure . . . You know what she does? She collects cats, man; and squirrels; and birds with half a leg missing. But she doesn't keep them."

They were all right ahead of Ranald now, although the trees still hid them. He burst through that last screen and came out only a few running steps from them. Maybeth and Letty stood back by the side of the road with the opened packs, and one blanket that had been tied up to make it into a sort of packsack. Between the girls and the trees Tom stood facing Rob with perhaps eight feet of space between them. Rob's back was arched; the narrow, tight muscles of his shoulders under their shirt were thrust forward. Tom was stiffly upright and pale, with the sweat rolling down his face. In his hand he held his revolver, pointed at Rob.

"Go ahead," Rob said. "Let's see you shoot me. You've been talking about it long enough—"

Running at full speed, Ranald came between them, turning his upper body toward Tom just as the revolver went off. The battering-ram impact of the heavy revolver slug high on his left side spun him around. He tried to carry the spin on around in a full circle and stay on his feet. But his legs staggered and dropped him. He lay on his back on the soft roadside earth, looking at the clouds.

The blow of the bullet had left him without breath to speak. There were voices above him, and faces, looking down—Letty and Maybeth, particularly Maybeth. His eyes met hers. He could not remember a woman who had looked at him so.

Both she and Letty were kneeling over him, one on each side. Letty ripped his jacket and shirt open, popping buttons as if they had been sewn with paper.

"It's down there," said Letty, staring at his bare chest. "He needs a doctor. He's got to have a doctor, quick."

"I didn't," Tom was saying. "I didn't pull the trigger. I wasn't going to hurt anyone. It just went off. It—exploded. By itself. I wasn't going to shoot anyone. . . ."

"God . . ." Rob said. His voice was like the thick voice of a drunk. "God, you bastard . . ."

"We've got to get help," said Maybeth, looking up. "An ambulance!"

"Where's his motorcycle?" Letty asked. She had torn off a portion of Ranald's shirt and wadded it up. She was holding this against the bullet hole in his chest. "It's hardly bleeding at all. Maybe he's bleeding inside."

"Please . . ." said Maybeth, almost crying. She had lifted Ranald's head softly onto her knee and was trying to wipe dry his forehead with the edge of her skirt. "Please, will somebody please go get an ambulance?"

"It just went off," Tom said. "I was holding it like this—I didn't even have my finger—"

"Where's your cycle?" Letty asked over her shoulder. "Get on it and get going. Can't you see we need some help?"

"You don't understand. It's not supposed to go off unless it's cocked," said Tom. "Well, I mean you can pull the trigger, but unless it's cocked . . . I didn't have it cocked. I don't think I—"

"That iron's got to be back where we were camped. He walked here just now." Rob's voice was still thick, but sensible. "I'll go find it. I'll ride the thing."

"No, I'll go . . . I'll go," said Tom's voice, moving away. "It's just back around the curve, there. I'll ride up the other way to Medora. That's where the hospital is."

"You'll go someplace else . . ." said Rob, thickly. "You'll let him die—we all saw it, how you shot him!"

"No—I'm going . . ." There was a sound of boots running off. Tom's voice floated back. "Over the hill, there—

down a ways—a farm. Maybe you can get to their phone before—"

He did not finish, running off.

"The farm—you go, Rob!" said Letty. "You—" Her face jerked for Maybeth. "Run back to the camp. Maybe there's somebody still there, or still near, who can help. Get going, damn it, will you both?"

Rob turned and went running into the trees up the hillside.

"No," said Maybeth, not moving, "I won't leave him. You go. Hurry!"

Letty lifted the wadded shirtcloth from the wound. It had all but stopped bleeding. For a second it looked as if she were about to hit Maybeth with the fist holding the cloth. Then she shoved the cloth instead into Maybeth's hand.

"Watch him!" Letty said, and scrambled to her feet. She started off at a trot back toward the meadow.

Left alone with Ranald, Maybeth pressed the cloth gently against the hole in his chest and let her head drop until her face was hidden by the long mass of hair that spilled forward like a dark wave onto the leather-brown skin of his lean chest. He had recovered his breath now; and he felt only something like an emptiness, a heavy emptiness, where the bullet had gone in and stopped.

"Do not mourn," he said to her, a little faintly, "this is a great moment. I'm like the rest of them, after all. I did what any one of them would do."

She lifted her head and shook her hair back so that she could see his face, and he, hers. Her face was simply a face, now, but very still. She, who had been able to cry so easily, could make no tears in this moment.

"You'll be all right," she said. "Don't talk."

"I am all right," he said. "And why not talk? I came here knowing what would happen. Men and women do always the same things. It happened; and I will fall from the cliff now, leaving some other climber my handholds and my footholds."

"Don't talk like that," she whispered, as if her throat were raw. "As if it was nothing—as if you were just being wasted."

"That is man," he said, "who can waste himself. It's a gift. The small birds and all other creatures don't know how."

She twisted as if a bullet had just entered her own body.

"No!" she said. "Don't agree with me like that. You saved Rob's life with your own, and he isn't worth it!"

"There is no worth," he said. "What is paid to God, or paid to Caesar, has only the value the giver gives it. A man must choose which one to pay, though, even though he's like me and needs neither of them. I was wrong about that. I had to choose; and I chose to pay the least foolish of the two."

"No!" she said. "No—you saved someone's life. You threw away your life after all this time to save somebody else. Because you love people, you really do. You just won't admit it."

"Do I?" he asked. "Even if I do, it doesn't matter. Man loves man. They love each other—that's the important thing, even when they don't know it. Look at them; they love each other even when they hurt and kill each other. It's their pride. Which is why they will accept no god-help."

She shook her head.

"All this," she said, "just to satisfy yourself! All this!"

"No, no," he said. "To find home, again. I was a wanderer and I've discovered my own place, again. I was a stranger and I've found my people. You—and Dave, and Rob and Letty and Tom and all the others."

He closed his eyes for a second, looking for the image of the green clearing and the log houses, but they were gone for good. He felt Maybeth's hands, suddenly frantic on his face.

"No," she was saying. "Don't . . . hold on. . . . They'll have help here in just a minute. . . ."

He opened his eyes.

"I'll have to be going now," he said. "Walt is down by the river. Go to him."

"Walt!" She went suddenly from her knees to a squatting position with her feet under her, ready to rise. "He's probably got things in his pack. Maybe he knows—where is he?"

"You remember where Dave and you and I came first to the edge of the river," he said. "Close to there. Go there and call him. He'll hear you."

"Oh, yes—" She started to rise, then stopped. "But I can't leave you."

"It makes no difference whether you leave me or not," he said.

"It does! But—" She looked back toward the meadow and the woods. "If Walt can help . . . I've got to go. Maybe he knows something about medicine, or he was a medic in the army once, or something. Don't move, I'll be right back—"

She started to rise. He caught her arm with surprising strength for a wounded man and held her for a moment while he spoke.

"I'll lie still a while," he said. "But things don't hurt me easily. It takes more to kill me than most imagine. If we don't speak again, remember to trust yourself as you would have trusted me."

"Don't talk like that!" She pulled away and he let her go, to her feet and running back toward the meadow. He lay still for a little, listening until the intervening trees softened the sound of her footfalls.

The sun was warm upon him, the heavy emptiness was only a little larger within him. He rose on his left elbow, rolled to his side, and climbed to his feet. For a moment he swayed and tottered, a little off balance. Then he put out one foot before the other and began to walk.

He went in the same direction in which Maybeth had left, running. But once more, his path was a straight line, and

soon it took him away from the road and back into the trees
of the hillside. He walked more surely now, and faster.
Soon, he began to run—at first only at a slow trot, staggering a little, but then with more speed and balance.

Still, it was a slow and clumsy pace he made, compared
to his earlier soaring run. The easiness was gone from his
coursing. His legs, which had been weightless and instinctive, now were heavy and needed to be driven, one past the
other, by the push of his will. At the same time, it was not
all work and weakness. The sun flicked at him through the
treetops, the breeze cooled his face, and the woods gathered
around him as he went. He passed through the trees above
the road by the meadow, hearing Maybeth, now out of sight
toward the river, calling for Walt, and Walt answering.

He ran on, leaving the meadow and the two of them
together, behind. A Western song sparrow flew past him,
perched on a low-swung sugar maple limb and watched him
pass, cocking its head at him.

He ran on. Angling downslope now—until the straight
line he followed once more intersected the road, so that he
crossed it and went on into the woods on that same side as
the meadow had lain, a way back. He could hear the river
growing louder, now, as it swung in toward the road and
him; and the angle of the ground on which he ran bent into
an upslope, for he was coming close now to that point of
land from which he and Maybeth and Dave had looked
beyond to river and road running side by side toward Medora.

The heaviness was larger in him now; but now it made no
difference. He had had some doubts earlier, but now he
knew that even the stubborn will to live could be slain. He
ran now almost as he had run before, not as lightly but
nearly as fast as he had run to meet the slug from Tom
Rathkenny's revolver. The woods swam past him and the
song sparrow flew steadily to keep up with him.

Now, the meadow was more than a short distance behind
and the heaviness in his chest was grown large enough to

make him stagger again for all the length of his strides and his speed. It was done now. To stop would end it. He could hear not only the river loudly now but, even more loudly, Dave, whom he had caught up with and was now passing, above, and out of sight among the trees.

He passed Dave and saw the end of the woods, the edge of the cliff overlooking the partnering of river and road. His head spun, and his chest felt as heavy as if it contained a cannonball. He staggered to a stop and dropped to his knees at the edge of the cliff, looking out through a screen of low bushes and popple saplings at the road below. Dave, below and a little behind him now, had begun to sing:

> *"There was a rich man and he lived in Jerusalem.*
> *Glory, Hallelujah, hi-ro-de-rum."*

He seized the pencil-thin stem of one of the saplings to hold himself upright on his knees. For a moment doubt chilled him with something like terror; but his body cried the truth to reassure him. It was a hard body to kill; but there was a limit to any flesh and bone and the cunning toughness of a thousand years. This last run had finished what the revolver bullet had started; and the cliff that only he could see was growing misty and insubstantial before his inner vision, as the life-hold of his will upon its craggy surface slackened.

He swayed on his knees, still managing to stay upright; and caught hold of another popple stem with his other hand to support himself. The song sparrow perched on a narrow young limb not a foot from his eyes.

"Gods," he said, "I am overdue, long overdue, but I won't disappoint you. Watch me fall, like the others."

". . . *Now the poor man died,*" Dave was singing as he strode along the road down below, his voice growing stronger as he drew level with the high point where Ranald knelt above him, *"and his soul went to Heavenium."*

"Glory, Hallelujah, hi-ro-de-rum.
He danced with the angels till a quarter past
elevenium.
Glory, Hallelujah, hi-ro-de-rum."

"Gods," murmured Ranald, "mourn that you can only fly; and were not born a human who knows what it is to climb."

He swayed, almost going down, but held up by his grip on the saplings. Dave was almost in sight now; and as Ranald held grimly on, the foreshortened, pack-laden figure came into view below, emerging by the river, singing . . .

"Now the rich man died and he didn't fare so
wellium.
Glory, Hallelujah, hi-ro-de-rum.
He couldn't go to Heaven, so he had to go to
Hellium.
Glory . . ."

Ranald held to the saplings, watching Dave move off along the road, singing. A little way farther on he stopped, abruptly, both singing and walking, and stepped over to look down into the waters of the river by the bank.

"Now," said Ranald to himself, but unheard to Dave as well, "all men and women do the same things, time after time—only perhaps, just once, my brother . . ."

Dave started to turn back to the road, taking up his song again. But he broke off and swung once more to face the water. His hand went into the right-hand pocket of his Levi's and came out with something which he threw, arcing, out into the middle of the stream. It twisted and glittered like a metal snake as it flew; and a fraction of a second after it had entered the water there was no sign it had ever existed.

Ranald let all the breath out of himself in a deep sigh. He

loosened his grip on the popples, and his cupped palms slid down their lengths, roughened and stained by sap from the young torn bark, as he fell forward onto the ground between them. With a last effort, he rolled over on his back to hear Dave's song more clearly as it moved off in the distance.

"Gods . . ." Ranald said; but that was all.

Above him the song sparrow looked down at him, then threw back his head, exposing the white blaze on its chest like a star of great worth, a medal of immeasurable honor, to the hot midday sun.

"*God is Man and Man is God,*" sang the song sparrow above Ranald, "*and I am a Bird!*"

Far and farther away, as the world closed in about Ranald, so that the sun was very close above his head and the song sparrow perched almost on the threshold of his mind, the last of Dave's song chanted faintly to his hearing.

> "*Now, the moral of this story is riches are no*
>   *jokium.*
>   *Glory, Hallelujah, hi-ro-de-rum!*
> *We all will go to Heaven for we all are stony*
>   *brokium.*
>   *Glory, Hallelujah, hi-ro-de-rum . . .*"

—And farther, fainter yet, but invincible still, as Ranald let go his last hold on the cliff and began to fall, the closing chorus followed him down. . . .

> "*Hi-ro-de-rum! hi ro-de-rum!*
> *Skinna-ma-rinky-doodle-doo!   Skinna-ma-rinky-*
>   *doodle-doo!*
>   *Glory, Hallelujah. . . .*"

GORDON R. DICKSON

☐	53567-7	Hoka! (with Poul Anderson)	$2.75
	53568-5		Canada $3.25
☐	48537-9	Sleepwalker's World	$2.50
☐	48580-8	The Outposter	$2.95
☐	48525-5	Planet Run	$2.75
		with Keith Laumer	
☐	48556-5	The Pritcher Mass	$2.75
☐	48576-X	The Man From Earth	$2.95
☐	53562-6	The Last Master	$2.95
	53563-4		Canada $3.50